NEIGHBOUR FROM HELL

Neal Bircher

Edition 1.0

Copyright © 2021 Neal Bircher
All rights reserved.
ISBN: 8469052678
ISBN-13: 979-8469052678

NEIGHBOUR FROM HELL

1. Frank

Nick glanced over at the speedometer; it hit seventy-five before Jason dropped down a gear and braked for a mini roundabout.

"Right at the roundabout, please."

Jason threw the car to the right, its tyres squealing in protest. Then he raced up through the gears, flashing past blurred rows of parked cars on either side. "Goes well, doesn't it? You've got to say, the 325i is one hell of a piece of kit."

Nick hadn't really wanted a lift back from their couple-of-beers-after-work gathering, but Jason had insisted. Nick was aware that he was gripping his seat with both hands. "You need to go left here and then right at the end of the road."

He made himself release his grip on the seat to take his phone from his pocket.

"I'll text Alyson to tell her I'm coming."

"Lucky girl; give her one for me, mate!"

Getting a lift. Back soon. Shall we go to the pub?

Alyson got straight back.

If you're not too drunk already.

"Left here; nearly there."

Jason swung his car into the turning and looked quizzically at each side of the street.

"Is this where you live?!"

"Yeah, turn left at the top there and it's on your right."

"You live in a council house?!"

"Yep, well - ex …"

Jason mouthed an exaggerated laugh as they passed a car on axle stands in a driveway.

"Ha! Bloody hell, Nick - I hope you don't have an old mattress on your front lawn."

1

Nick rolled his eyes. "It's alright living here, actually. You'd be surprised."

"I'll take your word for it, mate."

"Just there on the right, thanks."

Jason pulled half onto the footpath outside Nick's house and slammed on his brakes.

Nick got out of the car. "See you next week. Thanks for the lift."

"No problem, mate … Ha-ha! Council house scum!"

Jason closed his window, revved the engine, and drove off - tyre-squealing into the distance. Nick trudged up to his front door shaking his head and mouthing "tosser" under his breath.

*

THIS CAN'T GO ON! They're all over the street. We've got to DO SOMETHING….

It's too MUCH. It's TOO MUCH. Somebody's going to die. Somebody's going FUCKING DIE!

*

Graduate trainees at CountrySafe Insurance tended, as anywhere else, to lead active social lives. And that, combined with their exposure to different parts of the company, as well as their reputations for hosting quality piss-ups and having lots of young and attractive friends, led to such events being very well attended.

The occasion was a joint leaving do for three former graduate trainees who had each been with the company for a couple of years, and the main event was to be a party at one of their student-style houses. It was to start at a pub called The Red Lion, where Nick had arranged to meet up with, among others, Pete Little - a techie who worked in his team. And Alyson was away for the weekend with her friend Sarah from schooldays, so he could stay out as long as he liked, lie in as long as he liked, and pretty much do whatever he liked - for the evening, and for the whole of the weekend. It had all the ingredients for a great night out ... but Nick wasn't sure that he could be bothered. He and Alyson had had a major boozy night at their local, The Star, the night before and then he'd had a heavy day at work that hadn't ended until after six o'clock. The usual Friday beer after work session in The Carpenter's Arms wasn't on because of the party, and so Nick had walked home, thrown together a quick cheese sandwich, and then jumped into the bath.

After a long soak during which he came close to falling asleep he'd put on some clean clothes and trudged downstairs ready to walk the five minutes to the Harlesham Road where he could catch a bus for a thirty-minute ride and then make a final short walk to The Red Lion. He did have other options: he could stay at home and either watch TV or do something useful, or he could walk to The Star or one of the other local pubs for a couple of pints. In his knackered state, either of those choices felt more appealing than the party. But he had told people that he would be there, and he didn't like to let anyone down.

He checked that the back door was locked, switched off a couple of plug sockets in the kitchen and walked through the living room. He was just closing the living room door behind him when he caught sight of the red light flashing on his answering machine. That landline didn't get used much anymore, except by older relatives. It was almost certainly Alyson's mum who'd left the message. It could wait; he closed the door and turned to his front door. But then he hesitated - it wouldn't do any harm just to listen.

"Hello? ... ... Nick? ... It's Frank. Not to worry ... I'll catch you another time ... I hope all's OK. Er, goodbye." Click.

Frank was Nick's great uncle, his mother's uncle. Nick visited him occasionally - he lived in Croydon, the opposite side of London - but he hadn't done so for quite a while.

A feeling of guilt shivered through him, and he picked up the phone ready to call Frank back. But then he had a better idea: he could go over and visit Frank the next day. Yes, that would work … although not very well with a raging get-home-at-four-in-the-morning party hangover. Fuck it! It wasn't as if the party was going to be a life-changing experience; he could make do with a few pints in The Star and an early(ish) night.

*

"Those dogs were just gorgeous," cooed Sarah. "I could have so easily brought one of them home with me."

She and Alyson had spent the day at a health spa before dining at her favourite Italian restaurant and having a couple of drinks in her local pub, where they had befriended a gay man with two miniature dachshunds. They had now returned to her flat and started on the Prosecco.

"Yes, they were sweet. And the guy was so camp! Why is it that there are there so many gay people in Brighton?"

"I don't know. It goes back centuries apparently. All part of the liberal arty thing I guess."

"He was sweet, but such a stereotype, with the dogs and the campness and all of those girly hand gestures. Doesn't it get a bit wearing in that pub when it's full of them?"

"Not really" said Sarah unconvincingly, "it's not a gay pub as such - just gay friendly, like most of them around here. And it just so happens that lots of gay people drink there. It makes a change from getting chatted up by arseholes, and the lesbians are OK; they're not so predatory as blokes - most of them aren't, anyway."

"So, anyway - how's Stephen?" asked Alyson tentatively. "You haven't mentioned him yet."

Sarah was single but had been seeing Stephen, who was much older - and married, on and off for a number of years.

Sarah took a sip from her glass. "Oh, he's good. He was here on Thursday. But, you know, he's away so much, always jetting here, there, and everywhere. He's at a conference in Dubai next week."

"Hmmm, I wish Nick could be a bit more ambitious sometimes. He's capable - I'm sure he's got more about him than most of them at that bloody place, but he's just not, I dunno, 'corporate' enough."

"Well, at least you've got him all to yourself. Anyway, how's that bloke at work? What was his name … Simon?" Sarah had a mischievous twinkle in her eye.

"Ha-ha," said Alyson, slapping Sarah's arm with a cushion. "He's only a friend."

"Yes, of course," said Sarah, smirking.

"At least we've got the house now," said Alyson, getting back to the subject, "but I don't want to stay there for years. I want to upgrade to somewhere nice, but Nick doesn't seem to care."

"No, you wouldn't want to live on that estate for ever would you."

"Umm … well, no – I wouldn't."

"You need to tell him."

"I do … at least I hint strongly enough but he doesn't take any notice."

"Well, at least he's kind. He doesn't get violent or anything, like certain people from the old days."

"Hmmmm," said Alyson, looking distant.

"He doesn't though, does he?"

"No, no, not at all. He gets quite opinionated and sweary when he's drunk, but not aggressive. He hates confrontation; in fact, he could do with having a bit more fight about him. I think it might be something to do with his past, you know - that business with his mate being murdered when he was still at school and then him being robbed with knives when he was at college. He doesn't like to talk about that stuff, and I think those things still affect him. It comes out a bit sometimes when he's pissed."

"Does he drink a lot then?"

"No, not really. Well, he doesn't get seriously drunk too much if that's what you mean. He drinks most nights though, but then so do I."

"Speaking of which," said Sarah, "more Prosecco?" And without waiting for a response, she filled both of their large glasses to the brim.

"When did that become such a thing - Prosecco?" said Alyson. "Why do all girlie night outs have to involve Prosecco nowadays? Look at us, we're bigger stereotypes than that gay bloke. We'll probably be crying in another couple of glasses."

"Yeah, could be. Well, slap me if I do. So, what about Nick - does he ever see anyone else?"

"Ha-ha, as if! Who would want him?"

The two of them laughed long, loud, and a bit unnaturally.

*

Nick felt some trepidation as he lifted the brass door knocker at his great uncle Frank's house. He rapped loudly three times, as Frank was in his eighties and hard of hearing. There wasn't any response at first; he knew there wouldn't be. He peered in through the door's frosted glass. There was a cold darkness and no movement. The door's pale green paint was decades old and was peeling badly; the off-white paint of the surrounding panels was little better. Nick was standing inside Frank's shallow open porch. He turned his back to the door and looked back down the narrow footpath that he'd just walked along. It was about thirty feet long and ended at a small rusty wrought iron gate that had scraped on the concrete when he'd opened it to enter. Nick had not been here very many times during his thirty-four years; he visited maybe once a year. In his memories, the gate changed from dark green to light green to black, but its paint covering had now given way mostly to rust. To the left of the path as Nick looked at it was Frank's overgrown front lawn, and to the right his empty tarmac driveway that clumps of weeds were sprouting through. At the end of the driveway a pair of gates matching the one at the pedestrian entrance were strapped together by a very used-looking bicycle lock. Separating Frank's garden from the quiet street outside was a low wall made of solid red brick. Nick turned back to face the house, constructed of the same solid red brick in the 1930s. He rapped three times on the door again. After another period of cold dark silence, he was beginning to regret his idea of a surprise visit when something made a sound inside and, peering through the frosted glass, he could detect movement - Frank was shuffling his way to the door.

The old door juddered open, and Frank peered around it. An initial confused look was quickly replaced with surprised smile.

"Hello!" said Nick.

Frank had been 'Uncle Frank' when Nick was a child, but as an adult that hadn't felt right anymore, but then nor had 'Frank', so Nick no longer called him anything at all.

"Hello," said Frank. "I wasn't expecting to see *you*!"

"No, I got your message last night and thought I'd …"

Not appearing to hear him, Frank beckoned Nick to follow him through the house to the 'back room', which was a small sort of living room where Frank watched TV, received visitors, and spent a large percentage of his time.

Nick sat on one of the room's small upright floral-patterned cloth sofas whilst Frank made them each a mug of tea in his kitchen. Little had changed in this room during Nick's lifetime. The sofa - or 'settee' as Frank would call it - had always been there, along with two matching armchairs. That three-piece suite surrounded a coffee table that also hadn't changed, nor had the standard lamp - including its lampshade - behind the armchair that Frank always sat in, nor his bookcase, nor probably most of the books that were crammed into it. The gas fire in its fireplace was the same as well, as were the two black and white framed photographs on the mantelpiece above it of Frank, and Frank with his wife Margaret. Margaret had died thirty years ago.

Frank and Margaret didn't have any children and Frank had lived alone since her passing. Nick could remember Margaret's death. At least, he could remember meeting her when he was very young, and he could remember something serious going on when he was about four that was clearly for adult interest only. It had been for him to infer what had actually happened.

He stood up to have a bit more of a look around the room. The hatch through to the kitchen on the wall that had been behind him when he was seated brought back memories of food dishes being passed through it, but was firmly shut today and, he suspected, always now.

Frank came unsteadily back into the room, carrying a tray containing two mugs of tea and a plate of Digestive biscuits.

"Do sit down," Frank commanded, as if Nick had been waiting for permission to do so.

Nick did as he was told and Frank placed the tray down on his coffee table, shoving out of the way his copy of the *Daily Mail*, opened on the racing pages.

"So, did you drive here?" asked Frank.

"No, I came on the Tube … well Tube and a bit of train."

"Oh, how long did that take then?"

A five-minute conversation then ensued in which Nick had to explain his rationale of Tube/train vs. car travel. In short, although it probably took a little longer, he found the Tube and train experience much more enjoyable, and he spent much of the time reading. Frank didn't particularly seem to get it but didn't argue.

"So, did you sell your car then?" asked Nick, referring to the lack of Nissan Micra in the driveway.

"Yes, I had to give up driving you see." Nick knew that; Frank had told him the last time that he had visited, nearly a year before - but the Micra had still been there then.

"I'm eighty-four now you see; my co-ordination isn't what it used to be." Nick knew both of those things as well.

"Bob's nephew had it. I didn't get much for it but at least someone's getting use out of it."

Bob was Frank's friend of many years, pretty much his only friend. Nick had met him a couple of times, many years ago.

"Yeah, that's good. And speaking of cars, how's the Bond?"

"Eh? Oh, it's still there in the garage. I haven't done much with it lately."

The Bond was a car that Frank had owned since long before Nick was born, a 1967 Bond Equipe. It had been Frank's only vehicle for many years, and he'd kept it once it had been replaced as his main vehicle by more modern cars. Nick had spent literally hours sitting in it as a child.

"Do you want to have look at it?"

"Yeah, why not."

"We'll have a wander out there once we've had this cup of tea then."

It was after another cup of tea and an hour and a half by the time Nick and Frank did actually put on their coats and head outside, during which time they had discussed a range of topics including football, which Frank didn't really follow very closely anymore but Nick did, cricket, which Nick didn't really follow but Frank did avidly, relatives that they both knew, and acquaintances of Frank that Nick on the whole had never met. Although feeling a little guilty that he was getting bored, Nick had prompted the move to the garage.

Frank collected the garage key from his kitchen and led Nick towards his front door. On their left they passed the door to Frank's 'front room'. Nick had hardly ever been in there, and probably not at all for about twenty years. It had a polished wooden floor with a large rug on it and a lot of quality wooden furniture. It was a dining room that had been kept 'for best'. It was hardly ever used even when Margaret was alive and since her death even Frank only went in there rarely, mainly to keep it clean and polished. On their right, near the front door and on its own tiny table was Frank's 1980s Trimphone - a collector's item nowadays Nick wondered; it was Frank's only phone, he didn't have a mobile.

"Ken and Irene moved out you know?"

Nick knew that Frank's neighbours, Ken and Irene, had moved as Frank had told him on each of the previous two times that he had visited.

"Yes, you said."

"There's a coloured family moved in there now. I don't really have much to do with them."

Nick knew both of those things too.

Once at the garage door, Frank faffed around with the lock for some time before enlisting Nick's help in dragging open the sagging double doors.

It was Nick's first sight of the Bond in years, and it was something of a disappointment. Its white bodywork was coated in a thick layer of black dust, and it was slumped down on four near-flat tyres.

"I haven't really done much with it lately," said Frank again, rather stating the obvious.

The Bond took up most of the garage but stashed around it were pieces of wood, hardboard, random lengths of metal pipe, and other bits and pieces that had been kept in case they were ever needed. They were all coated in the same thick dust that covered the Bond and were joined together by forests of cobwebs delicately spun by generations of spiders over many years. The garage was dark and smelled musty. The Bond was parked nose in, tightly against the left-hand wall. On the right-hand wall at around head height were two layers of wooden shelving stacked with tools, bottles, oil cans, containers filled with nuts, bolts, screws, and all the other things that get squirrelled away in garages and hardly ever used. It was a tight squeeze as Nick made his way to the Bond's driver's door and tried the handle. The door was locked.

"Here, I've got the key." Frank handed the key to Nick and then launched into a coughing fit brought on by dust that they had disturbed and that was now floating around in the dank air.

The door resisted being opened at first but then emitted a squelching sound as whatever grime build-up had been holding it in place gave in to Nick's endeavour. Nick squeezed himself into the driving seat. Its black vinyl felt cold and brittle and let out little crackling sounds as he settled into it. He pulled the door closed and placed his hands on the wooden steering wheel. Inside the car the dust was not quite as prevalent as in the rest of the garage, but the musty smell was worse. Nick gazed over the Bond's wooden dashboard, round instruments, 'organ stop' switches, and its wobbly chrome gearstick with polished wooden knob. The dashboard's lacquer was peeling, the instruments were shrouded in dust and their chrome surrounds corroding, and the gear knob was coated in mildew. But none of that mattered. Nick pushed himself back in the low bucket seat. That dashboard, those instruments, that gearstick, the gear knob, the wooden steering wheel, had all been explored by him when he'd first sat in that same seat thirty years before, and again twenty-nine years before, and then a year later. His impression was that from the ages of about four to fourteen whenever he'd visited 'Uncle Frank' he'd spent most of the time sitting in this same seat getting excited by the same things that were exciting him now. It was an old car even then, but a hand-built rare British classic, and that had appealed to Nick even as a small child. He only remembered travelling in it once when Uncle Frank had taken him for a local drive, when he was maybe eight years old. There was a photo somewhere too from around the same time of him sitting in the driving seat with his brother James as his passenger. Uncle Frank was still working back then. Nick didn't know exactly what he did, but it was something in Lloyds Bank. Nick closed his eyes and … and then Frank was banging on the window.

Nick turned the handle to wind down the window. It was reluctant to move, and its mechanism made a disconcerting grinding noise as it did so.

Frank had his 1960s foot-pump in his hands. "We could pump up the tyres."

Nick took the hint. He got out of the car and placed the old pump first at the front right wheel. It took twenty minutes or more to get all four tyres back to full pressure and it was hard work. They all needed a lot of air and the two on the left-hand side were tricky to get to. Frank kept offering to help but he struggled for breath just by speaking, so Nick declined any assistance. By the end Nick was grubby and exhausted, but the Bond looked better for his efforts - not quite so down in the dumps. The improvement put a smile on Frank's face.

"I should get it cleaned up really," he said.

"Can do it next time I'm over; maybe start it up as well."

Frank nodded. "I should get the battery on trickle charge … and put a drop of fresh petrol in it."

For that moment, as Frank and Nick looked in at the old car from outside of the garage, they both probably believed that those things might actually happen.

"You've always liked that car haven't you," said Frank. "I'll have to leave it to you in my will!"

Nick responded with a slightly awkward chuckle, not catching Frank's eye.

The two men locked up the garage together and it was time for Nick to be on his way. Frank saw him off from the gate.

"Let me know when you are coming next time," Frank called after Nick. "I'll do you a bit of lunch."

"Will do ... cheers!"

Nick fastened up his coat. It was starting to get dark, and the temperature was dropping. There would probably be a frost during the night. He broke into a jog. He was smiling; he was glad that he'd decided to visit Frank. Frank had no close family and other than Nick's parents - who now lived in South Africa and rarely returned to the UK, Nick was the only relative who ever visited him. He resolved to do so again soon and to do so more often in the future.

*

The Star was the nearest pub to Nick and Alyson's house - a ten-minute walk away. They had gone there on the first night of their first day in their house and over the course of the following two years had become regular customers. The Star was old and 'traditional' with a lounge and bar that were accessed through separate external doors. The bar was large and divided into front and rear sections, between them featuring two pool tables, two dart boards, two TVs, and a juke box; it had a lino floor throughout. The lounge was much smaller than the bar, had a carpeted floor and lots of polished wood, but no pub sports, music, or TV. The Star was a classic 'old man's pub' with very much a working-class clientele. There were regulars in the bar and regulars in the lounge but rarely did any of them cross over to the other side. The lounge customers were charged two pence more per pint than their bar-dwelling counterparts. Nick loved The Star. He would take its authenticity any day over the more polished offerings of a chain pub or bistro. Alyson wasn't quite as keen, but she did enjoy it; it was a place that the two of them could relax, and where she wasn't concerned what she was wearing. In the early days, very few of the locals had spoken to them but in time, partly through them both playing pool and Nick joining in the winner-stays-on sessions, they had made a number of friends there.

One of the first to be friendly towards them was Len Phillips. Len was in his late fifties and a self-employed builder. He drank in The Star more nights than not, sometimes alone, often with one or two of his workmates. He spoke a lot of his grown-up children and of his wife but seemed happy enough to leave her at home most nights. "She likes her soap operas; I like the pub."

Tonight was a Sunday - a quiet one, not a darts night - and Alyson, Nick, and Len sat around a table-for-four. Alyson had asked Len for advice about getting their driveway re-surfaced and after Len had gone into far too much detail about each of the various options, Nick was getting agitated. He knew that whatever the options were Alyson was sure to choose the most expensive, and he was also bored of talking about driveways.

"Did we tell you that those miserable people from opposite us have moved out?" Nick asked, knowing full well that they had.

Nick and Alyson's house was on the inside of a sharp bend and three houses on the outer side of the bend faced it. All contained people who kept themselves to themselves. The house that Nick referred to was the one that was directly opposite their driveway, and its occupants were a sour-faced recently-retired couple who never spoke to them but who constantly peered out from behind their curtains. To the left of them from Nick and Alyson's direction was a house containing some Polish people who never spoke to anybody, and to the right was an older lady called Joyce with whom Nick and Alyson had exchanged the odd wave or 'hello' but no more conversation than that.

"Yeah, you did. Nosey bastards weren't they."

Alyson chipped in. "Certainly were. We could never leave the house without them peering through the curtains."

Len continued, "Remember that time I came round to do your fence posts?" They did, it was the only time he'd been to their house. "Couldn't get enough of it could they?"

"Miserable sods though," said Nick. "I never saw either of them smile, and they never spoke to us - not in the whole two years."

"Apparently they'd been there for forty years," added Alyson. "Hopefully we'll get someone nicer next time."

"Any idea who's moving in then?" asked Len, looking Nick's way.

Nick shook his head. "No, no idea."

Len had a view on who it might be though. "It'll be pakis. Always is nowadays, it's getting worse than fucking Southall around here."

Alyson caught Nick's eye and grimaced.

Nick thought for a moment and then spoke.

"I certainly hope so; their kids are always well behaved. Much better than having some scumbag like that Billy Grindle over there."

Billy Grindle was a well-known shaven-headed pasty fourteen-year-old who lived on the estate. He was assumed by most to be responsible for just about all of the crime in the area.

Len nodded and gave a small shrug of his shoulders. His expression seemed to possibly say, "Yes, I suppose you could have a point." He picked up his pint of bitter and took a long swig. Nick and Alyson both pick up their lagers and did the same.

*

"How many was that then - six … seven? Probably six - spread over a few hours though. So not so bad. Heavy day tomorrow; gotta be up early. Need to stop doing this. Booze-free day tomorrow - definitely. STARVING! Just do myself some toast and sit down in front of the telly for a bit before I turn in. Will get to bed by one o'clock. Just the one more can with it, no more than that … definitely no more than that."

*

2. Tricia

Nick and Alyson had visited the Isle of Wight five times during their seven years together, sometimes camping, sometimes staying in B&B accommodation. This time it was the latter and they had enjoyed, as Nick put it, a weekend of 'sun, sea, Sandown, and shagging' … plus of course a fair bit of booze. It being November though, their exposure to sun was limited and they hadn't actually got in the sea, but the excess of the other activities ensured that they were both completely knackered by the time they got back home late on the Sunday afternoon.

"I wonder if we'll have someone new living opposite us," said Nick as he turned the car into their estate. It was the third time that he'd said it over the course of the weekend.

They turned the final corner that brought their house into view as well as the house opposite. And that view told them that the front 'garden' of that house (which was a patch of concrete with a small circular rose bed in the middle) was full of people. There were maybe twelve of them, mainly young men, and most of them clutching cans of lager.

"Shit!" said both Nick and Alyson.

Nick pulled the car into their driveway and switched off the engine. There was loud music coming from the 'party' opposite.

"Not looking promising," said Nick.

Alyson shook her head.

They both got out of the car, took their luggage from the boot, and made their way hurriedly into the house. Once inside they went up to their bedroom to peer over the road though the net curtains.

Most members of the gathering opposite seemed to be aged seventeen to twenty. One though was younger - maybe ten or twelve, and one was older: "Dopey Dave's there, look," said Nick. 'Dopey Dave' was a local 'character' – a podgy man in his late twenties who lived on the estate with his parents and spent much of his day wandering around doing very little. Neither Alyson nor Nick had ever spoken to him.

They weren't doing much, just standing around on both the concrete and the rose bed, most of them drinking, half of them smoking, and a few of them talking. Under the front window of the house was a large ghetto blaster that was providing the music, and just along from that, sitting on the step of the open front door was a woman - the only female among the gathering. She was older than the others, maybe late forties; she was overweight, had straggly black hair, a ruddy complexion, and face that looked as if it had seen a lot of life - and quite likely a lot of alcohol. She wore loose-fitting baggy clothes - blue trousers and a dirty-looking white top - and had a cigarette in one hand and a can of lager in the other.

"I guess that she's our new neighbour," said Nick.

"Looks like it. Let's hope that the rest of them aren't all her kids," quipped Alyson, attempting to be light-hearted despite the horror that she felt inside.

"I think I already prefer the miserable old fuckers who were there before," said Nick.

Over the course of the next hour or two they unpacked, had some food and showered. Each time either of them was in the bedroom they glanced apprehensively over the road to see what was happening and each time they were disappointed to see that nothing had changed. Neither mentioned anything to the other.

By eight o'clock they were ready to do what they'd always planned to do, which was to walk to the pub for a couple of pints to round off the weekend. They exited their front door with trepidation - but all was quiet and there was nobody in the garden opposite. The front door of the house was open but there was no talking or music and no evidence of the earlier gathering beyond some crushed lager cans on the floor and a flattened flower bed.

Nick and Alyson's moods were immediately buoyed.

"Maybe they were just helping her move in or something," said Alyson.

"Let's hope so," said Nick taking Alyson's hand ... something that he didn't do very often.

Three hours and four pints later Nick and Alyson were on their way back from the pub. The Star had been busy as it was darts night, and there had been a good atmosphere. They'd told Len about their new neighbour and her gathering of youths. Len had just tutted and shaken his head in a 'what's the world come to' kind of way.

As they walked back, again hand in hand, they were in good spirits.

Alyson turned and kissed Nick on the cheek. "Do you want to have sex when we get in?" she asked coyly.

"What? Haven't you had enough over the last two days?" said Nick, "I'll see what I can do!"

They quickened their pace; in no time they were again rounding the final corner to bring their house into view and ... the crowd was back.

"Shit!"

They slowed and walked dejectedly into their house, both looking out of the corners of their eyes towards their new neighbours. It seemed to be the same gathering as before and the ghetto blaster was back too, playing loudly to the street.

Nick and Alyson climbed naked into bed together and then laid on their backs staring up at the ceiling. For fifteen wide-eyed minutes they listened to music interspersed with snippets of conversation and the occasional shout. "Fuck off, you cunt!" was followed by a raucous round of laughter.

And then the music stopped.

Alyson grabbed Nick's hand.

A few minutes passed with only the noise of voices, before … the music started up again.

For maybe half an hour the 'party' continued, and Nick and Alyson continued to lie there simultaneously getting both stressed and drowsy.

Then the music stopped again.

Nick listened to the babble of conversation, on edge, waiting for the music to re-start. There were sounds of some of the people walking away, although the babble didn't seem to get any quieter.

Some more people left. Somebody called "See ya!"

There was more laughter, which was loud but muffled; they'd moved inside the house.

Then an argument kicked off. There was sweary yelling from at least two men and a woman. That went on for a few minutes before the front door of the house was closed and again only muffled noise could make its way to Nick and Alyson's bedroom.

Peace.

It was two minutes before the door opened again. More music, more voices. Then the door closed once more, and the sound of footsteps followed, and then faded. It was twelve-thirty; Nick and Alyson were both still staring at the ceiling.

Nick realised that he must have dozed off. "Have they gone?" he said. But Alyson was asleep. He looked over at the alarm clock. It was just after two o'clock. He felt a horrible combination of tiredness, stress, and that special drained feeling that only waking up after a small time of sleep following a few hours of drinking can bring. And the inside of his mouth also tasted and felt the way only such circumstances can bring - dry, stale, and somehow furry. He clambered out of bed and stumbled on heavy weary legs to the curtains. The streetlamp outside the house opposite lit the still scene with a faint glow; it all looked so peaceful.

Nick got back into bed and quickly fell asleep, not waking until the shriek of Alyson's alarm clock awoke him from his nightmares at six o'clock.

*

"Not looking good. The fucking STATE of her too! Better not have those wankers around too often. Miserable old fuckers there before weren't so bad after all. FUCK! Just what we fucking need - fucking chav scum all over the street. I need another drink."

*

Nick drew up his chair at the canteen table. He was with three colleagues, and he was the last of them to sit down. He usually ate with brash go-getter Jason Barker and mild-mannered Martin Broome, both of whom were - like him - project managers, and all of them worked under the same boss, called Tony Clarke. A number of others joined the three them for lunch from time to time and today it was Annette Price who had worked with Nick for a long time and was in effect his deputy. Nick and Annette had become good friends over the years and at times in the past their relationship had stepped over the boundary to beyond mere friendship. On the one hand Nick enjoyed it when she joined them as she had a great sense of humour and always livened up their conversation, but on the other he didn't because she was also an attractive woman, and that meant that Jason felt the need to show off even more than usual.

As Nick joined his colleagues, he got the impression that they had been talking about him, and Jason immediately confirmed that to be the case.

"We were just saying about your Porsche, Nick. I haven't seen it for ages. What have you done with it?"

"Still got it," said Nick. "It's in my garage; I hardly ever drive it nowadays to be honest."

"I don't get you," said Jason. "You have a Porsche in the garage, and you drive around in that silly little three-wheeled van. What's that all about?"

Jason's eyes darted from Annette's to Martin's and then back to Annette's as he sought approval of his observation, or better still guffaws of laughter. They each looked down and picked up a forkful of food from their respective plates.

"Well, in its own way, it's actually more fun than the Porsche. And it's interesting but not showy," said Nick.

That concept wasn't something that Jason would ever comprehend and so he changed tack. "Well, I don't say I blame you keeping it hidden away, living where you do." His eyes darted between Annette's and Martin's again as he went on, "Did you know that he lives in a council house?"

Nick rolled his eyes. "*Ex*-council house, Jason. But anyway, what's wrong with that?"

Jason smirked. "What's wrong with it is the swarms of chavs roaming the streets looking for stuff to steal or smash up - like a Porsche, for example."

Had this same conversation taken place just a week earlier then Nick would have strongly defended his community, insisting that he and Alyson were very happy there and that all the people around them were good neighbours. And for the two years that they had been there, since buying the house and moving from their tiny, rented flat near the centre of Norling, they had indeed been mostly happy. But given the arrival of the new woman across the street such protestations would have felt a little hollow. So, he confessed.

"Well, most people are really good, but we had a new neighbour move in over the road at the weekend and must admit I'm a bit concerned about her."

"Go on," said Jason, eagerly.

Nick didn't immediately answer. Instead, he briefly switched into daydream mode, musing that there had to be more to life than drifting along doing what he was doing, where the least dull parts of the day were those part-spent talking bollocks with the likes of Jason, and where some dullest aspects involved having to 'compete' with him. This was a common thought for Nick, and it was getting ever more so. He wasn't going to be able to resolve anything just now though. He snapped back into the present.

"Well, don't take the piss, but she seems to fit the stereotype that you attribute to everybody on the estate - you know: fags, bad teeth, slobby clothes - and on Sunday night she did indeed have a swarm of chavs all over her front garden."

"Ha-ha, told you!" said Jason, full of glee.

Martin and Annette meanwhile carried on eating without comment.

"It was hopefully only a sort of house-warming thing," said Nick. And he so wished that he really did believe that to be the case.

Over the following weeks, it did indeed turn out that the gathering over the road from Nick and Alyson's was not just a house-warming, and similar 'events' began to occur every few days. The format was similar: lots of youths milling about generally smoking and drinking, and often with a musical accompaniment provided by the same ghetto blaster. The woman of the house - the lady in her forties with the straggly black hair - was always there too, normally taking up her position in her doorway with a cigarette in her right hand and quite often a can of lager in her left. Nick and Alyson learned that her name was Tricia and that she lived there with her son, who was the youngest of the youths in the gathering - a particularly miserable looking ten-year-old called Damian. The gatherings varied in size, the number of attendees usually being somewhere between five and fifteen. They varied in timing - they could happen any day of the week and usually late in the afternoon or during the evening, but they could also sometimes start as early as ten o'clock in the morning. And they varied in duration, sometimes ending almost as soon as they started and at other times going on all day or deep into the night.

One time, as Nick got to the end of his walk home from work, he was relieved that there were only two people in Tricia's front garden. As he got closer, he could see that those two were Damian and another boy of similar age. He could also see that the fence that separated Tricia's front garden from the footpath outside was no longer there - it was instead scattered in pieces all over the concrete, and out into the footpath and roadway beyond. Damian was holding one of the slats from the fence like a walking stick. As Nick passed, the boys glared at him as if accusing him of doing something wrong, before Damian threw his walking stick up onto the roof of his mother's house where it slid down the tiles and lodged in the guttering.

November became December and winter whether set it, but Tricia's gang were not deterred. Christmas came and went; they even turned up on Boxing Day. Whatever the size, timing, or duration, there was always something unsettling about the gatherings, even though they didn't have any real effect beyond the apparent threat of menace. It seemed that many felt the same way, as Tricia quickly became the main talking point of any of Nick or Alyson's conversations with neighbours.

Ted Davies came over for a chat one day. He and his wife Jean, who were both in their early sixties, lived on the same side of the road as Tricia and four houses to the left from Nick and Alyson's point of view. Nick and Alyson had first met Ted soon after they'd moved in when he had come over to introduce them to the informal neighbourhood watch scheme that he administered. Nick and Alyson hadn't signed up to the scheme but often spoke to Ted and Jean, who were reserved but friendly characters. They had moved into their council house thirty years previously but had since bought it and proudly kept the house and its gardens in pristine shape. Ted was worried about Tricia and her gang and wanted to get Nick and Alyson's views. "I don't know what we are going to do about it," he proffered. The implication seeming to be that 'we' included Nick and/or Alyson and that there might be something that they *could* do. Cups of tea were shared but no plans of action were forthcoming from any of them.

Nick and Alyson's adjoining neighbours were Danny and Brenda. Danny was of Indian descent (and his real name was Gulshandeep, but he never used it) and Brenda was white; they had four sons aged between ten and sixteen living with them in their two-bedroom house. Danny was a self-employed motor mechanic and Brenda worked as a cleaner in a local school. Danny was, as often, working on a car in his driveway one Saturday afternoon when he called Nick over to ask what *he* thought of Tricia.

"She's from the travelling community," Danny said, assuredly. "Mess with her and they'll all be onto you."

"Well, let's hope it doesn't come to that."

Danny winked. "If it gets too bad, we'll sort her out."

That begged a question or two, and Nick asked one of them. "Who do you mean will sort her out?"

Danny touched his nose. "We'll sort her out, don't you worry."

Nick left it at that.

Harshad Ranganathan was a slightly aloof character of around fifty years of age who sometimes spoke to Nick but had never spoken to Alyson. He lived two doors to the right of them with his wife Meena (whom neither of them had met) and a daughter of about twenty who was there on and off. They also had an older son who had fled the nest. Nick was out cutting his hedge when Harshad came by.

"What do you think of our new neighbour then?" was his opening gambit.

He and Nick then shared their very similar concerns about Tricia being in their habitat. Harshad had a further issue though.

"Her son - that horrible little shit - he called me a 'paki'."

"Really? You could get the police onto them for that kind of thing."

"Nah, no point in doing that - would only make things worse. I wouldn't mind but I'm not a bloody paki anyway, I'm Indian!"

It was often hard to tell whether Harshad was joking or serious.

Joyce, the woman who lived in the house adjoining Tricia's, had been there for more than forty years and had been alone since the death of her husband ten years ago. Although Nick and Alyson hardly knew her, when they came across Joyce in their local shop, she too was full of Tricia talk, with tales of bangs and crashes, screaming, swearing, and 'dreadful music' coming through her walls, day and night. "What do you think?" she pleaded. "I'm going to get onto the council and complain."

Regular visits from the police were another aspect of Tricia's presence. They tended to arrive every three or four days and would disappear inside Tricia's house for some time, usually when she was alone or with her son, rather than when the crowd was gathered in her garden. Nick and Alyson didn't ever call them, and they wondered who did.

So, life was changing as a result of Tricia's arrival. Nick and Alyson may have got to know some of their neighbours better, but overall, their home was getting to be a decidedly less pleasant place to live.

*

Nick donned his coat and went out to the back garden. He scraped his old wooden chair into position and sat down. He could smell cigarette smoke wafting through the fence from next door and he knew what that meant. He opened his can of lager, quite loudly.

"Evening!" said Colin, from the other side of the fence.

"Evening," Nick replied. "How's things?"

Nick and Alyson's neighbours to the side that they were not adjoined were Colin and Janet, and they lived there with their four young children – including a baby. Janet was not un-friendly but was quiet and seemed shy, as well as being occupied with the children, and Nick and Alyson hardly knew her. Colin was quiet too, but these late-night chats had become something of a habit for him and Nick. Nick often went into the back garden for a drink when Alyson was either working or watching a TV programme that he didn't like, or had gone to bed, while Colin came out for a smoke and sometimes a drink to, as he put it, "get away from a houseful of screaming kids."

"Knackered. What about you?"

"Me too; had a day full of meetings and then had to get some actual work done. How about you – been anywhere interesting?"

Colin worked as a chauffeur for a private hire company.

"Nope – Coventry. Had to pick up a bloke and take him to Gatwick."

"Nice!"

"Did you see her over the road again today?"

"No, what happened?"

"Loads of them over there, drinking and pissing about. I got home about three o'clock and they were all there staring at me like fucking morons. Janet said the music kept the baby awake all morning. Dickheads."

"Shit. No, I didn't get home until late. She was just sitting on the step on her own in her dressing gown. She must have been freezing."

"Probably doesn't feel it with all that fat … and the booze inside her. Silly bitch needs putting down."

"Yeah. Maybe she'll drink herself to death, do us all a favour."

"Some hope!"

"Anyway, you're up late," said Nick. "Is it your day off tomorrow?"

"No, got to be up at five o'clock. I was just about to go in now, to be honest. I'd better leave you to it."

"OK, no probs. All the best; see y'later."

"Cheers."

Nick carried on drinking on his own. He beathed in the cold January air and relaxed back into his chair. The sky was clear, and he spent some time gazing up at the stars. It was quiet too. His garden was a nice place to be, such a contrast from the stress of the front of the house when Tricia and her crew were in evidence … or even when they weren't but were inevitably going to return at some time. Not that he was free from their menace even now; the feeling of anxiety was getting to be always there; something bad might be just around the corner. He finished up his can. He pondered, as he often did, that he drank too much … and too often, and then went inside to get 'just one more'.

*

Nick turned the key in his front door and opened it gingerly. It was eight o'clock; he'd gone for a couple of pints after work with Martin and then walked the two miles home. He'd texted Alyson when he'd left the pub.

- Fancy going out to eat when I get in?

But her response hadn't been encouraging.

- Let's talk about it when you get here.

It sounded too much like a 'we need to talk', hence Nick's opening of the door gingerly.

Their ground floor was open plan, and upon hearing Nick come in, Alyson came through from the kitchen area into the living room to meet him.

"Hi," she said. And she stopped at that.

Nick hesitated. "Hi ... is everything OK?"

"Yes, well, no ... I have something to tell you."

They were standing six feet apart.

"Go on," said Nick.

Alyson cleared her throat. "Your Uncle Frank ... he died."

Nick felt two things at once, he felt the sickening numbing shock that the news itself brought on, but also felt a tinge of anger as he perceived a tone of glee in Alyson's voice - as if she was excited that she had something dramatic to tell him.

The two of them didn't move any closer.

Nick cleared his throat. "How did you find out?"

Alyson explained that Nick's mother had phoned the landline (from her home in South Africa) and that Frank had been found dead in his bed by his home help that morning.

Nick cleared his throat again. "Well, I'm glad that I visited him when I did."

He then went upstairs, sat on the toilet, and cried his eyes out.

It was a full ten minutes before he returned downstairs having dried his eyes and composed himself.

Alyson offered to make him some food.

"No, I'm fine, thanks. Let's go to the pub."

*

3. Colin

Nick enjoyed walking to and from work and he did it as often as he could. It took just over half an hour each way and as he rarely played any sport anymore, walking - this, plus going to pub/football/local shops - was pretty much the only real exercise that he got.

This evening he entered the final straight of his return from work and was confronted, as so often, by a noisy throng. It was much the same as previous times as Tricia was there, sitting smoking on her doorstep, Damian was there, as was Dopey Dave, and lots of others who were mostly both smoking and drinking. But there were more of them than there ever had been before - about twenty in total - and they spilled out over much of the street. They were being entertained by the usual ghetto blaster, but it was turned up even louder than normal. Nick judged, by the number of crushed cans and the general litter, that the 'party' had been in swing for quite some time. Two of the youths in the street had large knives on display and they seemed to be comparing them. Nick didn't feel directly threatened, but he did feel some anxiety as he passed by to turn into his driveway. He gave Tricia a little wave, but she didn't seem to see him. Nobody else appeared to take any notice of him.

He got inside and looked at his watch. It was just after five-thirty. Alyson would be home at about seven o'clock and she'd left him instructions to cook a curry that she had prepared the previous night. He really hoped that the crowd would disperse by the time she got there.

He had a shower and afterwards peered through the net curtain in his and Alyson's bedroom. The party was still going strong, and a number of the attendees were playing a half-hearted game of football with a beer can in the road.

Nick headed down to the kitchen and was there for the next hour, tending to the cooking, listening to 5 Live on the radio and drinking lager. As it got closer to seven o'clock, he became increasingly apprehensive. He went to the front door and peeped out. The party was still in full swing.

Seven o'clock came and went and Alyson hadn't arrived. Nick's anxiety level stepped up further. He wasn't worried about her being late as such - that was quite normal, it was just the anticipation of her inevitable horror at the sight of the gathering, as well as whatever else that its members might have in store for the rest of the evening.

Ten past seven came, and Nick heard the sound of Alyson's car pulling into the driveway. He went out to greet her at the front door, something that he wasn't sure that he'd ever done before. Alyson hurriedly got out of her car and locked it behind her.

"Looks like we are in for a fun evening," she said. But Nick was relieved to see that she didn't appear as stressed as he was anticipating.

"Yeah, well let's hope they don't stay for too long."

"She's like a bloody kid with a gang isn't she. She collects weirdos even more than you do."

"Maybe she's just lonely or something."

"Not surprised. Who in their right mind would want to be friends with that!"

They ate the curry in their kitchen, listening to some music, and sharing a large bottle of Cobra lager. Once they were done, Nick loaded the dishwasher whilst Alyson showered and changed, and by eight o'clock they were both sitting in their living room and painfully aware of the sound of the ghetto blaster across the street, along with increasing volume and frequency of shouted conversation and argument.

"So, are we going to the pub - or staying in?" asked Nick.

They decided on staying in, in order to keep an eye on what might evolve in the street, rather than leave their house, car, and garden unoccupied and exposed. They would need alcohol though. Nick looked for something to watch on TV while Alyson selected a bottle of red wine from her small collection in the kitchen.

They chose an hour-long documentary about Columbian drug crime. Nick turned up the volume, but both were still aware of the sounds from the street outside. Then, about half an hour in, the hubbub went up in volume; there was some kind of extra commotion going on. Nick went to the front door and opened it to see through their porch into the street. Alyson came with him.

Rob Stockdale was out in the street. Tricia's gang members were all watching him, and he was shouting at Tricia. Rob lived with his wife Michelle and their two children, two doors along from Tricia. He was a big muscular man with a big booming voice, and he drank in The Star, where he was known as 'Big Rob'. Nick and Alyson had got to know him and Michelle quite well.

They only caught the very end of what Rob was saying:

"And turn that fucking noise down - NOW!"

The ghetto blaster went off, the hubbub died down, and Rob stormed off into his house, leaving a parting remark of, "You lot are fucking scum, the lot of you!"

Nick and Alyson snuck back into their living room before anyone saw them watching.

"Well, that could be a result," said Nick.

Alyson topped up their glasses and they clinked them together. They got back to the documentary.

When their programme finished at ten o'clock Nick went up to the bedroom to check outside. He was optimistic that the crowd would have dispersed. It hadn't.

They watched *News at Ten*. In the middle of it the gang broke into a chorus of,

"We are the scum,

We are the scum,

Neighbour From Hell

We are, we are, we are the scum!"

"For fuck's sake!" said Alyson, "Fucking nightmare."

She glared into space and then slowly shook her head despairingly. "It's that poor woman Joyce I feel the most sorry for; it must be a living hell being next door to that lot."

She took out another bottle of red wine.

The 'singing' soon faded away. The singers were probably emboldened by alcohol, but not emboldened quite enough to risk incurring the further wrath of Rob Stockdale.

Nick dug out his *Father Ted* DVDs and they watched one episode. The gang was still there.

They watched another one. Still there. Briefly, the youths were all laughing, which was a rare thing.

Fawlty Towers. The wine was finished. They'd better not open another. They switched to lager.

They chatted. It was soon midnight. Still fucking there!

One more *Father Ted*. Then it sounded quiet. Nick stumbled to the front door. Peace.

They went to bed.

"Night," said Alyson. She kissed him on the cheek and turned away.

Nick lay on his back. *They'd better not come back*.

He was wide awake. He went to the toilet at one o'clock. He got a drink of water twenty minutes later. Then Alyson went to the toilet. He looked at the alarm clock yet again at just after two o'clock.

The alarm went off at six o'clock, as always. Nick jumped up and Alyson reached out to switch it to 'snooze'. Nick lay back down on his back; he was wide awake again and already well aware that he was going to have a terrible red wine hangover for the rest of the day. Alyson left for work, and he eventually arose two hours later. He looked bleary eyed over the road to Tricia's house. The word 'scum' had been spray painted in big white letters on the front of the house between the living room window and the large bedroom window above it. Nick thought that Rob might have come back and painted it during the night, but then he realised that the gang, or rather the 'scum' had probably proudly done so themselves. And in doing that Tricia's gang had a name for themselves which was to rapidly catch on. In no time just about everyone, including themselves, would be referring to them far less often as 'yobs', 'youths', 'chavs', 'wankers', or anything else, but instead as simply 'the scum'.

*

Frank's funeral was, understandably, a miserable affair. Nick's mother had flown over to do most of the organising, along with his 'auntie' Barbara, who was a cousin of his mother. His dad hadn't been able to make it due to work commitments and nor had his brother James, and in both cases that disappointed him. His mum was also not able to stay long and hadn't been able to find time in her schedule to make a rare visit to Nick and Alyson's home.

There were fourteen people there at the little chapel that was just around the corner from Frank's house. Bob was there - the neighbour who'd been Frank's close friend for more than fifty years, and he'd looked the most upset. Nick hadn't previously seen Bob for many years, and so it was hard to tell, but he formed the impression that Bob had aged a lot in the two weeks since Frank's passing.

The wake was held in the village hall. Everybody made small talk and ate sandwiches that Nick's mum and Barbara had prepared. The vicar was friendly and genuinely seemed to have known Frank, which surprised Nick. There were some cans of beer available - John Smith's - but Nick didn't drink anything as he was driving. He was very aware that he was still wearing his suit, something that he disliked doing at the best of times. He regretted not bringing a change of clothes in the car.

When it was time for him and Alyson to leave, Nick gave his mum a hug and mumblings were made by all three of them about next likely visits in either direction. Then Nick and Alyson said brief farewells to the remaining attendees and walked outside to their car. The village hall was just a minute's drive from Frank's house, and Nick made the brief detour to pass by. He slowed but didn't stop. He thought about his recent visit, his last cup of tea with Frank, and the old Bond in the garage. He wondered what would become of it.

Alyson saw a tear welling in Nick's eye and gave his hand a squeeze. He changed gear and pulled away. He felt empty; he would never be going there again.

It was around six o'clock when they got home. They got changed and headed straight to The Star. It was almost midnight by the time they left – an hour after the call for last orders. Back at their house they opened a new bottle of Baileys and polished off the whole lot before collapsing into bed at 3 a.m.

*

It was a rare treat for Nick to have time at home alone during the week, but he'd taken a day off as he had holiday to use up before the March end of financial year. He'd got up bright and early, determined to do something constructive with his time. He'd started by sorting out lots of junk that he'd accumulated in his shed, piling it into Alyson's car and then taking it to the dump in Norling. It was now eleven-thirty, and he was on the way back contemplating whether to make himself something to eat or to walk to one of the local pubs for lunch instead. A couple of weeks before, as he turned into his driveway, he had been pleasantly surprised by the sight of a young fox basking in the Spring sunshine, sleeping on his garage roof.

This time though what he saw on the roof was less pleasant, it was Tricia's son Damian with one of his mates. Nick pulled up the car and jumped out.

"What the fuck are you doing? Get off there!"

Neither of the two boys answered him. They both climbed down from the garage in their own time and then walked nonchalantly past him. Damian paused to pick up their football, which was lying in the driveway. He didn't look at Nick at all, whereas the other boy glared at him accusingly.

Nick watched the two of them amble out into the road where they started kicking the football about. He then turned to survey his garage. The garage had been built by the home's previous owner, and the frontage, including the door, consisted of horizontal wooden slats nailed onto a frame. Two of the slats were lying on the floor, and there were lots of football-shaped marks over much of the rest.

Nick turned and headed over to Tricia's house. The two boys carried on kicking their ball about, taking no notice of him. Nick knocked on the door.

Tricia answered the door quite quickly (which surprised him) and was wearing a dirty dressing gown, as often, but didn't this time have a cigarette or a can of lager in either of her hands. She eyed Nick disdainfully.

"Can I help you?" Her tone was confrontational, as it might be if a policeman or some other kind of official was on her doorstep.

Nick explained about the football, the damaged garage door, and the boys being on the roof. He started in a measured way, but his speech turned into more of a rant, and it ended with "and what are they doing here anyway - shouldn't they be at school?"

"He won't go to school - says he doesn't like it," said Tricia. "Yeah, I saw them on the roof; little bastards."

Damian and his friend carried on kicking their ball about. A car drove by, and the driver sounded his horn to

Neighbour From Hell

warn them of his presence. "Fuck off!" and "Wanker," they responded, respectively.

"Why didn't you tell them to get off then?" asked Nick. "They've probably caused hundreds of pounds worth of damage and if they'd fallen through, they could have killed themselves!"

"Might of learned a lesson then," said Damian's mother. "Nuthin' I can do about it, mate. Call the police if you've got a problem. They won't take any notice of me."

And with that Tricia retreated into her house and closed the door.

Nick turned and headed back to his house, not looking at either of the boys as he passed between them. He slammed his front door behind him, and once inside was fortunately out of earshot to hear Damian and his friend laughing their heads off.

Nick was still pissed off by the time that evening came around, and he felt the need for a drink. Alyson didn't want to join him because she had work to do, and so he went to The Star on his own.

He watched patiently as barman Michael diligently poured his pint of Guinness, concentrating on getting just the right height of head on it, and then drawing some kind of squiggle on the top as the final drop flowed from the tap.

Nick gratefully took the pint from him. "How much is that?"

Michael waved him away. "That's alright, mate. I'm getting this one."

"Are you sure?" asked Nick, surprised.

"Yeah, I've come into a bit of money." He smiled a big, satisfied smile.

"Oh - well done. Thanks very much," said Nick, as he lifted the pint of Guinness towards Michael.

"Yeah, the ald casino - won fifteen grand."

"Blimey! … Well, thanks again."

"Cheers, mate - no problem."

Nick turned and made for a small table where Len Phillips was sitting with Darren, one of the men who worked for him. He placed his free pint down on the table and pulled up a chair. Len and Darren were deep in conversation and didn't acknowledge his presence at first. He took a sip of the Guinness. Fifteen grand - that was a nice lump sum out of the blue. He couldn't help but feel a touch of envy for Michael for his windfall even though he was still no doubt much better off financially than Michael. And then he felt bad for the envy, after all the guy had just bought him a pint even though the two of them barely knew each other - he was fairly sure that Michael didn't even know his name.

"How's it going then, Nick?" asked Len, breaking away from his chat with Darren.

"Alright, thanks. And you two?"

Len nodded. "Mustn't grumble."

"Where's the missus, Nick?" chirped in Darren. He always asked the same question when he saw Nick without Alyson.

"She's got work to do. I thought I'd leave her to it."

The three of them took sips from their respective pints.

"He gave me this for free," said Nick.

"Who, Irish Michael? Yes, he won fifteen grand at the casino," said Len. "He's been buying pints for everyone."

"Fair play to him though," said Nick. "I hardly know him really."

"The rate he's going he won't have much of it left before long. He got them in for the whole pub on Friday. That's the problem with his sort - they're not likely ever to have any money and if by chance they do then they don't know how to handle it. It's wasted on them."

Darren had been staring into his pint. "Wouldn't mind finding out what it's like to have that kind of cash to blow though."

Neighbour From Hell

Darren, who was not blessed with great intellect, had only worked sporadically through his life. For the last five years he had been doing labouring for Len as and when Len needed him. His physical stature didn't lend him to the work - he was five feet two and scrawny - but Len liked his non-complaining do-whatever-needs-to-be-done attitude, and the two of them worked well together. Darren was forty-two years old, and he lived with his mum. He'd probably never had five hundred pounds to his name, let alone fifteen thousand.

Len on the other hand did have money. He wasn't what you might call rich, but his building business was doing OK, and fifteen thousand would have been the price of a fairly small job by his standards. He looked over at Darren and could easily have made a disparaging remark at his expense but chose not to. Instead, he trained his sights on 'Irish Michael'.

"Like I said, it'll be wasted on him. The way he's splashing it about he'll have none of it left in a couple of weeks. He's even packed in his job here, the prat. Tomorrow's his last night."

"Blimey," said Nick, "That sounds a bit rash. So, what does he do for his main living?"

"Thieving mostly," said Len, sardonically.

"Really?"

"Yes, he's always in trouble. Been around here for years. He was one of the ones questioned about that stabbing here last year, wasn't he? He didn't do it though. But he was putting the word about that he had done. I think he enjoyed the notoriety. He's full of shit; I wouldn't trust him as far as I could throw him."

Nick tried to look on the bright side. "Ah well, at least he got the drinks in. And maybe the win'll do him some good ... he might turn over a new leaf."

But Len was intent on bringing the tone back down again. "I doubt it. He'll probably end up worse off than if he hadn't won it. Wouldn't surprise me if he took to drinking even more than he does already and ends up dead in a ditch somewhere." And then he chuckled before smiling at Nick in a way that perhaps implied that he did really mean to be quite as miserable as he'd seemed.

Darren had returned to staring at his pint.

"Well - anyway," said Nick, "I had a little run-in with our friends across the street today …"

It was close to midnight by the time Nick left The Star, having drunk five pints of Guinness. He staggered slightly as he made his way home.

He texted Alyson.
QO?

Nick and Alyson had a few private text codes. 'QO?' meant 'fancy a quick one?' to which Alyson's reply tended to be 'as opposed to what?' which usually meant 'yes'. This time though she didn't reply at all as she was deep in alcohol-assisted slumber.

*

Nick's Reliant van had recently celebrated its fortieth birthday and was in very much 'used' condition. It never passed its MoT first time, but Nick liked to do what he could to give it a fighting chance, and this time he had set aside his Saturday morning to give it a look over. He checked the easy stuff - lights, horn, windscreen wipers and so on, and then jacked up the rear of the van to have a look at the back brakes. It usually needed something done to the brakes at MoT and although Nick was no mechanical expert, he could help to eliminate some possible issues.

Rob Stockdale walked by and paused for a chat.

"Alright, Nick - got trouble with the old Plastic Pig?"

"Hi, Rob. No, it's all OK. Just checking it over for the MoT."

"Why do they call them that then, 'Plastic Pig'?"

"Well, it's because they're made of plastic - well, fibreglass - and I think it's because the front looks a bit like a pig's face, particularly on the slightly earlier models than this one."

A black BMW convertible sped past: the driver was holding a mobile phone to his ear.

"That bloke always drives like a twat, especially around this bend," Nick observed.

"Him? Yeah, he *is* a twat - Bradley Mullen, your local drug dealer."

The BMW pulled in and parked half on the footpath in its usual spot about fifty yards along the road.

"Is he really?" said Nick. "He's a bit of a stereotype then with that motor!"

Bradley Mullen, early thirties, blond hair, tall and slim but muscular, crossed the road and walked into a driveway, mobile phone still glued to his ear.

"Yeah, that's his mum and dad's house. He's got properties all over the place ... and women."

"Well, definitely seems like a dick."

"Oh, yeah - he is."

"So, yeah, like I said. I think it's because they're plastic and the 'face' looks a bit like a pig. They're also a bit of a pig to work on, the way the engine's crammed in there, look."

"It's a Reliant Robin, is it?"

"No, it's called a Reliant Supervan III. It's the same as the one on *Only Fools and Horses*; it's the van version of the Reliant Regal car. They're older than the Robin and there were a lot more of them."

"I didn't know that. Well, rather you than me. Anyway, I'm off to the pub. Best of luck, mate."

Rob went to go but then he hesitated and nodded towards the roof of Nick's house. "You've got a loose tile on the corner there, mate."

"Yeah, I know. I need to get someone to look at it."

"I can do that for you."

"Yeah," said Nick, "could you?"

"Yes, sure. Are you around tomorrow?"

"Yeah, should be here all day."

"OK, I'll come over - probably after lunch. Should only take ten minutes."

"Brilliant, thanks … see you tomorrow."

"Right, I really do have to get going to the pub. Cheers, mate."

"Cheers; enjoy."

Nick was really pleased. He'd been meaning to get that roof tile looked at for ages.

With a smile on his face, he returned to the job in hand. He took off both back wheels and then, with a bit of help from a hammer and a large screwdriver, prized off each of the two brake drums. Then he went around to the driver's footwell, removed a little inspection cover in the floor that gave access to the brake master cylinder, and with some effort managed to unscrew its battered, grime-covered and corroded aluminium cap. The fluid level was a bit low, but he left it that way for the time being. He cleaned out the brake drums with a dry cloth, manually squeezed each wheel cylinder in and out a few times to see that they were all moving freely and then re-fitted the brake drums. Next, he did what he could to adjust the brake shoes, both for the handbrake and the main brakes, on both sides such that the two wheels seemed more or less balanced. This was never a particularly satisfactory process, but it might help a bit. Once that was done, he greased the handbrake cable and then dropped the van down from his trolley jack back onto its wheels. Finally, he topped up the brake fluid, replaced the master cylinder cap and inspection cover, and then went around all three wheels pumping the tyres up to the recommended pressure with his foot pump.

It had all taken just over two hours - including two tea breaks - and it had gone rather well. Wiping off his grubby hands with a rag, Nick stood back to admire his handiwork

- not that the van looked any different from how it had when he'd started.

"Awright, mate!"

Nick had been aware that Tricia had been standing in her doorway - adopting her usual smoking pose - for about the last thirty minutes, but now she was beckoning him over. Still wiping his hands on the rag, he wandered over to Tricia's front yard. There was nobody else about.

"Awright, mate. Got your little van sorted then?"

"Yeah, just checking it over for its MoT."

Tricia took a drag on her fag and then blew out the smoke. "I was wonderin' if you'd finished that if you could have a look at this for me."

Tricia was pointing to the Yale lock on the inside of her front door.

"What's wrong with it?" Nick asked.

"It's come all loose, look."

It had indeed. The body of the lock wobbled in Tricia's hand and all three of the screws holding it on were loose.

Nick had a look at it. "What happened to it?"

"My little shit of a son kicked the door in, didn't he?"

Nick looked at the door frame. The lock's slam plate had also come loose and there was a large crack running down much of the length of the door frame.

"What do you reckon?" said Tricia.

Nick nodded. "Yeah, I can have a go, but we'll have to repair the frame as well."

Tricia watched him expectantly. There was an element of pleading in her expression.

"OK, I'll get some tools," he said. "I'll see what I can do."

Five minutes later, Nick returned with his electric drill, a selection of drill bits for wood, a box of Rawlplugs and a tin of wood screws. "It won't be a perfect job," he said. "But it'll do you for now."

"Cheers, mate. Can I get you a cup of tea or something?"

Nick could see into Tricia's living room. The TV was on with the sound down low, the carpet appeared to have food ground into it, the small sofa and one armchair both had arms worn well beyond normal use and were both piled with assorted clothes that appeared to be awaiting cleaning. As well as being able to see the room, he could also smell it.

"No, I'm OK for tea, thanks."

He unscrewed the three screws that held the body of the Yale lock onto the door. Then he cut a Rawlplug into three slithers and placed one slither in each of the screw holes. Next, he returned the lock to its position and tightly screwed the original screws back into place. The lock felt solid. Nick was pleased with his effort.

"Let's try it out," he said. "Have you got a key?"

Tricia shuffled off somewhere into the back of the house. She returned with a pair of keys that she handed to Nick.

The keys were for the Yale lock and a mortice lock, and they were attached to a grubby chunky fob in the shape of a star and adorned with the words 'World's Greatest Mum' in pink. Nick chuckled inside at the irony.

The lock worked fine.

"Now let's have a look at that slam plate."

"The what? What's that?"

"This little metal bit here that the latch slides into."

"Oh, right, yeah. The little bastard buggered that up as well didn't he."

Nick took off the loose plate, selected two slightly longer screws than the ones that he'd taken out of it, and re-affixed it. It fitted nice and firmly. Perfect. All that remained then was the crack in the door frame. He drilled four holes deep into the wood and then put wood screws into them, pulling the separated splints of frame closely together. It was again nice and solid, and he stood back, once more pleased with his handiwork.

"There, that should do it. You might need a new door fame in time, but that'll help for now."

"Little bastard will probably break it again anyway. Then I'll have to get the council round to do it."

"Well, let's hope not. Let's just check it - you stand inside, and I'll open it with the keys."

Nick then opened and closed the door a few times, locked and unlocked it a few times, and pushed on it - although not too hard - while it was closed. It all seemed fine. He handed the keys back to Tricia.

"They're my spares," she said. "You can keep them if you like. It might be good for someone else to have a set for if I get locked out or something - you know, someone trustworthy."

Nick needed to very quickly think of a good answer, something better than just saying 'No'. He couldn't though.

"Er, no. No, I'd better not. Thanks." He handed the keys back to the 'world's best mum'.

Tricia didn't look particularly surprised - or offended. "Well, they are here if you change your mind. Might be useful for when I lock myself out. I sometimes do that when I'm a bit pissed."

Nick smiled politely.

"Well, that's all done then. Hope it's OK."

"Thanks ever so much, mate. Sorry I can't pay you nothing."

"No, no, that's fine," said Nick. "Have a good rest of your day."

"Cheers, mate. Goodbye!"

Nick felt good. He'd had a whole morning of doing blokeish weekend things that had gone really well, and he'd done a good turn for a neighbour - a neighbour that he despised. Plus, having Tricia think of him slightly less as being the enemy could only be a good thing. He went inside to clean up, make himself something to eat, and to tell Alyson about his new-found friend.

*

Colin had selected the bar at Norling F.C., the local non-league football club, as the venue for he and Nick to go for a drink, which was something that they had been meaning to do for a long time. Nick was a regular attendee at Norling games and many years before, Colin had played for the club. They took a cab - also Colin's suggestion, as Nick would have been happy to walk.

Nick hadn't been to the bar at the club many times, and whenever he had done it had been straight after a game when it was really busy. There was no game on tonight, but Nick was surprised by the number of people who were present, and he found that quite a lot of them acknowledged Colin and were keen to shake his hand. Nick began to understand why Colin was keen to bring him here. Colin ostensibly made little of the attention, but as the two of them got to the bar his disposition was as smiley as Nick had ever seen it.

"What are you having?" said Colin, pulling a twenty-pound note from his wallet.

They were served by a blonde woman in her mid-forties whose large breasts drew in Colin's eyes. He tried to flirt with her, and three times called her 'darlin'. He seemed to be hoping that she would recognise him as a former player, but she didn't show any sign of doing so.

Nick and Colin sat down at a small round table, each with a pint of bitter.

"You seem to have quite a few fans here."

The smile was still on Colin's face, much as he tried to suppress it.

"Well, I was here for a few years."

And then, right on cue, a man in his early sixties came up and shook Colin's hand. "Fuck me, Red Card, good to see you, mate."

The man had an Irish accent. Colin looked up at him. It wasn't clear whether Colin recognised him or not.

"Cheers, it's good to be here."

The man addressed Nick. "Could do with the likes of him here now, couldn't we? Bit of passion, unlike some of this lot!" He was gesturing towards the football pitch as he spoke, and he rolled his eyes.

Nick just nodded.

"Anyways, all the best mate - good to see you," said the man, before shaking Colin's hand and then Nick's and then heading on his way.

"Did he call you 'Red Card'?" asked Nick.

"Yeah, it was my nickname, 'Red Card Reid'; I got sent off quite a lot!"

Colin looked quite chuffed with himself.

"Ha-ha! You usually seem pretty laid back to me."

"Not always … and definitely not on the football field!"

"Shame I never saw you play," said Nick. "I started coming here about six or seven years ago soon after we first moved to Norling - when I got the job at Countrysafe."

"I was out of it long before that."

Nick took a sip of his beer. "Do they get good money then at this level?"

Colin shook his head. "I never got more than a hundred quid a week."

"That's not bad on top of the day job, especially for doing something that you'd do for fun," said Nick.

"Some of the other clubs in this league paid five hundred, even more for the best players," was Colin's reply.

"You must have enjoyed it though."

Colin looked as if he was about to say that he didn't, but then he checked himself. "Yeah, it was OK, I suppose, especially when we won. There's some real wankers in football though, especially some of the managers."

It didn't seem as if there was much fun to be had talking anymore about that, so Nick paused to think of what to say next.

Colin filled the void. "Did you see the jugs on that bird at the bar though? I could do something with them, I can tell you!"

That wasn't a topic Nick particularly wanted to explore either, but Colin was enthusiastic, so he went along with it for a bit. Soon they'd finished their first pints, and Colin offered to get them in - with Nick's money - in order to get another good look at the 'jugs' in question.

The pints flowed.

"Did you know that George Orwell used to live over the road from here? He was a teacher in Norling for a while, apparently," said Nick.

Colin gave a little laugh. "George Orwell, eh? There was a man who had it sussed."

Inevitably Tricia and the scum soon became one of their topics of discussion with Colin and Nick both recounting anecdotes of recent unpleasant events and wishing for Tricia's speedy demise.

"I don't know how they can afford all that booze," said Colin. "They're drinking all the bloody time, and I'll bet none of them are working - most of them aren't even old enough to work ... or drink. And God knows what drugs they are doing as well."

"Yeah," said Nick, "there's quite a nice smell of weed in the air a lot of the time; they're getting through a fair bit of that."

"Yeah, and the rest," said Colin.

"We're thinking of going to the council," said Nick. "Alyson phoned up. Apparently, their housing people can look into complaints about council tenants. You have to go in and speak to them."

"Don't you have to be a council tenant though? We get ours through an agency, and you're an owner, aren't you?"

"No, they'll speak to anyone, it seems. Do you fancy coming along if I get a meeting set up?"

As was his custom, Colin paused and took either a drag on a cigarette or a sup of beer before answering something to which he wanted to give a bit of thought. On this occasion, the beer was his only option, and he took a long swig before placing his glass back down on the table.

"Yes, OK - I'll come along with you, as long as I'm not working."

"Cheers. I'll get it sorted out then and I'll let you know."

Colin got pint number five in, and Tricia was pushed to the back of their minds for a while as standard subject areas such as cars, Premier League football, and complaining about their respective partners took over.

During pint number six they were joined by Colin's Irish 'fan', whose name turned out to be Dennis, and two more of his friends. The talk all turned to Norling games of old from Colin's playing days. Colin tried unsuccessfully to put on a façade of finding it all a bit tedious.

Dennis got the last round in at last orders, and half an hour later it was time to go. Colin and Nick stepped out into the night. Nick was keen to walk, but Colin was having none of it and again called up his regular taxi firm.

Nick was again keen to walk, but Colin was having none of it.

"Don't be such a tight-arse!"

"It's not that. I actually like walking — honest!"

"Bugger that!" He called up his regular taxi firm.

The cab arrived in no time and then took them on the ten-minute ride home. Colin had paid on the way out and tried to do so again, but Nick insisted. They got out and shook hands.

"Cheers, mate, must do it again some time," said Colin.

"Yeah, definitely," said Nick.

"Onwards and upwards, mate … onwards and upwards!"

"Yep. Sleep well, Colin; see you soon."

Then Nick made his way quietly into the house and up the stairs. He was feeling good. He'd really enjoyed the evening. He peered into the bedroom. Alyson was asleep. He could have climbed into bed and gone to sleep with a smile on his face. He decided to go back downstairs and round off the evening with a can of lager from the fridge.

*

"Fucking alarm clock! Shit! Fucking work. Gotta stop doing this. Should have gone to bed earlier, I was knackered enough. How many cans are there - five? Probably another one somewhere too. Let's take these through to the kitchen. Fuck there's another three of 'em. Feel SHIT! But going back to bed's even worse than going to work. Definitely have a day off the booze today … or maybe just a couple to help me sleep."

*

Michelle Stockdale, the wife of Rob, was a receptionist at Nick and Alyson's dentist. That's how they had first met her, and then when they moved into their house, they got to know her also as a neighbour, living as she did, a few doors along on the other side of their street. She had also worked briefly behind the bar of The Star, where she was efficient and friendly, but had soon stopped, apparently on Rob's orders, because he didn't like her 'flirting with the customers'. So, Nick had come across Michelle in a variety of circumstances, but as far as he could remember she had never knocked on his and Alyson's front door before. She had a worried expression, although her usual pleasant smile was still in place.

"Hi Michelle, is everything OK?" asked Nick.

She assured him that all was OK and after exchanges of pleasantries came to the purpose of her visit.

"Look, I'm really really sorry to have to ask you this, and feel free to just say 'No' - it's not a problem, but I wondered if you could lend me £20 - just until tomorrow. You see Rob's gone out with his mates straight from work and I've run out of nappies, and I really need some tonight …"

"Yes, of course," said Nick. He took out his wallet from his jeans pocket and handed Michelle a £20 note. He was careful that his body language wasn't patronising.

"Oh, thanks so much. Are you sure?" said Michelle. You see the credit cards are all maxed out and I usually have a bit of cash, but I had to pay the nursery this morning, and you know what Rob's like - if he has any spare money, he'll go and buy a car part or something."

Rob worked as a painter and decorator, although his own house was not in a great state of repair. His pride and joy was his Subaru Impreza and he spent much of his time working on it. He also spent a lot of time 'socialising'. Alyson had commented to Nick before that Michelle and their children, Archie, aged fourteen, and a two-year-old daughter called Kerry, didn't seem to feature highly on his priorities.

"Has he done that tile for you yet?" asked Michelle.

"Er, no not yet."

Michelle rolled her eyes.

"Are you sure that's enough?" said Nick. "I can give you forty if you like."

"Oh, no, no, that's loads thanks," said Michelle. "Thanks ever so much."

"No problem," said Nick.

"I'll bring it back over tomorrow. I'd better go back; I've left Archie in charge."

"No problem," said Nick - again. "And no hurry, it doesn't have to be tomorrow."

Nick was tempted to tell Michelle that she could keep the money. But he knew that she wouldn't do so. He also knew that she would indeed bring it back the next day as she'd said.

"Thanks again!" she called out as she ran back out of the driveway, rushing back to feed her kids, clean the house, take the dog for a walk, and then get herself to bed ready to do all of the same things the next day plus a day's work, which would all be accomplished with a smile on her face.

Nick looked on in admiration.

*

4. Brian

Pauline Fielding, a housing officer from Harlesham and Norling District Council, listened as Nick articulated the problems with Tricia and the effect that she was having on other residents. She nodded from time to time where appropriate and at all times maintained eye contact and a sympathetic facial expression.

Nick had contacted the council to arrange the meeting after Alyson had researched and found out what the processes were for raising issues with council tenants. Colin had come along as well, and several others of their neighbours had expressed support but weren't able to get to the meeting.

Nick went through a speech that he had prepared from his catalogued notes; he presented in a calm and factual manner. Colin listened throughout and nodded in agreement from time to time but didn't say anything.

When Nick had finished, Pauline Fielding picked up a note pad and spent a minute writing on it. She then read those notes out to Nick and Colin. They were a brief but accurate summary of what Nick had said, presented in an even more matter-of-fact style.

"Does that sum up your concerns?" she asked.

"Yep, pretty much," said Nick.

Colin nodded.

At that moment somebody else entered the room. It was a man in his mid sixties who wore a tweed jacket over a shirt and tie.

"Good morning, everyone," he said. He had an authoritative tone and a slightly posh accent.

"Hello Brian," said Pauline Fielding. "Please take a seat."

Pauline Fielding turned back to Nick and Colin. She spoke in her soft sympathetic tone as she complimented them on what they and other residents had done so far in terms of monitoring Tricia's behaviour and of involving the police. She recommended that they keep doing both of those things and, if possible, to do so even more than they had so far.

She then took out some leaflets and placed them on the table that they were all sitting around. She slid a copy each to Nick and Colin. The leaflet was titled "Forming a Tenants' and Residents' Association." She then told them about the history of tenants' and residents' associations in the borough, how many there were and some of their successes, as well as the processes of setting one up and running it. She talked of the rules and guidelines that the council applied to them and about how the police and local councillors were supportive and liked to get involved with them. She talked uninterrupted for a full ten minutes - ten minutes in which Nick's heart sank and sank. He was feeling that this was all that was on her agenda; she wasn't going to be offering them any help in getting rid of Tricia. Eventually she came to the end of her sales pitch. "So, do you think that this might be of interest? I really think that it could work for your community." She was looking at Nick.

Nick composed himself for a few seconds before answering. "Well, yes, it does seem like a positive thing to do. But I'm not sure how it will help deal with the problem that we have with this lady, certainly not in the short-term. Given all the issues that she's causing, both for council tenants and others, is there not something that you can do … move her somewhere else, for example?"

Pauline Fielding explained that the council had a duty to house Tricia and that to move or evict her would not be easy, especially as she had a child. She talked about Social Services and whether they should be contacted regarding concerns around Tricia's parenting.

"They are already involved," chipped in 'Brian.'

"Well, that's probably good to hear," said Pauline.

She then returned to the topic of the tenants' and residents' association, and how the first step to getting one set up would be to call a public meeting. She talked through the process of getting that meeting set up and of how the council could help with it. She also explained the etiquette of such a meeting, who should be there, what might be the agenda, and what the meeting should achieve. It seemed that the main thing that it should achieve was the election of a committee who would then run the association.

As she went on Nick developed a feeling of dread at the near inevitability of him becoming a member of that committee.

Pauline concluded with, "Well, what do you think?" She eyed the three of them in turn.

"I think it would be an excellent idea," offered Brian, "just what the community needs. I'd love to get involved."

"Good," said Pauline Fielding, turning her eyes questioningly to Nick.

Nick cleared his throat. "Well, er, under the circumstances, it sounds as if it might be the best option that we've got."

Then Colin joined in.

"Is that it?" he blurted. "This woman's ruining our lives and all you want to do is have another meeting? Perhaps you people from the council would like to try living opposite her and see how much you like it! See how you get on going six months without any sleep."

After a brief awkward pause, Pauline Fielding began speaking hesitantly in her same calm tone before Brian quickly interjected

"I'm sorry, I didn't catch your name." He was addressing Colin.

"Colin Reid … and who are you, if you don't mind me asking?"

It was a valid question and one that Nick too had been waiting to ask.

"I'm sorry: Brian Hart." He held out his hand and shook first Colin's and then Nick's. "I live on Connaught. We have a problem family of our own ... you've no doubt come across the lovely Billy Grindle."

Nick and Colin both nodded.

"Yes, we all know him," said Nick. "He's one of the regulars over at Tricia's too."

Brian went on to tell Nick and Colin how he used to be a councillor in the area, which explained his apparent familiarity with Pauline. He suggested that the three of them meet one evening for a chat. He said it with an authority that neither felt that they should refuse.

Pauline Fielding then said that she would put things in motion regarding getting the public meeting set up. There would need to be leaflets printed to publicise it once they'd agreed the time and place. She could get them printed but would need volunteers to distribute them.

And then they were leaving. Nick and Colin both shook hands with Brian and then watched as he unchained his old bicycle from a rail outside of the office. Their brief journey home (in Colin's car) was quiet: Colin smoked a cigarette while Nick sat back with mixed feelings. On the positive side, something was happening ... but he was going to be getting involved with a tenants' and residents' association, which was something that he would never have imagined or desired in a million years. And he certainly wasn't desiring it now.

*

Nick got in at eleven o'clock after going for 'a few drinks after work', and Alyson was sitting in the living room watching TV. She had her laptop open, and a glass of red wine in her hand. She turned off the TV and turned towards him.

"Your mum called."

That was unusual, Nick didn't speak to his parents particularly often, but when they called him, it was almost always at the weekend, and this was a Thursday night.

Nick frowned. "Anything wrong?"

Alyson put her glass down on her small side table. "Not particularly. They've got Frank's will."

Nick took off his coat and then sat down on the sofa - the sofa that Alyson wasn't sitting on. He was at the same time relieved that his mother hadn't phoned with bad news, saddened through being reminded of Frank's passing, and annoyed once more by the slightly smug way that Alyson was looking at him.

"I see. Did she tell you what was in it?"

"You got five grand …"

Nick nodded thoughtfully. That was nice of Frank.

"… and you also got his car."

"What, the Bond?" That was a bit of a shock.

"Yep," said Alyson. And she bit her lip before adding, "He left most of his estate to charity."

They both sat in silence for a minute before Nick said, "Well, five grand's a nice little bonus."

"Yes, it's OK. What are you going to do with the old car?"

"I dunno. I'll have to look into it."

"I wonder how much his house is worth. We could have done with a bit of that, instead of it all going to Dogs Trust or whatever."

Nick took a while to answer.

"Well, five grand's five grand. Shall we have a couple of drinks to celebrate our windfall?"

He got up and made for the fridge.

Alyson finished up her glass of wine. "No, you're OK. I need to be up in the morning. I think I'll go to bed."

Nick didn't answer. He got himself a can of Stella and a glass and returned to the sofa. Alyson closed down her laptop and went up the stairs.

Nick poured his Stella into the glass, took a large swig, and then sat back into the sofa. He thought back again to his childhood visits to 'Uncle Frank'. He could picture Frank in his driveway, holding his little dog - a Jack Russell named Kip, and he recalled again that one time that he remembered riding in the Bond. Frank was driving around his local streets and Nick was in the passenger seat; he could feel now the excitement that he'd felt three decades before. He could smell the Bond as it smelled back then. The images were in black and white and flickering like an old movie - an old silent movie. Frank was smiling. It occurred to Nick now that Frank was smiling because Nick was enjoying the ride so much; it hadn't occurred to him at the time, or at any time in between. Nick was smiling now but had a lump in his throat as well. He finished his Stella and got himself another one.

He wondered when Frank had written his will. When, on his last visit, Frank had seemed to half joke about leaving him the Bond, he had presumably already put that in the will - quite possibly many years before. He wiped a tear from his eye and turned his thoughts to the Bond in the present time. He wondered what he was going to do with it. He wouldn't be selling it, that was for sure. It would need some restoration, probably quite a lot. For a start, the white paintwork was in a poor state - should he keep it original and just clean it up, or should he get it re-painted? And if he got it painted, then what colour - keep it white, or change to red / green / blue, or what? But there were bigger concerns than the paint on the - mainly fibreglass - body: the engine would need some work, probably a re-build, and what about rust in the chassis? He thought about how much of the work he could do himself, what it might cost - that five grand would come in handy, and who could help him: Danny next door was an obvious candidate. He started thinking about practical considerations as well, such as how he would get it from Frank's house to his, and where he would store it.

He was soon full of enthusiasm. And by 2 a.m. when he decided to retire to bed after finishing his fourth can of Stella, he couldn't wait to go around to Danny's and get the project started.

*

Alyson was in a good mood. Nick was away in Dublin with some mates for the weekend and she had taken the opportunity to enjoy a bit of 'me time'. She'd got home from work quite early on the Friday night by her standards and relaxed in front of the TV getting through just one large glass of red wine before retiring to bed for an early night. She'd got up soon after eight o'clock the next morning and seeing that it was raining had decided to get a bit of work done. She and Nick had converted their back bedroom into an office for her use, and by nine o'clock she had showered, eaten breakfast, and was settled into it with a prioritised to-do list written out in front of her. Much as her work frustrated her - she felt that she was fighting a losing battle to break through a glass ceiling in a male dominated gung-ho City environment - she still kind of enjoyed the actual work and was happy to put the effort in to do well at it and, maybe subconsciously, to prove to 'them' as well as herself that she was as capable as anybody.

She worked solidly for four hours, only briefly leaving her desk twice to make cups of coffee, and she rattled through that list, getting stuff done that she'd been putting off for weeks. Throughout she had loud music coming through her headphones and hummed along, or even sang, most of the time.

By the time she decided to finish her work work for the day (there would still be non-work work to be done) the rain had long stopped falling and bright sunshine had taken its place. She went to the kitchen, made herself a small lunch, and then took it outside to eat on the patio in the sunshine, still playing music and singing along.

Her next task was a trip to Waitrose to do the weekly food shop. She was still humming happily to herself as she exited her front door and locked it behind her.

And then she turned and saw her car.

Thick swirls of loose mud were smeared over the windscreen. The same applied to the bonnet but there were lumps of mud as well. There were also big clumps of mud on the roof, and dollops on the ground all around the car that appeared to have fallen off it. The driveway itself was smudged with muddy footprints. Alyson looked out into the street and to the houses around her. There was nobody about.

NICK, THOSE FUCKING CHAVS HAVE WRECKED MY CAR - I'M GOING TO FUCKING KILL THEM. I'M CALLING THE POLICE

*

5. Joyce

Whenever Nick made that last turn of his journey home from work, his heart was slightly in his mouth. He would either be dismayed to see that there was a Tricia gathering happening or relieved that there was not. This time it was the latter, and he smiled at the sight of a clean empty street with the only person in sight being Tricia herself, occupying her usual doorway slot. He quickened his pace for the last minute of his walk and was just turning into his driveway when Tricia beckoned him over.

"Awright, mate!"

Nick reluctantly turned towards her. "Hi!"

"Nice, innit?" She nodded towards a pristine new larch lap fence bordering her property.

Nick wandered over the road. The fence was indeed very neat and as he got closer his nostrils were filled with the pleasant aroma of fresh wood preservative.

"Yes, very nice," he said.

"They done it today. And the concrete, look."

She pointed to the centre of her small 'garden' where the rose bed had been. There was now instead a circular patch of drying concrete, and Nick took in a second not unpleasant smell.

"They was all treading in the mud, see, and tramping it all around my house. So, I got the council out."

"Yeah," said Nick, "They've made a nice job of it. Did they do the door frame as well?"

"Nah, I forgot about that. I'll get them out again sometime. Let's hope the little shits don't bust up the fence again."

"Yes, er, hopefully not. Well, I'd better go, my tea's going cold."

"Yeah, don't you keep 'er waiting. See ya, mate."

Nick opened the door and was greeted with, "I see you were chatting to your friend over there."

"Yes, she's got a new fence - seems quite proud of it."

"I know, the council were there half the bloody day doing stuff for her."

"Yeah, they've filled in the rose bed with concrete too."

"Nice that they've got plenty of money to spend on her, but they can't send the police round when my car gets vandalised."

Alyson had reported her car incident to the police, and it had been 'noted'. She was hoping for more.

"It's not really the same thing," said Nick.

That was probably a mistake.

Alyson reddened and snapped back, "It's still yours and my bloody taxes funding that little shit of hers to smash things up, but we get fuck all help in return. Did you ask her about my car?"

"No, I didn't. I didn't think that there was much point."

"See, there you go again. You've got no balls, that's your problem."

Nick tried a bit of levity. "Well at least one thing's clear now: I was never sure whether to call her front a 'garden' or a 'yard', but now that it's all concrete it's definitely a yard."

Alyson's glare told him that he wasn't helping the situation.

"Your tea's in the oven," she said wearily. "You might want to do some gravy with it."

"Thanks."

"Don't mention it." And then she disappeared upstairs and slammed the bedroom door behind her.

*

Nick and Alyson filed apprehensively into their local church hall for the public meeting that would launch the tenants' and residents' association. It was the first time that either of them had been inside the building. There had been an awkward moment a couple of weeks before when Brian Hart was explaining to Nick where it was. "You know, it's the place where you go to vote," Brian had said. Nick had struggled to respond without it being clear to former councillor Brian that he hadn't actually voted since moving into the area.

It was surprisingly busy in the hall and very noisy. Nick and Alyson took seats near the back. There was a printed A5 sheet of paper placed on each seat and, like most others in the room, Nick picked up his copy and had a look at it. It was entitled 'Harlesham and Norling District Council Tenants and Residents Association Launch Meeting' and contained the evening's agenda.

INTRODUCTION - Harlesham Council Housing Officer, Mrs P Fielding

Welcome - Cllr. Gerry Caldwell

Questions to the panel:

(Pauline Fieling - Housing Officer,
Cllr. Gerry Caldwell - District Councillor,
Ms. Rashini Kumar - Tenants and Residents Assoc. co-ordinator;
Chief Inspector David Ball - Metropolitan Police Service (Harlesham)

Election of committee

ANY OTHER BUSINESS

Nick got over the typos and appallingly inconsistent formatting and learned two things: (i) Pauline Fielding was married, and (ii) the police were taking a real interest if they were being represented by such a senior officer. But what jumped out at him were the three words 'Election of committee'. His imminent probable membership of that committee brought him out in what would have been a cold sweat if it hadn't been such a warm evening. *Aaargh! What was I thinking!* He looked around the room. Alyson was sitting to his left, after her there was an empty seat, and beyond that the makeshift passageway along which more people were shuffling to get to the final seats at the back. There were windows high up in the wall of the church hall through which rays of the June evening's low sun shone, making it difficult for Nick to see the faces of the new arrivals. He turned his head back towards the front of the room. A gaggle of people stood talking, including in their number, Pauline Fielding, Brian Hart, a policeman in uniform, and a few others that he guessed must have included Rashini Kumar and Gerry Caldwell. Between him and them were six rows of ten seats which were mostly occupied, some by people that he recognised, but none by anyone that he knew. In the seven seats to the right of him in his row were just three people - a man in his mid-sixties and a man and woman each aged about forty. The three of them were talking to one another and they all looked very serious. There were just two more rows behind, and Nick turned to observe who was sitting in them. The rows were all-but full, mainly again of people that he didn't know, but one face did catch his eye - sitting right behind Alyson was Tricia! He nodded at her, and she gave a half-hearted smile back. He could see nobody else back there that he recognised. He'd been hoping that Colin would have been able to offer him some moral support, but he'd had to go to work.

The meeting had been due to start at 7:45, but it was just after eight o'clock when Pauline Fielding eventually turned to the assembled throng and, with some difficulty, got them to be quiet. She thanked everybody for coming and then gave an overview, much of which Nick wasn't able to hear due to a combination of Pauline not speaking very loudly, and people behind and around him mumbling to one another, mainly moaning that they couldn't hear. Annoying though it all was, it didn't actually matter to Nick, as Pauline's speech was the same one that she'd given to him and Colin at the council offices three weeks earlier. She ended by reminding everyone of the agenda and then introducing the other people who were at the front of the hall with her: Gerry Caldwell, Rashini Kumar, and … community police officer, Sergeant Alan Rose. She then apologised on behalf of the announced Chief Inspector Ball who apparently had to attend 'another engagement.' *Maybe the police weren't taking it quite so seriously after all.*

Finally, Pauline Fielding handed over to Councillor Gerry Caldwell.

He was in his early sixties, quite portly, and he wore a shirt and tie, dark blue blazer, and grey woollen trousers, all immaculately presented, and all very 1970s. He welcomed everyone again and spoke of the importance of tenants' and residents' associations and of his absolute belief in them. He spoke with much more authority than Pauline Fielding: he was louder, he projected his voice better, and he commanded the room's attention - the mumbling from the back rows all-but ceased. But Nick was very quickly bored. Gerry Caldwell's words were the usual bland positive politicians' guff. And it got worse when he alluded to his two fellow councillors in the ward who would have apparently 'loved' to have been there that evening but had other pressing Council business to attend to. He slipped in that the three of them were all Conservatives and went on to talk of how supportive his party was of communities such as this one. They would, he contended, fight on behalf of the community, putting in place the right policies to make this part of Norling a better place to live for everyone. Mutterings of discontent were heard at that point; Gerry Caldwell's party probably weren't as popular on the estate as they were in the ward as whole that had voted them in. And mutterings continued as he went on, and they did so because again, in typical politician style, he really did go on … and on - way beyond the point where anybody was taking any notice.

Nick was actually considering the possibility of giving up on the whole thing and running to the pub when eventually Cllr. Caldwell handed back the reins to Pauline Fielding. It was time for the questions to the panel session.

"Who'd like to ask the first question?" pleaded Pauline Fielding.

For a brief moment the hubbub came to a stop as members of the throng looked at one another and nobody put their hand up.

But then someone broke the silence … loudly.

"What I wanna know is what are you lot gonna do about all these bloody kids knocking on my door at half past ten at night and running off!"

The man was two rows in front of Nick and to his right. He was in his mid-sixties, thin, moustachioed, ruddy faced, and angry. He glared at the seated panel, looking for answers.

Pauline Fielding turned to Sergeant Rose and asked whether he "would like to take this one."

Sergeant Alan Rose nodded and slowly stood up. He asked the man his name - it was Derek Tindall - and he asked a bit more about the incidents that he was referring to.

It turned out that that Derek's door had been knocked on in the evening "two or three times" but that he hadn't reported it to the police because "you never do anything anyway". That comment prompted much murmured agreement in the room.

Sergeant Rose responded in a practised measured tone, and he diplomatically explained that the police could only respond to problems if people reported them. He

Neighbour From Hell

recommended that in future Mr Tindall should make notes of the details of such incidents - time and date in particular - report them to the police, record any given incident numbers, and pick up with him personally at a future tenants' and residents' group meeting if he hadn't had satisfaction.

Derek Tindall nodded and sat back, but he didn't look particularly satisfied with the response.

Suddenly another man piped up.

"It was the same with my van - ripped the whole bloody door mirror off, the little bastards."

He was in his late fifties, quite fat, with jet black hair ... and ruddy faced.

Nick looked around the room. The sun had dropped now, and he could see faces more clearly. It was apparent that a large portion of the audience was made up of ageing ruddy-faced angry men like this man and Derek Tindall.

Sergeant Rose again took the question. It transpired that the incident with the man's van had happened two years before, and that he knew who had done it - the son of a neighbour with whom he had had a previous argument. He hadn't reported it to the police because there was "no point". Sergeant Rose gave him the same advice that he had given to Derek Tindall.

The older man in the group to Nick's right looked to be itching to say something.

Murmurings got ever louder. A woman near to the front, and unseen to Nick, shouted out.

"Well, I reported it when they threw eggs all over my house and the police never bothered to show up!"

The hubbub cranked up a further level. The man to Nick's right seized his moment.

"I bet you would have shown up if their name had been Patel, wouldn't you!"

The man hadn't been as ruddy faced as the others up to that point, but as he spat out his words, he turned the colour of a tomato.

And then it became a free-for-all, with random rantings coming from around the hall - mostly from the angry old men. They moaned about the hedge not being cut in the park, they moaned about parked cars, they moaned about moving cars, they moaned about dog shit …

Nick wanted to tear his hair out. The whole point of all this was to get rid of Tricia!

And then Tricia had her say.

"There's too much crime around here, that's what the problem is, and no-one's doing nuffink about it!"

The room went quiet. Everyone turned towards Tricia. "That's right," said someone, "it used to be nice around here, but it's not anymore."

Nick had to say something. He addressed the panel. "To be honest, it was fine here until nine months ago, when it suddenly became a nightmare for a lot of us living on Hain Avenue."

But no-one was listening. By now everyone had an opinion that they wanted to share with the person next to them. The hubbub became an explosion of opinions. Nick looked at Alyson who shrugged and shook her head. He caught a snippet of Tricia's voice: "The snobs want to kick me out of my own home. It's disgusting; I haven't done nothing."

Pauline Fielding called order, and the hubbub did die down.

Then somebody completely new joined in. She was a few rows ahead of Nick and all that he could see of her was her head of long straggly greying dark hair. She sounded around fifty years of age.

"I think that we all need to remember that these young people are all human beings. Demonising them as 'yobs' is not at all helpful. We should think about what effect that sort of stereotyping might have on an impressionable young mind. What does it do to their mental health?"

The hall exploded with that grenade, and it seemed that just about everyone in the room felt the need to shout their view at the woman, or the panel, or the person sitting next to them. Nick leaned forward with his head in his hands. Alyson looked at him sympathetically and put her hand on his knee. The chaos continued all around. Pauline Fielding tried to call order again, but her pleas now had no effect at all. Sergeant Rose looked on despairingly; Rashini Kumar looked like a frightened rabbit.

Gerry Caldwell came to the rescue. "Order! Order! Please, ladies and gentlemen …"

And to the surprise of most people - at least certainly of Nick - it worked. The melee quickly died down to merely a scattering of murmurs. The wannabee Speaker of the House - even he seemed surprised at least at the speed of the response to his command - seized the opportunity to hold court again.

First of all, he thanked everyone for their contribution to the 'lively debate' in which, he suggested, 'many interesting points' had been made, demonstrating exactly why a tenants' and residents' association was exactly what the community needed. Nick began to fear the prospect of another rambling speech, but Gerry Caldwell was astute enough to realise that it wouldn't be in his interest to bore his audience still further. Instead, he quite soon uttered possibly the only words that could make Nick feel even worse.

"So, now we come to the part where we need some of you to volunteer."

At that point Pauline Fielding nervously resumed her duties and explained the nomination procedure. The committee would need to be made up of at least three people, although there normally tended to be between six and the maximum of ten. One of the members had to be the chairperson and another the vice chairperson. Each candidate had to be nominated by somebody, which could be themselves, and seconded by someone else. Then they could be voted in by a show of hands; at least three people other than the candidate themselves had to raise their hands in order for the candidate to be voted in. If there was more than one nominee for the chairperson or vice chairperson roles then each candidate would have an opportunity to briefly speak to the room to put their case, and then there would be a vote by a show of hands. If there were too many volunteers for the committee then there would be similar voting for those roles too, but Pauline Fielding said that it rarely, if ever, happened that there were too many volunteers. She described the procedure twice and then asked if there were any questions. There weren't any.

"OK, well if we are all ready to begin, who would like to put themselves forward for the role of chairperson."

Nick and Brian Hart had discussed this. Brian would nominate himself for chairman and Nick would second him, and then Nick would nominate himself for vice chairman and Brian would return the 'favour'.

Brian, who was sitting in the front row, put up his hand. "I'd like to put myself forward, please."

Pauline smiled and nodded. She looked around the room for any other volunteers, but there weren't any. "Thank you, Brian," she said. "Would anyone like to second Brian's nomination?"

Nick put his hand up. "I will."

"Thank you, Nick. Sorry ... remind me of your surname, please."

"It's 'Hale' - H-A-L-E."

Pauline turned to Rashini Kumar, who was taking the minutes. "Nicholas Hale, please, Rashini."

She turned back to the room. "And a show of hands for Brian, please."

About six people put up their hands.

"Thank you," said Pauline. "So, then - do we have any volunteers for deputy?"

Nick obligingly raised his hand at the same time rather hoping that someone else might challenge him for the position.

Neighbour From Hell

"Seconded!" yelled Brian Hart.

Pauline Fielding gave a polite smile. "And another show of hands, please."

Five people raised their hands, including Alyson. Nick didn't look around to see what Tricia's reaction was.

"Thank you, Brian and Nick," said Pauline. "We'll get your addresses afterwards if you wouldn't mind. Just come and see us at the front. The same applies to everyone who gets appointed to the committee, please."

Murmuring had returned as members of the audience quickly bored of proceedings. Nick picked up the words 'fucking stitch-up' from the older man to his right.

"So, who would like to join Brian and Nick on the committee?" Pauline Fielding asked.

There was a ten-second silence before the 'fucking stitch-up' man bellowed, "I would!" He looked angrier than ever. He was seconded by the younger woman with him, and voted for by the man with them, the man whose van had been vandalised two years earlier, and about six others.

"Thank you, sir. And your name, please?"

"Bert Walsh." He still looked as if he was seething.

Derek Tindall turned to Bert Walsh and gave him a thumbs-up.

"Go-on," said Bert Walsh. "You do it too."

Turning back to the front Derek Tindall called out, "Yeah, I'll give it a go", half waving his hand in the air and wearing a faux-resigned expression, as if his public had talked him into it.

"Thank you, Mr Tindall," said Pauline Fielding.

Bert Walsh seconded him, and a flurry of angry old men approved.

The next volunteer was a slim middle-aged black man whom Nick hadn't noticed up to that point as he was sitting near the front and hadn't said anything. The murmuring heightened again when he raised his hand and for a brief moment it appeared that nobody was going to second him. But then Brian Hart did the honours, and then four people raised their hands, including Nick and Alyson. His name was Aki Oduro.

Pauline Fielding's request for the next volunteer was met with no response.

"Surely someone else would like to volunteer?" she pleaded.

There was some discussion among the three people to Nick's right, and then the woman in that group put up her hand. She was seconded by Bert Walsh, and then voted for by the other man with her and three others.

"And your name, please, madam?"

"Susan Henwood," the woman said, timidly.

And that was it, there were no more volunteers. Pauline Fielding gave a short summing up, in which she explained that the committee would meet soon and that at their first meeting they would need to agree such things as a name for the association, ways of working, and frequency of future meetings - both for the committee and for all, and the assignment of the remaining two committee roles of secretary and treasurer. In any case though they had an obligation to organise a public meeting at least four times per year. Then she thanked everyone for coming, reminded the committee members that they needed to give her their addresses, and then said that she looked forward to seeing everyone again at a future meeting.

The throng began to make their way noisily towards the exit. Nick made his way towards the front and then had a thought. Cupping his hands in front of his mouth he called out, "We are off to The Star for a drink now if anyone would like to join us."

The committee members assembled around a table, where Pauline bustled around handing out pieces of paper for them each to write down their names and addresses. Nick nodded at the others who similarly acknowledged him back.

"I'd love to join you for a drink but need to be getting back, I'm afraid," said Brian Hart, "Maybe next time."

"No problem," said Nick, "… anyone else?"

Bert Walsh and Susan Henwood shook their heads, Aki Oduro was busy chatting to Pauline Fielding, and Derek Tindall seemed to have already gone.

Nick filled in his name and address on the piece of paper and placed it down on the table. He looked around the room. The 'officials' had all left, and only stragglers were still shuffling their way outside, still muttering to one another. There was nobody remaining that he knew.

"Might as well go," he said to Alyson.

She nodded in agreement.

They left the hall and turned right, in the direction of The Star, which was a five-minute walk away. There was nobody else from the meeting heading the same way; they had all either gone to the small car park or turned left, back in the direction of the estate where they all lived.

"Well, that's that done." said Alyson.

"Yup," replied Nick, pensively.

"One or two chavs on the committee," said Alyson.

"Yes, looks that way. At least Tricia didn't join! Did you see that Bert and Susan? I reckon they are father and daughter."

"Ha! Perhaps I should have joined."

"Yeah, maybe you should have … although you would probably end up killing someone."

Alyson thought about that for a moment. "Yes, you're probably right."

She put her arm through Nick's and walked the rest of the way without speaking, both looking forward to a drink.

The next day Alyson was hurrying between shops in Harlesham's mall when the sight of a distinctive shock of big red hair alerted her to the approach of Joyce, the old lady who lived next door to Tricia, who was making her way in the other direction. Alyson held up her hand in a greeting and mouthed 'Hello' as she normally would, but Joyce indicated that she wanted to speak.

"Hello. How are you?" said Alyson.

Joyce leaned on her walking stick and took a moment to catch her breath.

"I'm moving out tomorrow."

Alyson was shocked.

"Really? But you've been there about forty years, haven't you?"

"Forty-two years it'll be in August. August 14th, we moved in."

Joyce went on to explain how she couldn't cope with being a neighbour to Tricia anymore and that she was moving to a flat in Yiewsley - "I'll be closer to my sister." The council had been helpful in finding the flat for her and "anyway, I don't need to have a big house like that all to myself, it's more suitable for a family to live in."

The two women spoke for three or four minutes, the longest conversation they had ever had. Joyce had tears welling in her eyes throughout and by the end Alyson had a lump in her throat.

Alyson didn't believe the needing to be near her sister or feeling that she shouldn't have a house like that all to herself any more than Joyce did. She left feeling guilty that she hadn't paid Joyce more attention before, and angry that Joyce was having to leave a home where she could no longer be happy.

Alyson didn't do any more shopping but hurried back to her car, wiping tears from her cheeks as she did so.

*

A week after saying that he would do so 'first thing tomorrow', Nick's neighbour Danny came to assess his legacy from his uncle Frank, the 1967 Bond Equipe. Since having it delivered and parked up on the front lawn a few weeks before, Nick had washed the Bond, photographed it, and then started worrying about how much it might cost to get it sorted and back on the road. Danny took his time looking all around it, doing a fair bit of tutting as he did so.

"What did you say it was again?" asked the professional car restorer.

"A Bond," said Nick. "It's mostly Triumph based."

"Ah, yeah - I thought it looked a bit like the old Triumph Heralds."

"That's right. It's a sort of sport version really. The main difference is the fiberglass body. They were hand built at a factory in Preston."

Danny carried on looking around it, rubbing his hand over the paint surface, alternately nodding or shaking his head … and doing plenty more tutting. He came to a scripted chrome badge on the boot lid that spelled 'Equipe'.

"That's what it's called is it, a Bond Equipe?" (He pronounced it 'Ekwipp'.)

"Yes, but it's pronounced 'Eckeep' - it's the French word for 'Team'," Nick explained.

"French? It's not French though, is it?"

Nick hesitated. "No, they were made in Preston."

Danny got down on the grass and had a look underneath. He did so from the left side, and then the right side, then the front, and then the rear. Next, he stood up behind the car and rubbed his hand across the paint surface again, this time on the boot lid. He pointed out the crazing in the old paint.

"Looks like it's been hand painted at some time," he suggested.

Nick knew that it hadn't, it was the original paint and it had crazed because all fiberglass cars do in time. But he chose not to disagree.

Finally, Danny had finished his inspection. He stood facing Nick, looking thoughtful.

"Did you want to do a full restoration or an oily rag?"

Nick had given thought to this, the pros and cons of an 'oily rag' restoration, in which the car would be made to function properly but would still look rough and original - or 'patinaed', or a full restoration, returning it to near new condition. He talked about those pros and cons with Danny. The oily rag would of course be cheaper, and in a way, it could be more interesting (he was unsure whether he really did believe this or whether he was just trying to convince himself in order to save money), whereas a full restoration would cost a lot more, but the end result would look nice and be more valuable. He had decided that he wanted to change the colour of the car though from white to dark blue, so an oily rag wouldn't be enough.

"Could we do something in between - get it running and MoT'd and tidied up a bit, plus the respray, but not showroom? I want to be able to use it. What sort of money do you think that would be?"

After much frowning and sucking of teeth, Danny did a summing up.

"OK, so we are going to get the engine going, give it a full service, do the welding on the chassis, overhaul the brakes, paint it, and MoT … plus whatever other bits of tidying up we come across. But mostly leave it original other than the paintwork?"

"Yeah, that's about it. What sort of money are we talking?"

This was the moment.

Danny extended the drama with twenty seconds of nodding thoughtfully before finally delivering his verdict.

"Cash price, you are looking at two grand. Maybe a bit more for parts depending on what we need for the brakes and that."

It was Nick's turn to nod thoughtfully for a few moments before he responded. He was very pleased with that quote but didn't want to show it.

"Yeah, I can go with that. Yep, let's do it!" And he held out his hand to shake on the deal.

Danny said that it would take three weeks and he wanted half the cash in advance and the rest on completion. Nick got the thousand pounds in cash from his house and handed it over straight away, which surprised Danny.

Danny said that he would get his mate who had a flatbed recovery truck to collect the Bond the next day to take it to his workshop.

Nick waved Danny goodbye and went back into his house. Danny was local - not only did he live next door, but his workshop was just a few miles away - and he was cheap. But even more importantly, him restoring the Bond enabled Nick to get involved with the work himself as well. Nick felt some unease, knowing how Danny was unreliable and full of shit, but he was excited to be taking such a positive step towards progressing with the project.

He went into the kitchen and made himself a celebratory cup of tea.

*

Alyson enjoyed the evenings when she had the house to herself and the freedom to do whatever she wanted or to do nothing at all if she so chose. She might choose to do a bit of work, but only if she was in the mood to do so; there was something less work-like about doing work in the evening when there were no deadlines to be met and when nobody was going to be sending an email and expecting a reply. Sometimes she might do a bit of cooking - but fun cooking, such as baking a cake. She might write a letter - that was something that Alyson liked to do, write an old-fashioned long letter (albeit by email) to one of her friends, usually Sarah, and these evenings on her own were perfect occasions to do that. All of these activities were accompanied with music and usually two or three glasses of red wine.

Yes, Alyson really enjoyed these evenings on her own - or at least she used to.

Nowadays she didn't enjoy being in on her own at all. Since Tricia's arrival, she spent these evenings feeling ill-at-ease. If a crowd was gathered over the road, then she hated it, feeling their presence and sensing their menace even when she couldn't see them. And when they weren't there, she was waiting for them to materialise, and that tension of not knowing was possibly even worse than the knowing that they were there. She couldn't win.

These evenings she struggled to focus on doing anything, even her supposedly relaxing activities. Instead, she would sit down and watch any old shit on TV with the volume turned up loud to disguise any hubbub from over the road.

They were there tonight. The ghetto blaster wasn't there, so it was just the odd surge of voices or shouted obscenity that she got to hear over the TV. It wouldn't have been too intrusive if she hadn't been tuned into it, and it wouldn't have bothered her if it hadn't been a regular occurrence - a one-off party wouldn't be such an issue. At one time some voices came into her garden, two of the yobs chasing each other around and having a mock fight. Alyson heard them but didn't look out through the curtains. She got through her usual few glasses of wine quite early on. Then she switched to vodka which she drank far too quickly. She would never tell Nick that it concerned her so much; she wouldn't tell anyone … well, maybe Sarah. She was angry with herself for being weak, but she was more angry with the situation that made her feel that way.

Alyson eventually went to bed when the scum dispersed at 11:30. She needed to be up for work at 6 a.m. She lay there wide awake until she heard Nick's key in the front door. Then she immediately turned on her side and pretended to be asleep. By the time that Nick climbed into bed just minutes later she didn't need to pretend, she really was deep in a slumber that would last until her hungover rude awakening, five hours later.

*

6. Charlene

A week after Joyce had moved out, Nick returned from work to see that the doors and windows of her house were open and there was a pushchair outside.

"I have an idea," he told Alyson. "You know how when we moved in Danny and Brenda came round and gave us a 'welcome' card and a bottle of wine? Well, I wondered about doing something similar with whoever's in there - get them onside."

"You haven't just come up with that - you've been thinking about it, haven't you?"

"Well, yes. It might be good for us and, you know, it's a nice thing to do when someone's just moved in."

"OK, if you want. *You* can take it over though."

So, later in the evening Nick walked to the local shop and got two bottles of cheap wine, one red, one white, a box of chocolates, and a four-pack of Stella. When he returned, Damian was hanging around Tricia's yard with two other boys, so Nick went into his house and peered out of the curtains from time to time until there was nobody about. Then he nervously crossed the road. The front door of the house was now closed, and the pushchair had been taken inside. He got to the door and after pausing for a couple of seconds to question whether he really wanted to do this, rang the doorbell. There was no obvious doorbell sound. He could hear movement and muffled voices inside. He waited maybe thirty seconds, again considered turning and going home, but then knocked softly on the door. If nobody answered this time, then he would be off. The door flew open.

Before Nick stood an attractive woman in her mid-twenties. She was tall and slim and had long reddish-brown streaked hair, tied into a ponytail. She wore a low-cut light flowery summer dress, large circular earrings, a deep tan, and an impatient frown. She was chewing gum.

"Er, hello," said Nick. "I, er, I live over the road, and I thought I'd come over and say 'Hello'."

"What is it, Shar?" came a man's voice from behind her. *He* sounded even more impatient than *she* looked. The man then appeared at the door and glared at Nick questioningly.

"Er, hello. My name's Nick, and I er, live just over the road. I thought I'd come and say 'Hello'."

The woman kept on chewing. She and the man both looked confused.

Nick continued. "I brought these - a sort of 'welcome to the neighbourhood' present."

Nick held out his carrier bag of goodies, and the man took it and looked inside.

"Ah, nice one mate. Look, Shar - chocolates and booze. Sorry mate, what did you say your name was again?"

"Er, Nick." He held his out hand.

The man at first looked unsure as to what to do but then gave Nick's hand a brief shake.

"I'm Kevin and this is Charlene."

Charlene stopped chewing and parked her gum.

Nick turned and offered his hand and Charlene took it in her own soft dainty hand, looking a little embarrassed. But she smiled and her pretty, deep green eyes made his heart skip a beat.

"Fanks mate," she said.

And then followed an awkward silence which was broken by Kevin.

"So, where do you live then - over there?"

"Yeah, that one with the Golf in the drive. So, where were you b…"

"Waaaaaaah!" said a young voice from inside the house.

Charlene cursed and disappeared inside.

"Waaaaaaaaaaah!"

"What's wrong with you now?!" Charlene demanded, although she did so fairly quietly.

Kevin and Nick looked at each other both struggling to know what to say next.

"Waaaaaaaah!" came the young voice again, but louder.

"Waaaaaaaah!" came a different young voice from the same direction.

"Shit! Sounds like they're kicking off," said Kevin. "I'd better, er…"

"Yeah, er, right. Well, I'll leave you to it."

"Cheers, mate."

The door shut behind Nick and as he turned away, he heard Kevin ask the same "what's wrong with you?" question but with rather more urgency than Charlene had.

Nick trotted back.

"How'd it go?" asked Alyson.

"OK."

"Just, OK?"

"Yeah, it was fine. Their kids kicked off though and they had to go. So, I didn't get to speak to them for long."

"Doesn't sound too promising. How many kids are there?"

"Dunno; I didn't see them."

"Hmmmm, but the parents were friendly enough?"

"Yeah, they seemed fine. Kevin and Charlene, they're called." He didn't mention anything about low-cut dresses or deep green eyes.

"Well, they can't be as bad as Tricia. Let's just see how it goes."

"Yep, let's see how it goes."

*

Nick wasn't listening to what Jason was saying, but he did wonder what the book was that he had in his hand. He wouldn't ask though as it was probably related to the subject about which Jason was subjecting him to a monologue: some kind of company coaching programme for people seeking promotion. Jason's keenness could be wearing at times, but Nick found it much preferable to the negativity of so many people in the workplace. That was probably His number one pet hate in the corporate world – miserable whingers. He thought about that for a moment – tolerating the lesser of two evils was about as good as it got. *There must be something more!* He suddenly sensed that Jason had noticed that he wasn't paying attention and so he focussed and looked him in the eye.

Jason continued, "… Grade three, Nick - that's proper senior management. Decent bonuses, company Five Series - why wouldn't you?"

They were in Nick's 'pod' - a sort of doorless mini office a bit like a cubicle in a Dilbert cartoon, and it was early. Nick had just settled in and turned on his computer ready to catch up on emails and ease himself gently into his working day, when Jason had turned up full of over-enthusiasm for this scheme that he had become aware of the previous afternoon. It was called 'Propel', which was enough to put off Nick on its own.

Jason was still going on. "It's for high-flyers only, and it's specifically designed for progression from grade four to grade three. It takes about eighteen months, and you are all-but-guaranteed a three at the end of it. I've got a slot in Tony's diary later on; we're having a chat about getting me on it. You wanna get him to put it in your objectives."

And right on cue, Tony Clarke appeared.

"What are you two up to now? Do you spend all of your time in here, Jason?!"

"Well, you know - just giving Nick here a bit of advice."

"You're like a couple of little old ladies you two. Do you go home together at the end of the night as well?"

"Not likely", chirped Jason, spotting an opportunity. "He lives in a bloody council house!"

"Really?" asked Tony, turning towards Nick.

"Yeah, well ex-council …"

"Bloody hell, Nick - what's next, a sixty-inch telly and all-inclusive package holidays in Benidorm?!"

Jason cringed a little as he thought of his own sixty-inch TV and upcoming all-inclusive package holiday, albeit in Mexico.

Tony went on, "And what about those cringy slogans on the wall, have you got one of them? Nothing says 'chav' like a piece of inspirational wall art!"

"I can assure you that I don't have anything like that," answered Nick.

Jason cringed again thinking of the lavish '*Live, Love, Laugh*' script with which he and his girlfriend had recently adorned their living room wall.

Tony turned back to Jason. "You put something in my diary for later?"

Jason got out of his seat looking slightly flustered. "Yes, eleven o'clock - is that OK?"

"Do you want to do it now instead? I've got ten minutes."

"Er, yes, sure." Jason was ushering Tony out of Nick's pod as he spoke.

Nick caught sight of the title of the book that Jason was holding. It was *How to Win Friends and Influence People* by Dale Carnegie. No doubt he was planning to brush up on his favourite passages before his meeting with the boss. He wouldn't be getting the chance to do that now though.

The two of them walked away.

"What was it - 'Prolapse', or something like that?"

"No, 'Propel'."

"What's that?"

Nick sat back in his chair. He would be annoyed if Jason was promoted ahead of him, but he wasn't going to be begging to be asked. Or maybe this coaching thing could be interesting? He logged on to his email. There were eighteen messages but all of them looked work related - nothing social. He got up and made his way to the coffee machine.

*

Sunday night was darts night at The Star, and it meant for a big crowd and a good atmosphere. It also meant that Monday morning often began with a hangover for Nick and Alyson as, although neither of them played darts, they were more often than not tempted to round off their weekend with a few drinks with some of their fellow regulars.

This time the place was already busy when they arrived, and two darts matches were in play - one in the front half of the saloon bar and one in the rear part that also contained the pub's two pool tables. Nick went through to chalk his name onto the 'winner stays on' blackboard, then he and Alyson sat at a table back in the front half with a couple called Richard and Carol. Richard and Carol were in their fifties and had no children. They both had professional jobs, but drank quite heavily, most evenings - more often than not in The Star. Nick and Alyson regularly joined them, especially on Sundays. They'd already had quite a few drinks this evening.

As Nick and Alyson neared the end of their first drink, Len came in, along with a friend of his called Doug. Doug was older than Len, in his mid-sixties, and he was miserable and opinionated. Much as Nick got on well with Len, he was disappointed when the two of them found chairs and then pulled them up to turn their group from a four into a six.

Rob Stockdale was there too. He was propping up the bar, but in time came over to get a view of the darts and stood next to their table. He saw Nick sitting there.

"Alright, Nick!"

"Hi, Rob. How's things?"

"Good - good, mate."

There was then a pause of about five seconds when both men knew what the other was thinking.

"So," said Nick, "are you still OK to sort out that roof tile sometime?"

"Yeah, yeah, of course mate. Are you about this week? I'll come over one evening."

"Of course, whatever day suits you."

"OK, no problem. I'll come over - probably Tuesday or Wednesday."

"Cheers, thanks."

The front door then creaked open loudly. It always creaked loudly; Nick was sometimes tempted to bring in a can of WD40 to try to shut it up. In walked a man that he didn't know well, but he did know that his name was Harry. Harry was in his fifties, he was tall, and he was black.

"Oh, it's gone dark in here," said Len.

They all looked up, and Doug tutted.

Harry started pushing his way through the crowd towards the bar. He caught sight of Len and gave a friendly wave.

Len waved back. "Alright, Harry."

The door creaked open again and a large Asian man entered. He was about forty and wore a black turban.

Doug looked up and rolled his eyes. "Oh God, that's all we need, a fucking Muslim."

Rob Stockdale heard him and put his hand on the Asian man's shoulder. "Eh, Ranj," he said, "Doug here thinks you're a Muslim."

'Ranj' turned towards Doug with a big smile on his face. "No, not me mate, I'm a Sikh. We had problems with the Muslims long before you lot did!"

Doug just grunted and Ranj continued on his way to the bar.

Doug turned back to the table. "He'll probably blow the place up now."

"No, he won't. Didn't you hear him? He's not a Muslim," said Len.

"To be fair, he probably wouldn't blow the place up anyway," said Richard.

"Not so sure about that," said Doug. "I wouldn't trust one as far as I could throw him - nor any other of the coloureds for that matter."

"Careful," said Richard, "you'll get yourself into trouble saying things like that."

"You can't say anything these days," grumbled Doug. "It's political correctness gone mad."

"Some of them are OK, to be honest. The one in my local shop's alright," offered Len.

"Why wouldn't he be?" said Richard. "To be fair though, it has all gone too far. To my mind there's nothing wrong with saying things among friends. I often say 'useless paki', don't I Carol - or 'U.P.' for short. But I'm not being racist, I just mean one of those crap Indian or Pakistani drivers, usually a woman in a Nissan Micra. Carol knows what I mean, so there's nothing racist about it at all."

"And 'nigger shit'," said Carol.

"You what?"

"'Nigger shit' - you say, 'nigger shit'," said Carol getting quieter with each repetition.

"Oh, yeah, that's another one," said Richard. "But it just means crap music by black people - nothing racist about that."

"NICK!" someone called through from the back of the pub.

Nick and Alyson picked up their drinks and went through to the pool tables.

Nick took on the incumbent winner whilst Alyson supped at her pint and offered him encouragement. He won that first game and then beat the next challenger, but after that nobody else wanted to play, so Alyson took him on. Alyson enjoyed playing pool and was quite good at it, but she rarely joined the winner-stays-on rota, it was all a bit too much of a blokey environment for her.

After four frames they were tied at two-all and considering playing a decider. But by then the darts matches were drawing to a close and plates of cheese sandwiches had been placed on tables for the players. To Nick there was no food in the world more appealing than a cheese sandwich after a few pints of lager when he was forbidden from eating it through not being a member of a darts team. Sometimes there were scraps left over at the end and the plates were handed around the general populace, but Nick could see tonight that the sandwiches were disappearing far too quickly for that to be an option. Suddenly he was starving.

"I'm hungry", he said. "Fancy going to the chip shop?"

There was a small fish and chip shop near to The Star, and on Nick and Alyson's route home. It closed at the same time as the pub stopped serving - eleven o'clock Monday to Saturday and ten-thirty on Sundays. And that was a blessing as far as Nick was concerned - had it been open on their walks home from The Star then it might have been too tempting to resist, but as they usually left about half an hour after last orders then he had probably been spared from piling on a lot of weight over the years.

"Can if you like. I don't want anything though." Alyson was always watching her food intake and was far more disciplined when it came to resisting such temptation than Nick.

And so, they made their way back through the bustle of the front of the pub. Len, Rob, Harry, and Ranj were engrossed in a huddled jocular conversation at the bar, which made Nick smile. Richard and Carol were loading money into the juke box, selecting lots of songs that they mostly wouldn't hear as the juke box would be turned off at the same time as the beer pumps. Doug was supping a pint at the table on his own. The door creaked open, and Nick and Alyson left unnoticed by any of them. They would be rounding off the weekend with a bottle of wine when they got home.

*

"Wankers! Fucking bunch of patronising twats. Take themselves so fucking seriously. It's only a fucking job, nothing more important than that. They haven't even got the brains or imagination to realise it. Fucking wankers. Wouldn't WANT their job anyway; got better things to do with my mind. If the money wasn't good, I'd be out of there tomorrow. Gotta get out anyway. Fuck 'em. Plenty of work out there. What's the time? Fucking half past midnight. SHIT! ... Need another beer."

*

Alyson liked that the bosses trusted her to work from home. They knew that she wouldn't take the piss, just like they knew - and liked the fact - that she wouldn't take shit from anybody.

She fired off an email, the last of ten in quick succession, sat back with a satisfied smile, and picked up her cup of coffee. There was only a third of a cupful remaining and it was lukewarm as she'd made it some twenty minutes before, but she sipped at it anyway. During her quick break she couldn't help but to wander through to the front of the house - hers and Nick's bedroom - to look out of the window and see what Tricia might be up to. Her heart jumped/sank at the sight of Tricia, as it always did. She was standing in her open doorway in her dressing gown smoking a fag. It was just after 11 a.m. But it wasn't just the sight of Tricia that set Alyson on edge: Damian was there as well - as usual, he wasn't at school. The window was ajar, and Alyson could hear that Tricia and Damian were talking to each other, but she couldn't tell what they were saying.

Neighbour From Hell

Damian kicked things around the yard, bits of wood and bits of plastic - no doubt parts of one of the many broken expensive toys that he had wrecked, and remnants of the new fence, which had lasted less than two weeks. The debris slid around on the smooth concrete surface that the council had provided, as indeed they had the fence. Alyson's blood pressure rose just viewing the scene and the apparent casual conversation going on between incompetent mother and wayward son that almost certainly didn't reference the latter's school non-attendance.

And then someone else came into the picture. It was an old lady, probably well into her eighties, who was walking with a stick and making slow progress. She was on Alyson's side of the street and passing from right to left from Alyson's point of view. Alyson recognised her but didn't know her to talk to and didn't know which house she lived in. Tricia looked up at the woman and then said something to Damian and the two of them laughed. Then Damian moved from the yard onto the footpath outside. He was directly opposite the old lady, who in turn was at the end of Nick and Alyson's driveway.

"Oi, Missus!" Damian called out. "You walk like you've got a fucking cock up your arse!"

He turned to Tricia for approval, and she fell about laughing. She laughed long and loud until her nicotine-coated lungs turned her laughter into a coughing fit. In the meantime, Damian looked back and forth between his mother and the old lady, his usual scowl replaced with a huge grin. He was very pleased with himself.

The old lady carried on walking slowly up the street.

Alyson took in the whole scene. She could feel the old lady's humiliation. She could see Tricia and Damian's jubilation. She was furious. She was torn between shouting at Tricia and Damian from the window, going outside and confronting them, or biting her lip. What she actually did was throw her (empty) coffee cup against the far wall of the room, smashing it to pieces, and run back into her office where she burst into tears.

*

Nick had a real lump in his throat. It felt as if he had lost a good friend, and that his community had lost something so much more.

*

The first meeting of the committee of the tenants' and residents' association took place on a Tuesday evening in the council office building where Nick and Colin had originally met Pauline Fielding and Brian Hart. Pauline had entrusted Brian with the key to one of its meeting rooms. As well as Brian and Nick, all of the other committee members turned up: the quiet black man, Aki Oduro; the shy white woman, Susan Henwood; and the two red-faced angry old men - Bert Walsh and Derek Tindall. The meeting was due to start at seven-thirty and everybody arrived on time.

After some introductions and handshakes, they all sat down, and chairman Brian gave a rambling opening speech before talking through the agenda.

"We have five items on our agenda: introductions - which we've done; we then have to choose a name for ourselves; then agree who will take on the roles of secretary and of treasurer. Next, we must select the date of our first public meeting, which will be back at the village hall; and then finally we need to plan how to communicate that meeting to all of our residents … plus of course any other business. We have an hour and a half. Hopefully, that should be more than enough but, if necessary, I am perfectly happy to carry on longer if we need to; is that the case for everyone else?"

Vague nods of heads and a couple of muffled grunts suggested that it probably was.

"Right then, what about our name?" asked Brian enthusiastically.

The estate that the association served essentially consisted of two roads, Connaught Avenue and Hain Avenue. Neither were avenues but were instead lollipop shaped, entering the estate as spurs and leading to something vaguely circular that met in the middle to form a misshapen figure of eight. Connaught Avenue was by far the larger of the two and sprouting from it were also two cul-de-sacs, Connaught Close and Hewens Close. So, there were some possibilities to explore for name inspiration. But Brian had a different idea.

"How about North Norling Tenants' and Residents' Association?"

Susan pulled a bit of a face, Aki nodded approvingly, and both Bert and Derek scowled.

"No, I don't like it," said Nick. "The two 'Nors' together sound a bit cumbersome, and anyway, we are a *part* of North Norling - we don't represent all of it."

Brian didn't look to be entirely in agreement, but he nodded. "OK, has anyone got any other thoughts?"

Silence.

"Let's look at the names of the roads, something like Connaught and Hain maybe?"

A lengthy discussion followed in which Nick and Brian explored various combinations of words, each incorporating one or more of 'Connaught', 'Hain', and 'Avenue', but nothing really worked. Aki nodded hesitantly at every suggestion, Susan looked frightened, Derek stared into space, and Bert shook his head in violent disagreement at everything.

"What about the park?" suggested Brian.

The local park - a large patch of grass with some vandalised swings and a slide in one corner - had entrances on both Connaught Avenue and Hain Avenue as well as the main Harlesham Road. It was called 'Hewens Park'.

"... Something like 'Hewens Park Tenants' and Residents' Association'," said Brian, hopefully.

"Yes, that works," said Nick.

Brian smiled with relief. "Well then, let's put it to a vote."

Bert Walsh made his first contribution.

"Bollocks!"

Brian responded. "You don't like it, Bert? What is it that you don't like about it?"

Bert Walsh looked exasperated. "Well, we don't live in the park, do we? We live in houses."

Another five minutes of discussion followed before Brian Hart exercised his chairman's right to put the decision to the vote.

"So, all those in favour, please raise a hand."

Nick raised his hand; Aki Oduro raised his hand; and Brian himself raised his hand.

"Thank you. Now, all those against."

Bert Walsh raised his hand; Derek Tindall raised his hand; Susan Henwood looked sheepish.

"Carried, by three votes to two. So, we shall be the Hewens Park Tenants' and Residents' association. Thank you."

So, at last, one decision had been made. Except:

"Sorry, Brian," said Nick. "I think that the 'Hewens Park' idea works, but 'Hewens Park Tenants' and Residents' Association' is a bit of a mouthful. How about making it just 'Hewens Park Residents' Association'? After all we're all residents, regardless of whether we are owners or council tenants or renting privately. It just sounds a bit, you know, more 'snappy'."

"Yes, I can see that," said Brian.

"Fucking typical!" said Bert.

"Quiet, Dad!" said Susan, confirming Nick's theory of the relationship between those two.

"Well, they're all the same. Us tenants have rights too, you know! Fucking waste of time."

And so, a further debate pursued, with Nick explaining that his point was exactly the same as Bert's, in that he wanted to show that 'residents' meant anybody who lived on the estate, and didn't differentiate, whereas 'tenants and residents' suggested a differentiation. Bert was not having any of it, Derek backed up Bert, Aki looked confused, and Susan looked embarrassed.

"OK," said Brian. "Let's put it to the vote."

Again, Nick, Brian, and Aki were in favour, Bert and Derek were against, and Susan continued to look embarrassed.

"Carried," said Brian, "by three votes to two. Now, onto roles."

As Brian had already been appointed Chairman and Nick vice-chairman there were just two other roles to fill, those of secretary and treasurer.

"So, would anyone like to be secretary?" Brian looked around hopefully, and everyone else looked at everyone else.

Then Susan raised her hand. "I could do that, if you like."

"Splendid," said Brian. "Anyone else interested?"

Nobody was.

"Well, I'll second that then. Congratulations Susan, you are the association's official secretary."

Nick wondered whether anybody else felt a little uncomfortable with the fact that the only woman in the group was the only person prepared to take on the role of secretary. He also wondered whether Susan had felt obliged to volunteer.

Brian carried on. "So, just the treasurer position left then. Who's good with figures?"

Everyone cast slight sideways glances and then looked at their shoes.

Nick was the first to speak. "Do we actually need a treasurer? I'm not sure that we are going to be doing anything with money are we?"

It was probably the first comment of the night that met with widespread approval. Brian was unsure and Susan looked a little miffed, but with Nick proposing the idea of no treasurer and Aki seconding, the motion was carried with no opposition.

After that the committee managed to agree a date for their first public meeting and Susan agreed to put together a draft leaflet publicising that event that the council would get printed for them. Nick offered to help her with that if she wanted.

"Right then," said Brian, still managing to sound enthusiastic, "…we come to the final item on the agenda, which is of course 'AOB'. Does anybody have any?"

Derek Tindall made his first contribution. "What's 'AOB'?"

"Oh, sorry," said Brian. "It's 'Any Other Business'."

"And we were supposed to know that were we?" said Bert Walsh.

There wasn't any other business.

"Well, just one thing left then. Which pub are we all going to?" said a still enthusiastic Brian.

The Royal George, always referred to locally as 'The George', was an early twentieth century 'old man's pub' not too dissimilar to The Star. Nick and Alyson went there occasionally when they fancied a change of scene. Nick and Brian sat at a small table each with a pint of Best in front of them.

"Well, that was painful," said Nick.

"Do you think so? I thought it went rather well," said chairman Brian.

Nobody else had come to the pub. Bert had shuffled out chuntering to himself. Susan had said apologetically that she'd better go with her dad. Derek had muttered something that sounded half-apologetic and then given a bit of a wave and hurried up to join his mate, Bert. Aki had said that he needed to get home but cheerily insisted that he would make sure to come along next time.

And so, Nick and Brian chatted. However, it was Brian who did most of the talking, referencing whenever he could his experience - and expertise - as a councillor. They talked of course about the other committee members and their respective attitudes, and about the estate that the association represented and some of its issues.

Racism was one of the topics.

"There's a family of them living opposite me, black as the ace of spades they are, but some of the nicest people you could ever meet."

But the biggest topic was inevitably antisocial behaviour.

"You know that woman in the first meeting who was bleating on about demonising the little blighters? Well, I was at one council meeting when some woman like that - hippy type - piped up about the human rights of one of these little scrotes. I said, 'what about the human rights of the old lady that he robbed - she didn't have any choice in the matter'. She didn't have an answer to that."

Nick wasn't sure whether the pub visit was any better than the meeting itself. He managed to get out of it after two pints.

"Must do it again," said Brian, reminding Nick of the dreadful truth that the public meeting was just a month away, and that the committee would be getting together in the meantime to organise it.

The next day Nick was playing back the events of the evening in his head on his walk home from work when the theme of racism again reared its head. The streets of the estate that he now represented were quiet from a traffic point of view, although not quiet enough to be safe for children to play in the road. That didn't of course stop them from doing so, and whenever Nick came across them it concerned him, given the speed at which some people - Bradley Mullen, for example - drove around the estate. It also concerned him that he had those thoughts, as he realised that it was a clear sign that he was approaching middle age.

This time, as he turned into Hain Avenue in the latter stages of his walk, he saw up ahead of him one child in the middle of the road and two others slowly circling him on BMX bikes. It was all that he could do to stop himself from tutting.

As he got nearer, he could see that the child in the middle was neighbours' Danny and Brenda's ten-year-old son Dhillon, and that one of the boys on bikes was Rob and Michelle Stockdale's fourteen-year-old son, Archie. The other boy was of Archie's age, but Nick didn't recognise him. He could also see that Dhillon was crying, and when he got closer still, he could hear the boys' 'conversation'.

The sound was coming from both of the boys on bikes, and they were chanting, "paki … paki … paki … paki …"

Nick had to forgo his usual reticence for confrontation, especially with youths on this estate. He ran towards the group, "Archie, what the fuck are you doing?! Leave him alone."

The two older boys immediately turned and cycled away but when they looked back over their shoulders, they were both laughing.

Nick had never really spoken to Dhillon, who seemed shy and kept himself to himself.

"Are you OK?" Nick asked.

Dhillon just snivelled and didn't look Nick in the eye.

"Come on, I'll walk home with you."

During the three or four minutes of that walk, Nick made a couple more attempts to strike up conversation, but Dhillon wasn't interested.

Nick knocked on the door of his neighbours' house, and Brenda answered - her large frame imposingly filling the doorway. Dhillon ran straight past her and disappeared inside.

"He was getting some grief from some older kids just up the road," explained Nick.

"OK," said Brenda with something of a 'so what?' expression.

"Well, er, I'll leave you to it then. Hope he's OK," said Nick.

"OK," said Brenda, again. And then she shut the door.

Nick left feeling a little perturbed. What next, go home or …?

He crossed the road and headed to the Stockdales' house. He felt that it was only right to tell Michelle what he'd seen, and if he did so now then she would be able to speak to Archie before Rob got home from work. He strode confidently up to the door and rang the bell. The door flew open straight away, and Rob stood there, holding a can of Stella.

"Alright, Nick."

"Oh, er, hi Rob… you're home from work early."

"Yeah, I had the day off. Been tiling the bathroom. What's up?"

"Oh, er, I thought I'd better tell you: I was walking home, and I saw Archie and another boy giving grief to one of the kids from next door to me."

Rob eyed him with the same kind of 'so what?' expression that Brenda had, but with slightly drunk overtones.

Nick continued. "They, er, they were calling him racist names."

Rob's expression changed marginally; it now had a touch of anger about it.

"Well, he's not here; he's out."

"Yes, well, I thought I should tell you."

"What is it, Rob?" called Michelle from somewhere deep in the house.

"Nothing!"

Rob and Nick then eyed each other for a moment.

"Right, anyway, I'd better be off," said Nick.

"Alright Nick," said Rob, and then he shut the door even more quickly than Brenda had.

Nick returned home disturbed. He knew that he'd done the right thing, but it seemed that he might have alienated two of his neighbours in the process.

*

Even as a child, Nick had noticed that the engines of fire engines when parked up at an emergency scene always sounded different from those of other lorries and trucks. If he'd ever cared to investigate why that was, he would have found out that their carburation was set to a fast idle speed in order for the engine's output to support extra powerful alternators required to supply their myriad of high consumption electrical equipment. He hadn't done that, but regardless, it meant that when a large vehicle pulled up outside his and Alyson's house one Saturday night, he knew instantly what it was. The glaring beams of blue light swooping across their ceiling would also have been a good clue.

It was rare for them not to go to the pub on a Saturday night but after driving out for a curry early on he and Alyson had come back home. Then, rather than going out again to walk to the pub, they had settled down to watch TV with a bottle of red wine, and when the wine was finished, they'd moved on to the lager. The evening was going well, they were both feeling good and were sitting next to each other on the same sofa. Sex was definitely on the cards, and Nick felt that it was likely to be one of those marathon sessions that only happened quite rarely.

The fire engine interrupted the ambiance.

Nick went straight to the front door. "Looks like it's bloody Tricia," he said. The vehicle was parked opposite his and Alyson's driveway, right outside Tricia's house. Some firemen were milling around, and other neighbours were appearing at their windows. There was no sign of any fire. Nick went out and walked to the end of his driveway, from where he could see around the fire engine to the front of Tricia's house. Tricia was there talking to two firemen. The blue lights' big beams flashed off every window in the street and noise of the high-revving engine bounced from every wall. It all created a dramatic aura but there didn't seem to be much urgency.

Colin came from his house and walked out onto the pavement, and Nick went out to join him. Alyson stayed watching from their open porch. One of the firemen who had been talking to Tricia came out into the road to get something from the cab of the fire engine. Colin spoke to him.

"What's she been up to now then?"

The fireman looked across to Nick and Colin and then walked over to them. Nick had a horrible feeling that he was going to give them a bollocking for being nosey.

"Do you know her?" he asked.

Tricia then noticed Nick and Colin there too and called out to them. "You see - I told you you should of had my keys, mate!"

"Sort of," said Nick to the fireman.

"Well, she's locked herself out. She said that she came out to put the milk bottles out and the door slammed behind her. There's no sign of any milk bottles though. She's been drinking."

The fireman was doing a very professional job of keeping a straight face.

Tricia called over again. "I was at the British Legion Club earlier, then I come home, and then I went to put the milk out and it slammed behind me."

Nick waived an acknowledgement to Tricia.

Colin spoke to the fireman. "So, she's gone to the pub and lost her keys then?"

"Yes, that looks about the size of it."

"Bloody nuisance, she is. Nightmare."

"You wouldn't know of anyone who has a spare set of keys?"

Nick shook his head. "Sorry, no. So, will you break in for her then?"

"No, we can't do that. OK, thanks guys."

Colin turned to Nick. "Calling the fucking fire brigade because she's lost her keys. Stupid bitch."

Then more blue lights came reflecting off the windows, and a police car sped into view. It pulled up next to the fire engine and the driver got out and went over to talk to Tricia.

"More bloody resources wasted," said Colin. "They should lock her up while they are about it."

Assisted by a leg-up from one of his colleagues a fireman climbed over Tricia's side gate to get into her back garden. A minute later he emerged from the front door. He called over to his colleagues.

"The back window was wide open!"

Within what seemed like seconds the fire engine was pulling away.

"Thanks, lads. Thanks ever so much!" called out Tricia to no apparent response.

Then Tricia went inside her house and the policeman left.

Nick turned around to see that Alyson had also disappeared back into their house.

"Ah, well," he said to Colin, "at least she's given us some entertainment!"

"Yeah, silly cow."

"I know she's a pain in the arse, but I can't help almost feeling sorry for her sometimes. Her life does seem pretty desperate."

Colin laughed and for a moment looked as if he was about to ridicule Nick's comment, but then he checked himself.

"Yeah, maybe you're right. In a funny way, maybe she's lonely."

"Yes, exactly. Anyway, I'd better be getting in. See ya tomorrow."

"Yeah. See you, mate. Onwards and upwards!"

Alyson was loading some crockery into the dishwasher. Nick picked up his lager glass and took a swig.

"Right then, where were we?" he said.

Alyson pushed past him on her way through the living room. "That fucking woman! I'm going to bed."

*

"Hi Danny!"

It was a rare thing to see Danny in his back garden and Nick had stopped his lawn mower to go over and speak to him.

"Oh, alright Nick."

The fire brigade thing gave Nick an excuse to start a conversation.

"Did you see the fire brigade out there last night?"

"No … what was all that about?"

"Bloody Tricia. She got pissed and locked herself out and phoned them."

"Fucking nightmare. She wants shooting - and it'll happen. She's pissing everyone off. My kids are scared to go out there."

"Well, hopefully we might be able to get something done with the residents' association. We'll see. Anyway, how's the Bond coming along - much progress?"

"Yeah, yeah - good."

"Oh, great. Have you been getting some of the photos?"

"Yeah, lots. They're not here though, they're at the workshop."

"OK. Let me know when I can have a look."

"Sure, we'll catch up. I'll take you around to have a good look at it."

"Cheers. Yeah, let's do that. Give me a call; I'm good any night this week."

"Sure, no problem. Well, better go mate; I need to get this barbecue sorted out."

"OK, see you later in the week."

"See ya, mate. Yeah, sure - I'll give you a call"

"Cheers." *Like fuck, you will.*

*

Nick stood in his driveway watching his Porsche being winched up onto a flatbed recovery truck in the road outside. He was keeping his distance from the winch's steel cable and wondering why the truck driver was winching the car when he could have driven it - force of habit maybe as most vehicles that he picked up would be crash damaged or broken down, not merely being transported to their owners who were reluctant to drive them due to expired MoT and lack of recent use.

At the other side of the truck Damian, Billy Grindle, and two others of Billy Grindle's age each looked on, with their usual unsmiling sneering gaze. Tricia and Charlene were watching too, each leaning against their respective doorways with fag in hand.

Once the Porsche was in place the driver went about securing it to the bed of the truck with some robust orange ratcheted straps. Nick walked around to the back of the truck.

"Are you selling it?" asked Damian.

"Yes, it's off to its new home in Gillingham," Nick replied.

"Nice car, mate," said Billy Grindle.

"How fast does it go?" asked an unusually talkative Damian.

"About a hundred and fifty," said Nick, phlegmatically.

Damian nodded an approval. He was impressed.

Neighbour From Hell

Billy Grindle looked on silently, and seeing him and the Porsche together, Nick suddenly realised that he'd given Billy Grindle a ride in it a couple years earlier when he'd been a wide-eyed twelve-year-old - two years before cynicism, thieving, misery, alcohol, drugs, and Tricia had to varying extents blighted both of their lives.

When he'd finished securing the car, the truck driver got Nick to sign some paperwork and then shook his hand and drove slowly away. As he watched the Porsche go, Nick felt that he should have been sad, but he wasn't. It had always been a dream of his to own a Porsche 911, and that dream had come true just over four years ago, but it hadn't been long before the car no longer excited him. In fact, he almost felt some sense of relief at it leaving his life, as if it had in some way become something of a liability.

Once the 'entertainment' was over, Damian, Billy Grindle, and their two companions wandered moodily away, heading in the direction of the park. Just Nick, Tricia, and Charlene were left.

Tricia called over to Nick. "You get a good price for it, mate?"

Nick walked over into her front yard rather than shout across the street. "Yes, it was OK. Should keep me in beer for a few weeks."

Then Charlene joined in. "Nice car that; I wouldn't have minded a go in that."

"You should have asked," said Nick.

And he was just trying to think of what to say next when Tricia interrupted his thoughts.

"Oi, leave him alone you dirty mare, he's a married man!"

Charlene smirked and took a seductive drag on her cigarette - at least that's how Nick saw it anyway.

He decided against pointing out that he wasn't actually married. "Well, I'd better go. See you soon." "Cheers, mate," Tricia and Charlene called in unison as he turned and walked away.

As Nick went back into his house, he felt good. He was buoyed by the friendly chat with Tricia and Charlene, and in particular by the thought that Charlene would have liked him to take her for a ride in a sports car, but he was also pleased with the rare non-confrontational exchange with scowling members of the scum. Maybe living opposite a nightmare family wasn't always quite so bad after all.

7. Len

"Shit, they're at it again," said Alyson.

Nick knew that Harshad and his wife were at it again, as he'd been lying on his back listening to them for ten minutes, hoping that they would stop, and hoping that Alyson wouldn't wake up.

"They've been at it for ages," said Nick.

"I must have been asleep," said Alyson. "He hasn't hit her, has he?"

"I don't think so. She seems to be giving as good as she gets."

Harshad's arguments with his wife were becoming a common occurrence. They tended to happen late at night and were conducted at high volume and always in their native tongue, not in English.

It went on, each of them yelling at the other, seemingly at the tops of their voices. It was stressful to listen to. Nick could sense that Alyson, like him, was staring straight up at the ceiling. It was a warm night, and windows were open, allowing the unwelcome sounds to drift in all too easily. There were bangs and crashes: objects were being thrown around. Nick wondered how much longer it could go on before he felt obliged to intervene. Alyson suggested calling the police. The exchanges were becoming ever more frantic. Nick said to wait a bit longer, it had been worse before - one time the Ranganathan's living room window had been smashed. Things were always quite normal though the next morning.

The volume seemed to crank up even further.

Nick and Alyson were both naked.

"It must be keeping everyone awake," said Alyson.

"Yeah. Poor old Colin and Janet. And what about the kids?"

It went quiet for a bit. Relief.

Then Harshad was shouting. There was real aggression in his voice; it felt as if violence was imminent. Then his wife's voice took over. She was shrieking; she sounded terrified … or furious. Then it was Harshad again, getting ever faster, and, if it was possible, even louder. Alyson reached over and held Nick's hand; he squeezed hers. Harshad was still going; he threw something to the ground.

And then there was another sound. It was a window being opened.

"SHUT THE FUCK UP, YOU FUCKING BLACK CUNT!"

Silence.

Nick and Alyson lay there tense and unmoving for a full minute. They were still holding hands.

Alyson spoke first. "That was Rob, wasn't it?" For some reason she was whispering.

"Yeah," Nick whispered back.

Rob Stockdale pulled his window shut and they heard him clatter its latch into place. There were no other sounds.

They waited a further thirty seconds before simultaneously turning towards each other. They were still holding hands, Nick's left hand gripping Alyson's right. They kissed.

"What's the time?" asked Alyson. She was still whispering.

Nick squinted and looked at the clock-radio behind her. "It's just after two o'clock."

"I'm wide awake. What shall we do?"

He put his right arm around her and kissed her again. "I'm sure we can think of something!"

*

The first proper public meeting of the Hewens Park Residents' Association took place back in the church hall where the launch meeting had been. After helping to arrange the chairs and then mingling with and chatting to some of the early arrivals, Nick took his seat at the front of the hall. There would be no 'officials' present this time; the committee members were on their own. Nick watched the people filing in and seating themselves, some alone, some in small groups chatting and chuntering. They all looked rather serious - there wasn't much laughing going on. The meeting was due to start at seven-thirty and when that time came the hall was rammed. There were a lot more people there than last time. Nick had felt increasingly nervous over the course of the six-week build-up since the first committee meeting. He questioned why he was putting himself through all of this.

At seven-forty Brian opened the meeting. He gave a 'short' introductory speech. It was planned to take less than five minutes, but it went on for nearly fifteen that felt to Nick like thirty. It was similar dreary stuff to Cllr. Caldwell's speech at the launch meeting. People did actually seem to be listening to his waffle about how important the association was and how great it was that it was bringing everyone together as a community, although towards the end some were starting to get restless.

Then it was Nick's turn.

Nick was to run a 'brainstorming' session in which to capture any topics that people wished the association should get involved with. At the end there would be a vote to choose the most popular topics in order that the association could focus on those first. Before that he gave a brief introduction of his own in which he light-heartedly reminded all of those present that the committee members were unpaid volunteers, and that the association was not in any way connected to any political parties. He also reminded everyone that a new committee would be elected after a year and that any of them might like to think about putting themselves forward when the time came. (He was already looking forward to that occasion.)

"OK, then," he said. "So, what we are going to do now is a brainstorming session. Remembering that what we are here for is to work with the authorities - mainly the council and the police - to help to make positive changes to the environment in which we all live, I want you to shout out the things that you think we should be looking at, and I'll capture them here on the flip chart. There are no right or wrong answers, so please feel free to shout out whatever you want … even if you think it sounds daft."

He looked around expectantly as lots of people shuffled their feet.

"Someone …?" said Nick. "What's going to be our first topic?"

And then it started.

"Kids driving too fast!" a woman blurted out from somewhere near the back.

"Thank you," said Nick, "Let's write that one d…"

"Yeah, it's like a bloody racetrack around here!" yelled a man from the front.

"Drug smoking in the park," chipped in someone else.

"Hang on," called out Nick. "Let's get one thing at a time."

But the people were gathering momentum.

"The park's rubbish - all the graffiti and vandalism; it's disgusting!"

"Bloody kids, they've got no respect nowadays."

"I blame the parents."

Neighbour From Hell

"The problem is all these women going to work nowadays. My wife stayed at home and brought my kids up proper."

"They should go to scouts - teach them respect."

"It's alright for you to say that - not everyone can afford to send their kids to scouts!"

"I bet they can afford to smoke though - and have a fucking big TV."

Nick tried again, "Can we just …"

"Yeah, and a dog - probably an illegal one."

"Police never come when you call them!"

"There's nothing wrong with dogs, it's the owners that are the problem."

"What about that van always parked outside my house? What's wrong with him parking it at his own house?"

That final comment came from behind Nick, in the committee seats. It was Bert's contribution.

"OK, OK!" Called Nick. "So, let me just capture those so far. I have three potential topics, I think: 'Condition of the Park', 'Traffic Calming', and 'Police Response'. Is that it?"

"Ha-ha - 'Police Response'! There *is* no police response, that's the problem."

"It was the same with my van - ripped the whole bloody door mirror off, the little bastards. Police didn't do anything. They didn't give a shit."

"Wouldn't happen if your name was Patel!"

"Yeah, just tell 'em it's racism then they'll be there quick enough."

Loud murmurs of approval.

"It's the ports, that's the problem. They haven't got enough staff to keep the drugs out."

"Yes, thanks," said Nick. "But that's probably a bit beyond our remit."

"Speed humps, that's what it needs!"

"Yes, thanks," responded Nick. "We've got traffic calming on the list."

"What's the point in us saying stuff if you are just going to tell us to be quiet?"

"Sorry, I wasn't …"

"Fucking speed humps! Are you going to pay for my exhaust when they rip it off then? What a load of bollocks."

"No, they're just going to let that bloke park his van outside my house. Is that your solution?"

"What about tenants?" shouted yet another angry old man, and he winked in the direction of someone behind Nick, that someone being Bert.

"Sorry," said Nick. "What do you mean?"

"What about tenants? Fucking 'Residents' Association' - aren't us council tenants good enough for you anymore?"

"No, that's the point. We are all residents," replied Nick, ostensibly keeping very calm. "It makes the point that we are all part of the same community; it says that we don't differentiate between different groups of people."

"Bollocks!"
"So, what are you going to do about the park?"
"The streetlight outside my house hasn't worked for three weeks."

"My mate had his tyres slashed last week in West Drayton."

"The litter's disgusting."

"What about the Muslims?"

"The kids have got nothing to do. They can't even play conkers nowadays because of bloody Health and Safety."

"National Service!"

"The police won't come round though, too busy driving their flash cars up and down the Harlesham Road."

"I blame the government."

"I blame the parents."

"I blame the schools."

"They were quick enough to fine me for doing 46 miles an hour in a 40 limit. There was no traffic about either. Ridiculous."

"My kids are scared to walk home from school."

"Motorists, see. We're an easy target."

"Drugs! That's the problem."

"Bob Cambridge, next to me – they tore up all of the daffodils in his front garden."

"And what about all the fireworks in the middle of the night? We can't do it for bonfire night, so why should they do it for Ramadan or Diwali or whatever!"

"Kids have got no respect nowadays."

"Very proud of his garden, is Bob. Makes a lovely job of it."

"Give 'em a clip round the ear - never did me any harm."

"Like with my van - ripped the whole bloody thing off the door, they did."

"OK," yelled Nick. "We seem to be coming back to these same three subjects, so that's good. It means we are clear on what are the most important things to people. So, now that we have those three high-level topics, let's work out what are the next actions that we would like to take to begin to address them."

Thinking on the fly, Nick applied a crowd control tactic to this next section of the meeting. He thought up a possible action, suggested it to the room, let them shout out whatever they wanted, and then wrote on the board exactly what he'd said in the first place. It worked a treat, and in not too much time at all he had a list of actions for the committee:

- Speak to council about the budget for maintaining / improving the park
- Come up with some traffic calming options for discussion at the next public meeting
- Get a police representative to speak and answer questions at the next public meeting
- Come up with some possible measures for reducing antisocial behaviour in the park, for discussion at the next meeting.

Nick rounded off by thanking the audience for their participation.

"… and so, I'll hand back to Brian. I look forward to seeing you all again next time."

There was no round of applause.

Brian then brought the meeting to a close with some characteristically dull words, but did manage to enliven things briefly by mentioning that he knew of a park where the hedges had been cut down to increase visibility in an effort to reduce antisocial behaviour. The raucous response from the people in the room made it clear that such a measure would not be welcomed at 'their' park.

When it was all over, everyone shuffled out. They were noisy and they were still chuntering. "Well, that was a bloody waste of time," said Bert, loudly, as he joined up with Derek and the man who had complained about 'tenants' being omitted from the association's name.

Nick could so easily have responded "thanks for your contribution, Bert", but he managed to maintain some professionalism, helped by the fact that, despite all the negativity, he had in a way quite enjoyed the evening. He'd been pleased with how he'd handled the chaos. He felt that he'd done a good job … not that anyone said so, or even acknowledged him on their way out.

Only Nick and Brian went to the pub again. On the walk there, Brian commented that the real reason that any of them were there was the collective feeling of helplessness in the fight against lawlessness and toothless authority. "That Billy Grindle has been arrested seventeen times, but he's never been charged with anything. That's why people lose faith in the system." Nick meanwhile moaned about what a miserable twat Bert was, and although Brian seemed to agree, he was much more measured in his language.

Brian got back to Billy Grindle. "The problem with these youths is they see the world as black and white: there's 'them' and there's 'us'. There are the people in their little gangs, and there's everyone else together against them in one great amalgam: their teachers, the police, the council, the residents' association - basically anyone in any kind of authority, plus the likes of you and me - you know, middle class people who do things like buy houses and drive cars that are insured. We are all just part of a conspiracy that they have to fight against, and there's no differentiator for them between any of us."

It was one of the few things that Brian said that Nick actually agreed with. "Yes, I think you're right," he said. "I know one time I was walking home from work in my office clothes and a bunch of them - not our lot, this was up near The Ram - started having a go at me, insisting that

I was C.I.D. and wouldn't believe me when I said that I wasn't."

"Yes, exactly," said Brian, "a bloke who works in an office or a plain clothes policeman, it's all another world to them that they just touch on from time to time. There's this invisible divide. They use it to absolve themselves of responsibility too. Do you notice how there's more litter in the streets on council estates? It's not because the council don't clean them as often; far from it – quite the opposite, in fact. No, it's because so many of these people see everything as somebody else's problem – the authorities, the 'posh' people. So, they don't pick up litter like people in nicer areas do – plus of course they drop more of it in the first place. You can't pretend these things aren't true; it's there right in front of us. They breed like rabbits too – it's all part of that lack of responsibility. You get the feeling that the human race is doomed!"

They arrived at The George and Nick selected a table while Brian went to the bar to get the drinks in.

Brian returned and placed their placed the pints on the table.

"I found it amusing how the first thing that they brought up was speeding cars," said Nick. "There isn't a community in the world that doesn't moan that 'they all drive too fast around here'. And then the same people always complain that their local speed cops are too strict!"

"Ha-ha! Welcome to politics," said Brian. "You'll soon get used to it."

Nick wondered whether Brian might be the one to tell him that he'd done a good job of controlling the baying mob, but it was not to be. In fact, he was soon onto familiar old ground "… family opposite me, as black as the ace of spades …" "… what about the human rights of the old lady that he robbed" …

Nick managed to make his excuses and leave after the one pint. He made his way hurriedly through the estate, unsure whether he wanted to be recognised by any members of 'his people' or whether he really didn't want to see any of them ever again.

*

"Oh my God, look at this!" laughed Alyson, looking out of the bedroom window.

Nick did as he was told and saw that what Alyson was drawing his attention to was Charlene apparently asleep, lying on her back on a sun lounger in her front yard. She was wearing only a pristine white bikini that contrasted starkly with her deeply bronzed - and perfectly toned - body whose ample application of tanning oil glistened in the hot sunshine.

Nick feigned shock and then nodded. "Hmm, yes, very nice!" he said.

"Oh, for God's sake," said Alyson. "Don't these chavs have any shame? So, you'd go for that, would you?"

Nick played along. "Well, er …"

"Oh Nick, you are such a wanker."

And then she slapped him on the arm, but they were both laughing.

"Ow, that hurt!"

"Serves you right."

"I'll bet *she* wouldn't do that."

"Why don't you go and find out."

"Actually, maybe she would … that wouldn't necessarily be so bad."

And then Tricia appeared at her door, fag in hand, as ever.

"There you go," said Alyson, "if you like your chavs so much, why not give her a go?"

"Now, come on - my standards might be low, but even I have limits."

Alyson hit Nick again, but this time much harder.

*

Len Phillips was sitting at a table in The Star on his own. He'd got there early when the place was all but empty and then sat supping away at his beer observing the scene as it began to fill up. The front bar had quite a few people in it now and in the back where Len was, a number of men were playing pool. Len sat slowly mixing drinking with thinking and with people watching. He recognised most of the men playing pool but didn't know any of them well enough to exchange much more than a greeting. That suited him; he was quite happy to be alone with his thoughts for a while. He pondered that he'd been drinking in The Star longer than most of the pool players had been alive.

It was all men in that part of the pub apart from one woman, who was in her early thirties, bottle-blonde, and called Julie. She was the girlfriend of one person in the group that Len couldn't stand, a forty-year-old shaven-haired stocky EDL-supporting stereotype called Greg who enjoyed a bit of football trouble and was quite good at pool but not as good as he thought he was. Greg and Julie were both drunk, and annoyingly so. Greg was showing off both to Julie and to his mates, and Julie was giggling like a schoolgirl. Two 'men' who looked to Len to be about sixteen were putting some songs on the juke box - some dreadful rap stuff that he also couldn't stand - Karen's 'nigger shit' reference from a couple of months before came back to mind. Two drunk men in their mid-thirties propped up the back bar, next to the pool tables. He didn't recognise them, but he was confident from their fight/drink worn faces, cocky body language, and steely but put-upon dark eyes that they were travellers, or 'fucking pikeys', as he would put it.

Len pondered the sort of thing that supping four pints alone in a pub makes men ponder. He asked himself why he never felt comfortable in his own environment anymore. And, also no doubt aided by the four pints, an answer came to him. The kids, the music, the attitudes, the 'in-crowd' - he didn't fit anymore. He was no longer part of it, as he was on the way out: his life was largely behind him. It was something of an epiphany, but not a good one. He was glad to see Nick and Alyson heading his way.

Nick went to the bar to get a round in.

"How are you two getting on with your yobs over the road?" Len asked Alyson.

"Shit!" answered Alyson. "We haven't had the fire brigade out lately but there's still scumbags all over the street every other night."

Nick brought the drinks to the table - a pint of lager each for himself and Alyson and a pint of bitter for Len. Then he headed to the juke box which had just fallen silent, on his way nodding a 'hello' to Rob Stockdale, who had just come in and was standing at the bar. Nick put on six songs, an odd mix of three each from two of his favourite bands, The Sweet and Carter USM. By the time he returned to the table his first selection *The Six Teens* was halfway through - a rich slice of boisterous glam rock topped off with Sweet singer Brian Connolly's mournful yet melodic vocals swirled around the big pub, unnoticed by most of its occupants.

"They were from round here, you know - The Sweet," said Len.

"Really?" said Nick. "No, I didn't realise that. I knew there was a punk scene - The Ruts and The Lurkers were both local, weren't they. And Gary Numan wasn't far away. But, no, I didn't know about Sweet."

"Yeah, that Brian Connolly - used to see him in all the pubs. He was a right mess by the end."

"They were huge though, weren't they?"

"Oh, yes. They were superstars - all over the world. And the band 'America' - remember them?"

"What, as in 'A Horse with No Name'?"

"That's them. They were from Hillingdon."

"Really? I'd assumed they were American."

"They were. They were sons of U.S. airmen based at South Ruislip."

"Interesting."

Len took a sup of his pint." Anyway, Alyson says that you're still having problems with your woman and her yobs across the street."

"Oh, God yes. I'm thinking of getting some six-foot gates put in."

"Good move. What type are you going to get?"

"Dunno yet. If I do though, would you be interested in fitting them for us?"

"Yes, of course - if the price is right. Ha-ha!"

"Cool," said Nick, "I've been growing the privet hedge either side of the drive really high to stop the little shits jumping over it, but it would be good to get the gates to match."

Len looked over to the bar and saw that the travellers were getting ever more drunk, and that the silly Julie was talking to them, giggling and spilling her cocktail in the process.

The Six Teens had finished and the "Have a good time all the time" sample from *This is Spinal Tap* heralded the start of Carter USM's musical comment on pop decadence, *Do Re Me, So Far So Good*.

"Do you remember these?" Nick asked Len.

"No, not sure that I do."

"Carter USM, or 'Carter the Unstoppable Sex Machine' - there were two of them, Jim Bob and Fruitbat … plus a drum machine. They were really big for a while in the nineties."

"Ah yes, I remember them being around. Not sure if I could name any of their songs though."

"Yeah, they had loads of good stuff. They even headlined Glastonbury in 1992. People like Van Morrison, Kirsty MacColl, Lou Reed, James, and Blur were lower down the bill, and …"

CRASH!

They all look up to see that EDL Greg has smashed one of the travellers across the bar sending pint glasses in all directions. In an instant the room erupts. The second traveller grabs a bar stool and swings it at Greg's head. Three of Greg's mates pile onto him. Julie screams. The first traveller emerges shakily from behind the bar and smacks a punch into the mouth of the nearest person. Chairs are flying; glasses are flying. Carter's raucous 'Do Re Me' chorus fights to compete with the noise. Nick, Alyson, and Len get behind their table and edge into the corner of the room. More people pile in - there are fifteen or more in total. A pool cue is broken in half. Bits of glass and blood splatter across a pool table. One of the travellers is on the floor and someone is kicking his head. Carter play on.

And then things slow down and some of the combatants stand back. Two of his mates hold Greg back from steaming back in, and Rob Stockdale emerges holding a battered traveller in each arm. Rob makes his way towards the front of the pub, dragging his captives with him as the melee falls to near silent admiration. The door swings shut behind Rob as Carter's Jim Bob delivers his song's final embittered roar – "SO FAR, SO GOOOOOD!"

Ten seconds later Rob returned rubbing his hands together as the sound of a howling police siren announced that The Sweet's *Blockbuster* had arrived. A round of applause rang around the whole pub.

Some people were brushing themselves down; some were putting chairs back into place; others were nursing their injuries; Julie was crying; Greg was shouting at her. The barman was pulling a free pint for Rob.

"Shit!" said Alyson.

"Like a scene from a bloody Western," said Len.

"Blimey; I've not seen anything like that in here before," said Nick.

"Nor me," Len reflected, "at least not since the 1970s. Fucking pikeys; they're no good to anyone – got no morals whatsoever."

"True," said Nick. "If there's one group that it's OK to be prejudiced against it's got to be them. Although, in fairness it wasn't actually them who started it."

"No," said Len, "it was that prat, Greg. But they would have done had they thought of it first. Anyway, are you OK, Alyson? You look a bit pale."

"No, I'm fine," replied Alyson with a touch of sarcasm, "There's nothing I like more than a good punch-up at the local."

"Anyway, where was we?" said Len.

"Music," replied Nick.

"Yes, you missed out Scouting for Girls," said Alyson.

"Eh?" said Len.

"They're from around here too."

"Well, Ruislip," said Nick.

"Yeah, that's around here."

"Well, sort of."

"Oi, Oi, you two, let's not have a fight about it!" said Len with a grin. "What are you both having? I'll go and get the beers in."

*

Nick answered the front door to find an excited-looking Brian Hart waiting for him.

"Hello, Nick. I do hope I'm not disturbing anything?"

"Er, no, not at all. Um, come in."

Nick showed Brian through to the living room.

"Your wife not about?" Brian asked.

"She's upstairs doing some work. Can I get you a cup of tea or something?"

Brian took his seat on the sofa as he replied. "No, no, I'm fine thanks."

Thank goodness for that.

Brian continued. "I came to speak to you about the burglary at number 83; did you hear about it?"

"No, I didn't." Suddenly Nick was interested.

"Well, there's a woman lives at number 83, and it seems that she was burgled. But what makes it interesting is that it was our friend Billy Grindle that did it."

"Oh, brilliant! So, has he been arrested then?"

"No, I don't believe so - not yet anyway. But apparently a neighbour saw him leaving the premises."

"Interesting. When was this then - last night?"

"No, yesterday afternoon – broad daylight."

"So, he actually broke into a house in broad daylight?"

"Their shed apparently. They seem to think that he might have taken some tools. I don't really know all of the details."

Nick felt somewhat deflated; this wasn't quite such a dramatic burglary story after all.

"Anyway," said Brian, enthusiastically, "I thought maybe we should go round and speak to her."

Nick froze. His natural inclination when somebody asked him a favour was to say 'yes', but it was easy to resist doing that this time.

"Erm, has she reported it to the police?"

"I don't know, but they are probably not even going to call around, are they? I thought it might be a good thing for the committee to get involved and show some interest."

"I see. So, how did you get to know about it?"

"Susan told me. She knows the woman; their kids go to school together it seems."

Nick frowned. "So, if she's already spoken to Susan then why us as well?"

Brian pondered that one for a moment before coming up with, "Credibility. They see us as being in charge - which is fair enough as it's true, basically."

Nick had to get out of this. "I don't know. I'm not so sure that it's what the committee's for."

"No, it's not - necessarily. But, you know, it might be good for the image - supporting people in the community when they have a problem."

Hmmm, and how's that going to help us get rid of Tricia?

"I'm not sure," said Nick, I think we might be overstretching our remit." He was proud of that phrase, it wasn't the sort of thing that he would normally say, but it would probably resonate with Brian. "And it could do us more harm than good if we mis-set expectations by getting involved in things when we can't really help."

Brian looked disappointed. "No, no, fair enough, if it's not for you."

"No, it's not really for me I'm afraid. Sorry. Feel free to go by yourself if you like. I don't have a problem with it, I just don't … well, as you say, it's not for me."

"Yes, I might just do that; I'll give it some thought." Brian then relaxed back in the sofa, the main purpose of his visit over with. "Actually, you know, I think I will have that cup of tea if it's still on offer."

Nick thought for a second. "Er, actually, I'm supposed to be calling my mum at, er," he looked at his watch - it was seven forty-six - "at eight o'clock … you know, in South Africa."

"Oh, no, of course then - let me leave you to it," said Brian, now pulling himself up from the sofa. "Gosh, what time must it be over there now then?"

"Oh, er, good point. It's, er, I get always get confused what with British Summer Time and all that. They are usually not too different from here - an hour either way, something like that."

Nick saw Brian through to the front door.

"Are you absolutely sure that I can't persuade you?" asked Brian as he stepped outside.

Yes, I'm absolutely fucking certain!

"Thanks for asking but, like you say, it's not really my kind of thing."

"Ah well, never mind. Not a problem; I'll let you know how I get on."

"Yes, do. All the best then, Brian. Bye!"

Nick shut the door and looked up to the heavens in relief. Then he moved to the foot of the stairs.

"That was Brian Hart," he called to Alyson.

"Yes, I know. That's why I stayed out of the way."

"Good move. This bloody committee thing is getting to be more hassle than it's worth."

*

"Fucking burglary - my arse! Fucking bunch of kids. All as bad as each other – that Billy Grindle, and all the rest of that lot outside her house. They need machine-gunning, the whole fucking LOT of 'em - do us all a favour; make the world a better place. Fucking morons."

*

Nick looked out of his bedroom window and saw that Danny was in his driveway next door working on a car. *Great, an opportunity!* He hadn't seen Danny for quite some time; it was almost as if Danny was avoiding him. He ran downstairs and then edged out of his front door. He felt some trepidation, which annoyed him - if Danny was messing him around then it should be him feeling uncomfortable, but he didn't ever show any such signs.

Danny was leaning under the bonnet of the car that he was working on, a Ford Fiesta. He didn't look up as Nick sidled up and stood to the side of him.

Nick coughed, and then spoke, "Hi, Danny!"

Danny turned his head warily and then put on a big, forced smile. "Hello, mate!"

"Hi," said Nick. "What's the problem with this one then?"

"Customer's car; it's got a misfire. That's the problem with these, they've got rubbish electrics."

"Really? I thought that was Italian cars."

"No, Fords as well. They use poor quality rubber in the insulation, you see."

Danny then went on to explain why in his view Fords were poorly made all round, and to talk about the problems of this particular car, and also about its owner and how she was a regular customer who only ever trusted *him* to work on her car. None of this of course was of any interest to Nick, but he had to half listen to it before Danny ran out of waffle. When that eventually happened, Nick was able to pose the question that Danny undoubtedly knew was coming.

"So, how's the Bond coming along then?"

Danny stood up from leaning on the Fiesta and rubbed his oily hands in a piece of rag. "Yeah, really well. We've got it all stripped down ready. Going to be doing the engine work next before it goes into the paint shop. You know, it's better to do all the work before it's got new paint, so it doesn't get scratched or anything."

"Great! That's good. How did you get on with getting all the parts?"

"Yeah, yeah. Got all those." Then Danny thought for a moment. "Except for the master cylinder - they sent the wrong one. They sent one for a Riley car."

"Did they?" said Nick. "I thought the brakes were all standard Girling parts."

"Yeah, yeah - Girling, but this one was for a Riley. It had a bigger barrel, so it wouldn't fit. No problem though, we sent it back. Should have the new one next Tuesday."

"Sounds good. So, can I come around and get some photos? Remember - I want to keep a record of the restoration as it progresses."

"Yes, of course, mate. You can come and help out if you like!"

"Well, seriously, yeah, I'd love to help if I can do something useful."

"No, I'm only joking, mate. I wouldn't make you come and work on it; you've got me to do that."

"Well, like I say, I'd be happy to. But either way, I'll come and get some photos. Are you there this weekend?"

"Er, no, leave it a couple of weeks. You see, it's in the back unit at the moment and it's a bit crammed in there. We'll get it back to the main workshop ready for the painting, then you'll be able to get a proper look at it."

"OK, we'll do it in a fortnight then. But can you get some photos of it for me on your phone in the meantime?"

"Yeah, yeah, sure mate. But not on this phone though, the photo quality's not much good - I've got a digital camera at the workshop. I've already done some photos. I'll get them over to you."

"Oh great! But get some on the phone too if you can, and you can just text them to me. I'm not bothered about the quality."

At that moment, the front door to Danny's house opened and out stepped his wife, Brenda. She looked as miserable as usual. A smell of cooking wafted past her ample form - a not particularly pleasant smell of cooking.

"Hi," said Nick.

"You still trying to get him to do that old car of yours? Rotten as a pear, he says it is."

Then she turned towards Danny whose head was back under the Fiesta's bonnet.

"Danny, your tea's ready. Need to come in now."

"Yeah, alright. I'll be in now."

Brenda closed the door behind her. Danny didn't look up from under the bonnet.

"OK, I'll leave you to it," said Nick. "Let me know when I can come down … when it's convenient. And don't forget to send me those photos."

"Sure, mate. Yeah, I'll get them over to you."

Nick trudged back home, not so much wishing that he hadn't come to speak to Danny, more wishing that he'd never met him.

*

8. Rob

The six-foot-high wrought iron gates that Nick had bought from a company on the Internet were very cheap, but as far as he could tell they were well made, and he was really pleased with them. Len had then installed two wooden posts and hung the gates, leaving Nick with the simple task of painting them. The bare-metal gates had been in place for two weeks when he set to work on a Saturday morning with his big tin of black Hammarite paint and a selection of brushes bought at the local £1 shop. It was half past nine when he started his work, and he was hoping to be finished by lunch time.

He placed some newspapers on the ground under the gates, weighed them down with stones and then opened the paint and got to work on the bottom rail of the first gate. Throughout this procedure he was aware of Damian lurking on the footpath at the other side of the road. And then Damian was suddenly standing next to him.

"Awright, mate. You painting your gates then?"

Nick looked up at the boy standing with his hands in his pockets.

"Yeah, that's right."

"I'm waiting for my dad."

"Oh, right - are you staying with him for the weekend?"

"He was supposed to be here at eight o'clock. I don't think he's coming. He often doesn't pick me up"

"Er, oh dear. Can you phone him?"

"He's not answering."

Damian started to cry.

"Well, let's hope he comes along soon," said Nick.

"NICK!" It was Alyson at the front door. "Got a cup of coffee here for you."

"OK, thanks." Then he turned back to Damian. "I'll, er, I'll see you in a few minutes."

But when Nick came back from his first coffee break Damian was gone.

Half an hour later another boy came and spoke to Nick. Nick didn't know his name, but he was around the estate most weekends offering a car cleaning service. He had a home-made trailer attached to the back of his pushbike, containing a bucket and all of his cleaning materials. He seemed to do a good trade. Ted Davies over the road was one of his regular customers. Nick had got the boy to clean Alyson's car once, but he didn't do a particularly good job of it, so he hadn't asked him again.

"Hello sir, do any of your cars need cleaning?"

"No, thanks," said Nick, "they're all OK at the moment."

"I could do you a good discount on doing more than one if you want."

"Thanks, but no. It's not the money - I just don't need them done at the moment. Anyway, how's business?"

The boy then proudly told Nick about his growing list of regular customers and then about the different cleaning products that he used and experimented with, and the pros and cons of each one. He waffled on a bit, and maybe ten minutes had passed by the time Ted Davies appeared at the end of his drive and waved, and the boy headed over to his first booked customer of the day.

Nick was able to get back to his task in hand. But not for long - as once he had provided the car cleaning boy with water for his bucket and access to his car, Ted Davies wandered over for a chat. That chat inevitably covered the topic of six-foot gates and the unfortunate need for them, before moving specifically to Tricia and the scum and what misery they and their like were causing to the neighbourhood. Right on cue, an old Vauxhall Astra drove by at speed containing four youths, one of whom threw out debris from a fast-food chicken meal. A polystyrene container and some greasy wraps of paper swirled around following the car briefly before distributing themselves over several gardens; a pile of chicken bones stopped just where they landed - in the middle of the road, and an empty cola bottle bounced along the footpath before entering Ted's driveway where it hit the side of his car and then came to rest.

"Makes you despair for humanity," said Ted.

Ted then went away collecting up the debris to place in his bin. He'd been talking to Nick for maybe twenty minutes.

The postman was next. He was their usual one, a man of about sixty called Mike. His chat lasted only a couple of minutes though as he had work to be getting on with.

At halfway through the first gate, Nick decided it was time for another coffee break. When he came back out to continue his 'work' his heart sank at the sight of some of the scum hanging around. He positioned himself on the inside of the gate that he was painting in order that he could keep an eye on them. There were seven of them in total and as Nick carried on with his painting, they did what they always did, which was essentially nothing. They stood mostly in the middle of the road with one or two from time to time drifting into Tricia's front yard. Tricia didn't make an appearance but that didn't seem to bother them. None of them spoke to Nick and they didn't seem to speak to one another much, saving their energies for intermittently kicking stones around, smoking, and glowering at every driver that passed, each of whom had to slow down and turn to avoid inconveniencing the gang. An exception to this was Derek Tindall who drove through looking angry without slowing down at all - if anything he appeared to speed up. Several scum members had to jump out of the way at the last second in panic, and all turned and yelled after Derek, furious that he had challenged their authority and caused them to look uncool in the process. Nick managed to make his smirk not too obvious.

The scum wandered off to make a nuisance of themselves somewhere else soon after that, and with no other visitors, Nick had a clear run at his painting, managing to complete the first gate in time for his lunch.

When Nick returned from his lunch break there was a police car parked outside Tricia's house. There was nothing unusual about that and so he got back to the task in hand. Bradley Mullen soon drove by at his usual speed and with his phone to his ear, as ever. The developing angry middle-aged man side of Nick wished that the driver of the police car had been outside of Tricia's house to see him do it ... or even better, that the scum were still hanging around so that he might have hit one of them, or had something thrown at his car, or both. Bradley Mullen parked up and disappeared into his parents' house. Then, while Nick was still having thoughts of harm coming to Bradley Mullen or to the scum, he looked up to find a policeman standing over him.

"Oh, er, hello."

"Hello, sir. Put some new gates up, have you?"

"Yes, er, yeah - you know, sort of rounds off the driveway nicely."

"It's alright. I understand exactly why you've got them. How are you getting on with your neighbour over the road?"

Nick put down his paintbrush and stood up to address the policeman who introduced himself as "P.C. Bailey".

"Well, you can probably guess," said Nick. "It's not exactly fun having her over there - her and her friends."

And yes, P.C. Bailey could indeed guess what it was like. Well, he didn't need to guess, he explained, as he and his colleagues were being called out to come and see for themselves, more often than not by Tricia herself. Nick relaxed. P.C. Bailey came over as a nice enough bloke and seemed keen to chat. Nick was usually supportive of the police, but his past experiences hadn't always been positive.

He told P.C. Bailey about some of the incidents that had taken place since Tricia's arrival, some of which he was already aware of, and some that he was not. He was quite candid about acknowledging that she was a nuisance - along with her 'gang' but didn't give away anything more that he might know about her.

"I pity you guys having to deal with them all the time though," said Nick. "And what about the famous Billy Grindle; I'm guessing that you've come across him quite a bit."

P.C. Bailey rolled his eyes. "The problem is with some of them," he said, "is that you know what they're up to, but it can be difficult to get enough evidence for the CPS. They don't like locking up under sixteens if they can help it either."

His words were quite diplomatic, but his frustration was obvious.

"What gets me," said Nick, "is that they cause so much misery for so many other people, especially those who have lived here all of their lives. The poor old lady in that house over there had been here more than forty years, but she's gone because she couldn't take it anymore."

P.C. Bailey nodded. "A lot of them do turn around, to be fair. They get to seventeen, eighteen and get jobs and girlfriends and tone it down. You'd be surprised."

"Well, we can hope."

Nick talked to P.C. Bailey about the residents' association. P.C. Bailey encouraged him to make the most of that and shared his opinion that if the community and authorities pulled together, things really could work.

"I've got similar problems where I live," he said. "There's whole gangs of them about, day or night. But there's not enough people prepared to do anything about it."

He looked sad about that, and the thought that a policeman might feel powerless to tackle the problems in his own environment sent something of a chill through Nick's spine, contrasting with the warm feeling that P.C. Bailey's words had been giving him up to that point. But overall, the chat was a really positive experience. P.C. Bailey really did seem to care, and he really did seem to believe that there was hope for things to get getter. He'd also managed to help Nick feel that his own contribution had value.

"Don't forget," said P.C. Bailey, "make a note of everything - times, dates - everything that happens. And keep letting us know. Even if nobody comes out, it's all there on file and it helps to build a picture."

Nick thanked him as he left. "See you again ... although, in the nicest possible way, hopefully not too often!"

P.C. Bailey laughed and waved a measured but cheery goodbye.

As he drove away Nick found himself thinking - and hoping - that that was somebody who wasn't going to be only a constable for very long. That conversation had taken up another twenty to thirty minutes, but it certainly wasn't time wasted as far as Nick was concerned, and he returned to his task with renewed vigor.

He achieved a solid two minutes of further painting before his next visitor materialised, which was Harshad from the house next to Colin's.

"Hi, mate. Nice to see you're hard at work."

Derek Tindall drove by again, hands gripping the wheel. He stared ahead looking just as angry as he had done when the scum had been there earlier.

"Oh, hi Harshad. Yeah, just getting a bit of paint on them."

That opening gambit from Harshad was of course only an excuse to get onto the subject of why the police had been talking to Nick, and hence another lengthy conversation on Tricia and the scum ensued. Harshad had a social awkwardness about him but was always up for a chat with Nick, and usually a long one. "You collect weirdos," Alyson had said, "because you are too nice to them." But Nick didn't mind that - surely it was a good way to be? So, he tolerated Harshad - even perhaps enjoyed the fact that Harshad found him accommodating enough to want to be friends. All the same, after half an hour, he felt the need to more than strongly hint that "I'd better be getting on with my painting", and ten minutes after that, Harshad did eventually make his way back home.

It was after three o'clock, and Nick got his DAB radio from the house to listen to 5 Live's afternoon football commentary while he 'worked'. He quite enjoyed painting at times, especially when he could transform something from looking scruffy and dilapidated to nice and shiny and new quite easily. That worked with a door, for example. But wrought iron gates weren't quite the same: much as the work was needed, the gates didn't look particularly better having their colour changed from the dark grey of their bare metal state to the mottled black of the Hammerite. The fiddly intricacies of the ironwork made the whole process rather tedious. He was therefore actually grateful for the various interruptions that had broken up his day. None of the usual neighbours that he might have expected to come and have a chat - Colin, Danny, Rob, or Michelle - had been about, but the thought of the mixed range of people who had - Damian, the car cleaning boy, Ted Davies, P.C. Bailey, and Harshad, put a smile on Nick's face. His next visitor was less of a welcome sight.

Nick was painting from the inside of his second gate when he became aware of a large group of youths approaching from his right - past Colin's house. He assumed that it was the usual gathering heading for Tricia's house and followed his normal approach of not looking at them and carrying on with what he was doing. But he was quickly aware of a close presence and looked up to see Billy Grindle at the other side of the gate looking down at him. The other youths all came to a stop, amassed behind Billy Grindle, and they looked on expectantly. There were more of them than usual, possibly twenty in all. Nick recognised most of them as regulars at Tricia's gatherings.

"Hello," said Nick to Billy Grindle, standing up as he did so.

Billy Grindle glared out from under his hoodie. "Someone said you've been grassing me up."

That took Nick by surprise, and he took a few seconds to come up with a suitable response. He had no idea what Billy Grindle was talking about but thought it was likely to be something to do with his visit from P.C. Bailey earlier; he'd probably been seen by one of these paranoid clowns who'd put two and two together to make five.

"Grassing you up for what?" he replied.

Billy Cowan sneered. The cynical miserable Billy Grindle, not the wide-eyed boy who had so briefly made a re-appearance when Nick's Porsche was being taken to its new home.

"A burglary. People say you've been saying it was me."

Ah, the burglary! Well, yes, of course Nick had mentioned Billy Grindle's name in relation to that, and for a fraction of a second he felt bad for doing so. But then of course *everybody* had mentioned Billy Grindle's name in association with that burglary, and in any case, he'd almost certainly done it.

Nick had an idea. "Sorry, who are you?"

That wrong-footed Billy Grindle. He seemed to think for a moment, and then he spat on the ground. The assembled throng shuffled their feet. Billy Grindle glared at Nick and gave a big smirk for the benefit of his followers before turning to walk on in the direction he had been travelling.

"Do you know who did it then?" Nick called after him.

Billy Grindle only half-turned his head back towards Nick. "Of course not."

"Well let me know if you find out, won't you!"

The youths all shuffled off in the direction of the park, following their 'leader', and Nick was left bewildered. He was angry at the arrogance of the obnoxious little prick, and he was always angered by people who saw 'grassing up' as being a bad thing - surely it was the right thing to do for anybody with morals. But on the other hand, he was quite pleased with himself for the way he'd handled the situation, pretending not to know who he was had quite taken the wind out of Billy Grindle's sails. Nick wondered about the prospect of reprisals, but he was fairly confident that there wouldn't be any.

He didn't get any more 'visitors' after that and eventually finished the task that he had intended to take the morning at five o'clock, just in time to miss his usual Saturday afternoon viewing of *Final Score*. He packed up his things and headed into the house. He'd hardly seen Alyson, who had been working in her office, and he readied himself for a "what the hell have you been doing out there all day" conversation, for which he would be happy to provide a comprehensive answer.

*

Nick had been at a pub in Ealing for a large Thursday night work gathering to celebrate a couple of birthdays and somebody leaving. It had started early, and the beers had flowed fast. At nine-thirty he was flagging and had decided to head towards home to finish up locally. He'd texted Alyson from the bus to see if she wanted to join him at The Star, but he'd just got the answer:
No. Got to be up early for work.

He'd got to The Star just after ten-thirty, had a quick couple of pints at the bar, and then bought a bottle of Heineken to drink on his walk home. During that walk he'd deviated via the kebab shop and was just now finishing off his large doner with extra chilli sauce as he got to the gates of his house.

"Awright, mate!"

Nick looked over to see Tricia in her doorway, one arm leaning against the door frame the other sporting a cigarette - her usual pose. He ambled over towards her and as he did so he noticed that Charlene was also standing in her doorway, which was next to Tricia's. She was also leaning on her door frame and smoking. Both were wearing dressing gowns, but that was the extent of any similarity in their appearances. Tricia's filthy off-white gown was tied tightly around her overweight frame, and she would almost certainly have been wearing it all day, whereas Charlene's silky blue number hung loosely around her slender body and was open at the front revealing that underneath she was, as often, wearing only a bikini. She had probably just put it on after yet another session on her sunbed to top up her deep perma-tan.

"Been out on the town then, mate?" asked Tricia.

Nick still had the greasy wrapping paper from the kebab in his hands but had finished the contents.

"Yeah, been into Ealing for someone's leaving do." He slurred his words a little.

"Had a bit to drink, haven't you!"

"Yes, had a few beers."

"Your wife not with you?"

"No, she has to be up early to get into London in the morning."

"Well, she won't thank you turning up at midnight pissed-up and smelling of kebab, will she?"

Tricia cackled and then burst into a coughing fit.

Charlene meanwhile gave a little smirk and took a long drag on her cigarette.

Nick thought that Charlene was looking particularly alluring tonight. That could have been partly due to the amount of beer that he'd drunk and partly due to the comparison with Tricia, but mainly it was because she really was very attractive.

Tricia recovered from her coughing fit. "You can always come over here if you want a drink and a laugh, mate. Just as long as you bring a bottle with you!"

Charlene spoke for the first time. "Yeah, she's anyone's for a bottle of vodka!"

Tricia cackled again. "Shhh!" she said, and then she started to laugh and cough again.

"Well, anyway, I'd better go," slurred Nick, and he gestured a little wave as he turned away.

"Night, mate," said Tricia and Charlene in unison, making Nick wonder whether either of them could remember what his name was.

Nick crossed over the road.

Tricia's voice cackled after him. "He's not going to be getting it tonight, is he! Hahahahaha!"

*

Exactly two weeks after Danny had told Nick that he would be able to come and see the Bond 'in a couple of weeks' the two of them bumped into each other in the local shop. Nick had just picked himself up a four pack of Stella for the evening as he was going to be watching football on the TV, and as he walked up to the counter there was Danny buying some fags.

"Oh, hi Nick. How's it going?"

This time Nick didn't beat about the bush.

"Yeah, all good, thanks. So, shall I come up in the next day or two to have a look at the Bond, then?"

"Yeah, sure," said Danny, with no hesitation. And then, "Not just yet though. Stuart's gone and parked his van over the doors to the back garage, and he's gone away … and we haven't got a key."

Nick had no idea who 'Stuart' was or even whether he actually existed, and he had his doubts as well about the said van, or even the 'back garage'.

"OK. Do you know how long he's away for?"

"No, he didn't say - the wanker! I'll let you know." And with that Danny scurried out of the shop.

Nick turned back to the booze aisle and got himself another four-pack of Stella.

*

Alyson was in a good mood. She had left work early and she drove from the station in her usual enthusiastic style. It was a hot day, and she had both front windows open in her car; sometimes she preferred the wind in her hair to the chill of the air conditioning. But her good mood instantly evaporated as she turned the final corner of her journey. First, she heard the music from the ghetto blaster and then Tricia's house came into view. The scum were out in force, boys and men standing around drinking in Tricia's front yard, but they were also spread out over the street, maybe thirty of them in total. But worse than the sight of the yobs was the state of the street itself; it was a carpet of broken glass - bits of smashed beer bottles covering the entire width of the road surface for a stretch the length of three or four cars. Tricia surveyed the scene with indifference from her usual position in the doorway sporting her customary lager can and fag combination.

Alyson's blood boiled to the point that she wanted to drive straight into the crowd. She almost did. Blasting on her horn she swerved towards her driveway, crunching glass under her tyres, and causing scum members to nonchalantly edge out of her way, glaring smugly at her as they did so. The big gates at the top of the drive were flapping wide open which angered Alyson still further but at least meant that she didn't have to stop to open them. The car's front wing made contact with the left-hand gate as she sped into the driveway throwing it back hard on its hinges from where it bounced back in time to make contact too with the rear wing as the car passed. Alyson slammed on the brakes and the car skidded to a stop in front of the garage. As she hurriedly closed the car's windows, she heard a sarcastic "Oooooh!" from a small number of the scum, but not many of them - most were too lazy to take notice of or interest in anything. She ran to the house, fumbling with her keys as she first unlocked the porch and then locked it behind her, and then did the same with the main front door. She then threw herself into the front room and crashed onto one of the sofas. Her hands were trembling as she dialled up Nick on her mobile.

She screamed into the phone, "THIS CAN'T GO ON! They're all over the fucking street. We've got to DO SOMETHING!"

Nick attempted to calm Alyson, but to no avail; she carried on yelling.

"It's too MUCH! It's TOO MUCH! Somebody's going to die. Somebody's going FUCKING DIE!" And with that she threw the phone down and let out a yell loud enough that the scum would have heard if not for the volume of their music.

Alyson hid herself away in her office at the back of the house for the next hour or so. The noise from over the road continued to permeate and keep her blood simmering. But then there was a change. She could hear a man's voice and he was shouting. The ghetto blaster went quiet. She went through to the front of the house and looked out of her bedroom window. And what she saw was good. Rob Stockdale was in the middle of the street holding a large broom, and he was yelling at Tricia. Alyson couldn't make out exactly what was being said but the conversation was all one way: Rob was shouting, and Tricia was looking sheepish. The scum were all looking at

Rob too, as was Charlene, from her doorway. Alyson edged open the window in order to be able to listen, and at the same time Rob threw the broom down onto the road and bellowed "NOW FUCKING GET ON WITH IT!"

Rob then stood back with his hands on his hips and watched as Tricia, in dressing gown and slippers, came nervily out into the road and picked up the broom. The scum looked on silently; the scene felt to Alyson like a classroom when a teacher had lost their cool with an infuriating pupil.

"Go on then," said Rob.

And slowly Tricia began to sweep pieces of glass towards the side of the road. Not quite as slowly the scum all began to drift away towards the park. Alyson clapped her hands loudly in Rob's direction. Rob turned around, gave her a thumbs up and winked. Charlene then emerged with a broom of her own and started to help Tricia.

"Every fucking bit of it, Tricia, or I'll be shoving it through your letterbox," said Rob.

Alyson smiled and went back into her office. At last, somebody could stand up to those wankers.

When Nick got home, he found Alyson still on edge, despite the positive turn of events, and seeming to be blaming him for the scum's activities. They ate some food together enveloped in a tense atmosphere and then started on a bottle of red wine in front of the TV.

At eleven o'clock Alyson went up to bed as she had to be up early for work in the morning, and so Nick put on his jacket, took a can from the fridge and headed out into the back garden. He sat down in his usual chair by the fence. "Are you there, Colin?"

Colin drew on his cigarette before replying in his normal soft tone. "Yes, I'm here."

Nick opened the ring-pull on his lager can. "How's it going?"

"Same as ever. What about you?"

"Yeah … did you see all the mess that the scum made earlier?"

"No, what happened?"

"I didn't see it, but apparently they smashed loads of beer bottles all over the road. Alyson went mental when she came across it, she phoned me up at work like it was my fault! Rob made Tricia sweep it all up with a broom though, which I wish I'd seen."

"Brilliant! No, I didn't get in until late … fifteen-hour shift again."

"Fair play to Rob though, he had a real go at her, Alyson said. Sounds as if she was crapping herself."

"About time somebody sorted her out. What with that fucking lot and everything else I haven't had a decent night's sleep for months. Not going to end well, that business – that, I can promise you."

Nick took a long swig of his lager. "They called me over when I came home from the pub the other night, Tricia and Charlene."

"Really? She's a bit of alright that Charlene, isn't she?"

"Yeah. They were both quite friendly, to be honest."

"Perhaps that Tricia's after your body!"

"Blimey, that's a horrible thought. They say, 'any port in a storm', but there are limits. Charlene did say that Tricia is anyone's for a bottle of vodka, but I'm not sure there'll be too many takers."

Nick looked up to the clear sky and shivered. It was a cold night and winter was just around the corner.

Colin took a final drag on his cigarette and then scuffed out the butt on the concrete with his shoe. "Well, better be going. Got to be up at five-thirty."

"You going a long way tomorrow, then?"

"No, they've got me in the office doing the controller thing. I do it once a week. A 'development opportunity' they call it. Load of bollocks."

"Ah, well, makes a change, I suppose."

"Yeah. Sooner do without it though. See you, then."

"Cheers. Sleep well."

Nick stayed out there on his own. The cold didn't bother him, and nor would it have concerned him if it was raining. But actually, he didn't much enjoy these moments on his own, certainly not as much as he used to. Whenever he was alone in the quiet with his thoughts now, he was aware of an anxiety - a tension in his stomach, gnawing away at him. Why? Was it work - Alyson - the scum - the residents' association? He felt that it was always there. Maybe he should do something about it. Talk to someone, people would say. Who … Alyson? He smirked. That wasn't going to happen.

He finished up his can. *Maybe get just one more.*

*

"Haha! The little shits get some comeuppance at last. That's the floodgates opened now. There's going to be some more of that. Haha! Stupid bitch and her little shits. Maybe next time get that glass rammed down their fucking THROATS! Ha! I'll fucking drink to that."

*

Nick and Alyson tended to go out for a meal together about once every two weeks, and more often than not it was to the same restaurant - The Spice Tandoori, about a thirty-minute walk from their house. Tonight, they were in good spirits and were finishing up their drinks after the meal.

"So, it really does look as if the tide might have turned, doesn't it?" said Alyson, returning to a topic that they'd covered at length earlier in the evening.

"Certainly hope so - two whole days and no sign of them. Rob really is a hero, isn't he!"

"Ha-ha! Well, he will be if it has actually done the trick."

Nick had ordered the bill and it was taking ages to arrive, but it wasn't bothering him; he was happy to finish up his drink at leisure. A weight had been lifted.

"So, what shall we do now?" asked Nick.

Alyson looked at him quizzically; the answer was fairly obvious.

"Shall we go to The Star for a couple?"

"Yep," said Nick. "And then what?"

Nick was looking into Alyson's eyes. She knew what he meant.

"Go home, of course."

"And?"

Alyson brushed her hand on Nick's as she fixed her gaze on his.

"Well, we could go to bed and have sex."

She leant forward and kissed him and then they clinked their glasses together.

"Yeah, I suppose so - if you want to," said Nick.

Alyson playfully slapped him on the nose, just in time for the waiter to appear at the table with their bill.

They would indeed be having sex when they got in, as well as something else that they hadn't been doing much recently: they would sleep well for the whole night afterwards.

*

"Alright, Nick!"

Danny was at Nick's front door looking bubbly and enthusiastic.

He had a package in his hands – something wrapped up in a bundle of newspaper.

He handed it to Nick. "Have a look at that!"

Nick unravelled the newspaper to reveal a pristine gleaming chrome car hub cap that glinted in the low evening sunlight. It seemed to be from his Bond, although it felt lighter than he remembered.

"Nice," he said. "Is it one of mine?"

"Yeah, we've had them all done."

"You had them all re-chromed?"

"Yeah."

Cos you can buy new ones, you know – from Vietnam, I think they are, but they're quite cheap ..."

"No, no – these are the proper ones – this guy used to work at H.R. Owen doing the Rolls-Royces. He's doing all the chrome – badges, door handles – the lot. Not cheap, but really good. I thought you'd want to see it."

"Yes, looks great. No, I was going to say, those new ones don't have a good name. Apparently, they start to go rusty after a couple of months."

"Yeah, exactly. No, we wanna do this properly."

"No, that's great. It's good to see it. Nice to see that things are progressing."

Nick handed the hub cap back to Danny.

"No, you can keep that. I'll bring the other ones round; you can have the whole set."

"Right, OK, Er, thanks. Anyway, how's things otherwise?"

"Yeah, yeah – good, thanks. So, we've got all the parts coming and it's coming on nicely. Did you have the rest of the money yet, only it's cost a bit more than we thought and …"

"Er, yes, sure – no problem. I just didn't think that you wanted it until it was finished, otherwise …"

"Yeah, no, well it is finished now really – well practically. Only if you can though, no problem if you haven't got it. Or just some of it, you know – on account sort of thing."

"No, it's not a problem. When do you need it?"

"Just drop round the house sometime. Tomorrow? Just whatever you can. No worries if you can't though. We'll get it sorted for you."

"No, it's OK. I'll er, yeah. No problem."

"OK, cheers, mate. No worries. And, yeah, you can keep that. Show the missus; she'll be pleased with that, won't she?"

"Yeah, yeah. It's nice."

Danny turned to leave. "Cheers, mate. And don't worry if you can't …"

"Yeah, thanks. I'll bring it round. Bye for now."

"What did he want, then?" asked Alyson.

Nick held out the hub cap. "He brought this."

"Blimey, he's actually done something then. Looks nice."

"Yeah, it's good isn't it."

"Did he have anything else to say?"

"Er, no, no – not really. He's, you know, getting on with it. Says he's going to bring some more stuff round."

Alyson returned to what she was doing, and Nick went to the fridge for a lager. This time he hadn't asked Danny for any photographs. He hadn't forgotten, he just hadn't asked. He tossed the hub cap onto the sofa. It flew like a frisbee.

*

9. Derek

"Oi, Dave! Are you doing her yet?"

The question was directed at Dopey Dave who was chatting to Tricia on her doorstep. The member of the scum who had asked it was a blond-haired seventeen-year-old emboldened by alcohol and camaraderie. The three friends he was with fell about laughing. The ghetto blaster was playing loud, the scum - about twenty of them - had been drinking throughout the day and were standing around in groups of three or four in Tricia's yard and out across the street. Broken bottles littered the yard and spilled out onto the footpath and the street beyond.

"Leave him alone you little gay shit," spat Tricia.

Dopey Dave said nothing.

Damian sat on the kerb smoking a cigarette.

The blond boy staggered in Tricia's direction.

"Don't call me gay, you fat cow!"

His mates burst into hysterics. He took a long drag on his cigarette.

"Oi!" shouted Dopey Dave. "Leave her alone."

The blond boy half choked, and half laughed. Cigarette smoke billowed from his mouth and his nostrils.

Dopey Dave looked blankly back at him.

"Hahaha, fucking paedo," laughed the blond boy.

Tricia joined in again. "Don't call him a paedo, you fucking arse bandit!"

Dopey Dave threw his half-full can of lager at the group. It missed and clattered across the road, spilling its contents onto the tarmac.

"Fuck off Ryan, you fucking shit."

Dopey Dave advanced towards 'Ryan'.

Ryan spat in his face.

Dopey Dave took a swing at Ryan but missed and fell to the floor. Most of the scum laughed at him, including Tricia.

Dopey Dave got up and brushed himself down. He walked away. He was in tears.

Ryan laughed again.

His mates laughed.

Tricia got herself a fresh can of lager.

The rest of the scum got back to doing nothing.

Alyson had a pen in her hand. She gripped it so hard that it broke in half.

*

Nick knocked on his neighbours' front door. He somehow felt apprehensive, as if he was intruding. He had a brown envelope in his hand containing a thousand pounds – fifty £20 notes; that should have felt good – exciting. But it didn't, instead he felt flat.

The door flew open almost immediately and Brenda glared at him. "He's not here."

"No, I, er, it's OK. I've got some money to give him. He asked me to er …"

Nick held out the envelope and Brenda took it. The TV was playing loudly behind her.

"OK, I'll tell him."

"Right, er, thanks then."

"Cheers." She was already closing the door.

"Yeah, thanks, I …" The door was closed. Nick stood for a moment before turning and trudging back out of the driveway.

*

"Hi Sarah, Sorry that I haven't written for a while - but I know you'll understand why."

Alyson had spoken to Sarah on the phone a few times and the two of them had swapped plenty of texts, but she felt that it really was time - for the first time in many months - to sit down and write one of her email 'letters', which to her were something different from more casual types of communication - they were somehow more personal.

Alyson paused while she thought about what things she wanted to cover in the letter. She always went through the same process. She thought about what things she wanted to write about, then she wrote down some notes on a note pad, then she composed the letter - with much editing and re-editing - in a Word document, taking some time, often more than an hour. When she was completely satisfied with her composition, she copied it into an email and sent it.

She scribbled down her list of topics. It was quite a long list but with essentially only one theme. It took her maybe ten minutes to complete that exercise and when she felt that it was finished and she ready to start writing she had also finished her glass of wine. She was about to get another glassful but then instead turned to her desk drawer and her hidden vodka bottle. It was a half-bottle, and it was a nice one that she'd got from Waitrose; it was nearly full. She poured herself a generous measure into her wine glass.

"I hope all's well with you. Unfortunately, nothing's changed here."

She then went on to write about her recent Tricia experiences, which were of course mostly bad, other than the small chink of hope during the broken glass incident, "... There's a guy a few doors up from her called Rob - I've probably mentioned Rob and Michelle; he's a big bloke and a bit of an oik, but he's OK, and he had a real go at her and made her sweep it all up. They all disappeared for a few days and I really hoped that it might be a turning point but now they're back, as bad as ever."

She wrote about Nick and his involvement in the residents' association, and how that much as it might be well intentioned, she had no confidence in it achieving anything. She questioned, as she always did on her phone chats with Sarah, Nick's capability when it came to problems involving confrontation, "… it just frustrates me how he lets people walk all over him."

Alyson's words flowed as quickly as the vodka. She wrote of her desire to move away, but then of what effect Tricia and the scum's presence would have on the value of her house, and even whether they might prevent it selling at all. "And then there's the neighbours. Nick's entrusted that old car that his uncle left him to the Indian bloke next door and he's just a waster. I'm sure he's ripped him off. I don't know how much money he's given him, but I know that he's worried about it. The problem is that they live in the house that's the other half of our semi, and he's got this really horrible fat wife and four sons. So, if we fall out with them, how's that going to end? Honestly, Sarah, maybe I'm being irrational, but I really don't know how much more I can fucking take."

The letter was long and at times rambling. Alyson looked at her watch. It was after eleven o'clock: she'd been writing for more than two hours. The vodka bottle was close to empty. She read through the whole thing. It was good. It was very good, and it was emotional; it really captured everything that she was feeling. She was pleased with what she'd done. She wiped away a tear. She was aware that she was very drunk. She couldn't send the letter to Sarah; it wouldn't be fair. She deleted the Word document, switched off her computer and poured herself just one more glass of vodka - an extra-large one to polish off the remainder of the bottle. At least she would sleep soundly tonight … well, possibly.

*

Nick tended to go to ten or twelve Norling F.C. home games in a season. If, as was usually the case, they were Saturday afternoon games then he had something of a fixed match day ritual. He would leave home at around two-fifteen and at his brisk walking pace that got him to the ground a quarter of an hour before the three o'clock kick-off. Once there he would buy a programme and then slowly walk an entire circuit of the pitch before deciding where to stand to watch the start of the game. On occasions - some of the more competitive local derbies or the odd 'big' cup game, there were crowd segregation measures put in place, preventing his walkabout - the irrational tribalistic hatred of opposition supporters by a small section of followers existed as much at this level as it did with the big clubs. Either way, Nick never stayed in the same spot for the whole game and when he could, he would circumnavigate the pitch three or four times during the course of the afternoon. He usually got himself a burger shortly before the halftime 'rush', and more often than not a cup of tea during the second half.

There was something about the world of non-league football that he found fascinating and somehow invigorating. An amalgam of quirky features formed something that was unique and was apart from the rest of the modern world. And Norling F.C. was the epitome of a non-league football club. Its toilet facilities were sparse at best, one of the two small toilet blocks containing just a long concrete urinal and no hand washing facilities; the wind howled through it and winter resided there on all but the very warmest of days. The one small decaying stand with moss-covered corrugated roof had character, along with restricted views and limited weather protection. Amateurish pitch-side advertising hoardings for local garages and restaurants were mostly faded through being in place for years, if not decades. The lady in the 'tea bar' had been with the club since the 1970s, almost as long as the enormous urn from which she dispensed her steaming hot brews come rain or shine. The crackly tannoy 'entertained' throughout the build-up to the game and during the half-time interval, alternating between almost-impossible-to-decipher announcements and far-too-loud music played by a volunteer DJ who had a very limited selection of records. And then there were the local characters, screaming obscenities at seemingly every refereeing decision, every tackle, and every perceived indiscretion by players on either side. These were mostly older men who at every game stood in their same spot, normally alone, against the fence that surrounded the pitch. These men though were outnumbered by similar men who didn't shout so much but watched on their own or in small groups in near silence for much of the time, other than perhaps a little chuntering or chatting plus the odd eye-roll accompanied tut, and of course a cheer and clapping of the hands when their side scored. But perhaps the most surprising thing was the number of people - several hundred for each game at Norling and hundreds of thousands at similar grounds throughout the country. And not just older men either: groups of lads, families, gaggles of teenage girls - sometimes girlfriends or wannabe girlfriends of the players, who were of course physically fit and on a local scale, celebrities - and ageing 'grannies' in bobble hats and with pre-prepared flasks and sandwiches who were usually more knowledgeable about the club than anybody else there. And finally, from a people point of view, there were the various other 'employees', some paid, some volunteers, from the shouty football manager and his coaches, to the trainspotter-like programme seller, to the blazer-wearing directors and committee members, strutting around like royalty and retiring to their garden shed-esque 'board room' with invited guests after the game. This really was a world divorced from much of normal life and untouched by the march of time. Nick loved disappearing into it from time to time, and in a way it was something of a little secret, because despite the huge number of people taking part in little rituals like Nick's each week, and which others had done before them for more than a hundred years, most of the population at large never entered into this world, and many didn't even know of its existence.

And a bonus for Nick was that, unlike most people present, he left afterwards happy, regardless of the result. Although he preferred it if his adoptive team did win, they weren't 'his' team as such and so he really was able to just enjoy the experience of going to the game. He saw himself as a West Ham supporter, which was something that he had inherited from his father, or more from his grandfather, who lived in East London all of his life and sometimes took Nick to games as a young boy. Nick though was born and brought up near Oxford and as he got older, he felt a little uncomfortable that he followed a (relatively) big club, rather than the medium-sized club of Oxford United that was on his doorstep. So, in his teens he began seeing them from time to time which, besides anything else, was more practical than travelling all the way to the far side of London. Now though he rarely went anywhere other than at his new local club.

Today was Nick's first (and Norling's third) game of the new season. It was a warm August Saturday afternoon and he hurried, almost jogged, from his house in his enthusiasm to get to the ground. He was positively excited at the prospect of enjoying his live football passion for the first time in months. Such was his buoyant mood that his heart only sank slightly at the sight of Derek Tindall, who was out cutting his privet hedge with a pair of shears.

Nick waved politely at Derek as he approached.

"Alright, mate!" said Derek, dropping the shears down to his side as he paused his work.

"Hi! I'm good, thanks. You?" He slowed a little but had no intention of stopping for a conversation.

Derek though had other ideas.

"Saw you out chatting with your mate there the other day."

Nick had little option but to stop and face Derek over his half-trimmed privet hedge, which was the height of both of their chests.

"Which mate was that then?"

"You know, you was painting your gates - the darkie; Muslim or whatever."

Ah yes, of course, Derek had driven by looking angry when he was talking to Harshad the week before.

"Ah, yes - Harshad. I think he's a Hindu, actually."

Derek gave a dismissive 'Hmph'. "They're all the same as far as I'm concerned. I know you like to be friends with them …"

"I try to be friends with everyone", Nick interrupted.

"… but you don't understand. See you haven't seen it all change around here like I have. It used to be nice around here. It was a community. People lived here for generations: you had parents, grandparents, and aunts and uncles, and we all looked out for each other. You know I've lived in this road all my life?"

Nick shook his head. No, he didn't know that.

"I was born in number fourteen down the end there. Then we moved to number twenty-six because it had three bedrooms, and then when I got married, we came here. My wife Joan only comes from just over the other side of Harlesham Road. My brother still lives here too, in Connaught - number twenty-seven. It was all a big community you see. But now that lot have come in and upset the balance. Call me a racist if you want but I'm just saying it like it is. And it's not just the foreigners either - no disrespect, but it's you middle class types coming in too, buying up the houses."

Derek wheezed as he spoke and sometimes paused as he struggled for air.

"It's since Maggie Thatcher sold off the council houses, you have all these different factions. There's no respect. You wouldn't get all this dropping litter and smashing glass and all of that bollocks back then. There's just no respect anymore. All those scum that hang out over there by your house; got no respect; they want putting down. The lot of them."

It was Nick's turn to speak.

"But it's them that's causing all the problems, and they're all locals - and they're all white. So's Billy Grindle. He causes more misery on this estate than everyone else put together."

"But they wouldn't have been able to in those days. We wouldn't have tolerated them. We'd have sorted them out - given them a good kicking. Wouldn't have needed the police coming round here every two minutes - not that they do anything anyway."

"Well anyway, I'd better get going; I've got football to watch."

"Oh, right - you off to the pub then, are you?"

"No, no - Norling, I'm going to the game."

Derek's face brightened. "Really? I haven't been there for years. How are they doing nowadays?"

"Well, they're in the Conference South. They've only played two games this season and they won one and lost one."

Derek's expression turned wistful as he gave a little shake of his head. "Me and my brother used to go there as kids." He chuckled. "We didn't used to pay to get in, mind; we used to sneak in under the fence! ...Well sometimes we did anyway."

Derek gazed out into space as he recalled the memories from his youth. "They had a good team back then. They had this big centre forward, now what was his name? Must have been 1958 or 1959, thereabouts. Dawkins, that was him. Big hulk of a bloke he was … he didn't take any prisoners. Cor, them were the days. Do you go there often then?"

"Yeah, quite often," said Nick. "I used to go to league games quite a bit, West Ham mainly. But one time I went all the way over there, wasted the whole day and spent a fortune all for a crap nil-nil, and it occurred to me that I could just walk down the road and watch a crap game here instead. How about you - when did you last go?"

"Oh, blimey. Probably not since about 1975, if that. I didn't really go much after I got married."

"Well, it probably hasn't really changed since you were last there!"

"Ha-ha, no, I don't suppose it has."

"Well, I'd better get going; don't want to be late."

"Yes, you get going. Good on yer, mate. All the best."

And as the two men waved each other goodbye, Nick saw a big smile on Derek's face for the first time ever.

*

As often on a Monday, after a heavy drinking weekend, Nick had got up too late to walk to work, and so, at nine-thirty had just left the house in his van. He was less than a minute into the journey when the driver of a Transit van coming the other way flashed his lights and then waved him down. Nick slowed and pulled alongside the van which he could now see was not a van, but a tipper truck that was loaded with building equipment. Nick wound down his window. The man leaned out through his own window, he was about forty with sandy hair and a rugged complexion; Nick vaguely recognised him, but he wasn't sure where from. It was probably from a residents' association meeting. Nick steeled himself ready to receive a moan.

"You're the bloke that's got that car that Danny's doing up, aren't you?"

That was an unexpected line of conversation. "Yes," Nick said. "That's right."

"Well, did you know that he's left the workshop? … He's dumped all of your stuff outside for scrap."

Nick of course didn't know and given his startled expression and single word response of "Shit!" the man decided to fill him in on a bit more detail. He was a builder who rented the unit next to Danny's and on the previous Friday he had returned at the end of the afternoon to see Danny clearing out his possessions and locking up his unit. He'd given some story about choosing to go because of the owner of the site wanting to screw him over on a new leasing deal … "but I think he's full of shit. He's probably on the run from creditors; he usually is."

Nick nodded. He was trying to maintain a cool exterior, but he was panicking inside. "Thanks for telling me. I'll get down there and have a look."

"I'll come and join you if you like. I've just got to pick some stuff up from home - I only live just around the corner here; I'll catch you there."

"Er, OK - thanks. What's your name, by the way?"

"Lee". He leaned over and the two of them shook hands. "No problem."

Nick drove apprehensively on the short journey to Danny's unit. It was one of six clustered together around a yard on a small industrial estate alongside the Grand Union canal. A narrow tarmac roadway led from the entranceway, along the edge of the canal to the far end of the ramshackle estate where those six units were located. Nick steered his little van gingerly along that roadway, wary of the proximity of the drop into the murky water of the Grand Union. He rounded a bend and there was his Bond right in front of him. A triangle of land separated Danny's unit from the canal and on it were five cars all looking ready for the scrapyard. The Bond was possibly the worst of the lot.

Nick stopped his van, jumped out and walked hesitantly over to what had once been his uncle Frank's pride and joy. He stood and took in the scene for a moment. His hangover was catching up with him; the canal's putrid odour made him want to throw up.

The Bond was in a forlorn state. Its four headlights were missing, leaving dark gaping holes in their place. It had no windows, and it had no doors. As he got close, Nick could see that most of the exterior trim had been removed and a half-hearted attempt had been made at rubbing down the paintwork in preparation for the planned re-painting. He peered inside. The front seats had been removed from their runners but then crammed back into the car the wrong way up, and on the back seat were all of the car's windows. He went around to the rear of the car. Its two doors were leaning against the back bumper. He wanted to have a look in the boot, so he lifted the two doors and placed them against the side of Danny's unit. The rear lights, boot lock, number plate, and all of the trim from the boot lid had been removed. Nick lifted the boot lid to find that the boot was crammed full. There were the interior panels from the doors, the car's carpets, all of the lights, the number plates, and all the bits of exterior trim (none of which had been re-chromed), as well as assorted used paint tins and Frank's bottle jack, which had always been there. There was no sign of any of the new parts that Danny had supposedly bought. There were though four hub caps – four original battered and corroded hub caps. Nick picked up one of them, it was much heavier than the pristine example that he had at home.

A noisy diesel engine sounded, and Lee's truck pulled into the yard.

"It's a bit of a mess, isn't it?" Lee observed. "Can you recover it?"

Nick agreed that it was a bit of a mess and said that he didn't know whether he could recover it; that would depend on whether he could find anyone to help him.

"Fibreglass, is it?"

"Yep. Well, some of it - not the chassis or the doors or the bulkhead. So those are the bits that rust."

For the next few minutes, the two of them walked around the car looking at it and touching it and talking about what a wanker Danny was.

"You don't want to leave it here though," said Lee. "The landlord will have it down the scrapyard."

"No, I'll need to get it brought back to my house. I'll have to find someone to pick it up."

"Do you know Lawrence?"

Nick shook his head.

"That's his unit up the end there. He does breakdown recovery; he's got a flat bed. I'm sure he'll do it for you for not much."

"How much is 'not much'?"

"I dunno - fifty quid … a hundred at the most."

"That sounds OK," said Nick. "Have you got his phone number?"

"I'll speak to him if you like. You live next door to Danny, don't you?"

"I'm afraid so."

"I'll get him to bring it round in the next couple days, and I'll give the landlord a call to tell him not to scrap it yet."

They exchanged phone numbers and Nick thanked Lee for his help.

"I owe you a pint or two," said Nick.

"I might just take you up on that! Lucky I saw you really, wasn't it?"

"Certainly was. So, you live on the estate then, do you?"

"Yeah, I'm on Connaught. Lived there all my life. I'm three doors down from the house I was brought up in. My mum's still there."

"That's handy. Not a bad place to live, is it."

"Well, it's OK. Or at least it used to be. You've got that problem woman opposite you, haven't you?"

"Yes, certainly have. What about you – are you near the famous Billy Grindle?"

"Yeah, horrible little shit! My mum loves him though. He's always nice and polite to her; used to do shopping and stuff for her when he was younger."

"Blimey! Ah well, it takes all sorts. Anyway, thanks again. Can we sort out getting the car moved pretty soon? I wanna make sure it doesn't get scrapped."

"Yeah, sure. I'll give Lawrence a call now, mate. He'll get it round your house in the next day or two."

"Thanks. And thanks again for your help."

Lee gave Nick a thumbs-up and got back into his truck and drove off. Nick was left to continue to stare at the remains of his classic car. He decided to load what bits he could into his van. All the stuff from the boot went in easily enough but then he got the doors. It would be a tight fit in the tiny Reliant and he had to first remove the stuff that he'd just put in before maneuvering each of the two rusty old doors into the limited load space. It was a struggle and he wished he'd thought of taking the loose bits away when Lee was still there with his truck. But he got there in the end, by which time he was covered in dirt. He fired up the Reliant and drove slowly away.

He had been quite calm so far, but as he made his way home to offload the Bond bits into his garage and get a change of clothing, anger and frustration built inside him. He was of course angry with Danny for being everything that he'd always known him to be. But he was more angry with himself for taking the 'calculated risk' of going to Danny in the first place. Worse than the anger though was the frustration at the thought of all the I-told-you-so lectures that he would have to face from, among others, Alyson.

"Wanker!" He yelled at his windscreen.

But as he approached his house, he was aware of another feeling. There was actually some relief that the inevitable calamity had actually now happened; there was no more nervous waiting and desperately hoping that things would turn out OK. It was almost a relief that the hope was gone.

It was close to eleven o'clock by the time that Nick got back home, and he decided to do something that he hadn't done for years - he called in sick. Well, it was true - he did feel sick, as well as still quite hung over. He took off his grubby clothes and had a shower, his second of the day. Then he got back into bed where at first he lay staring at the ceiling stewing over Danny's treachery, but in time he managed to doze off. He was very quickly awoken from his shallow slumber by the sound of a commotion across the street.

He looked out of the window to see what was going on. There didn't seem to be too much to see - no gangs of snarling youths or bottles being smashed all over the street, just Tricia leaning out of her bedroom window and Damian in their front yard looking up at her. From the little that he could hear through the window Nick could tell that the two of them were arguing. He stayed behind the net curtain but reached his hand through to open the window a little to let some more sound flow in. As he did so, Damian turned away from Tricia and began to stomp out of the unfenced yard. Tricia called after him.

"Ha! Ha! Wet the bed, wet the bed, wet the bed!" She had a big grin on her face and was almost singing.

Damian picked up a stone, turned, and threw it at her. He then turned back, and Nick could see that he was crying. His mother called after him again.

"Oi, you little shit!"

And then she threw something down from the window. It was quite large and black and once it hit the concrete it broke into a lot of pieces that scattered around the yard.

Damian turned back to look, and his jaw dropped. He screamed at his mother.

"That's my Playstation, you fucking bitch!"

Then he turned and walked slowly off up the road sobbing, dejected, and looking as broken as the Playstation. Tricia lit herself a fag and blew smoke into the air as she watched him go.

That evening, Nick worked his way through quite a few cans of lager, and when Alyson went to bed, he ventured into the back garden to carry on. He took two cans out with him to save having to quickly go back into the house to top up.

"Are you there, Colin?" he called out as he took his seat.

There was no reply.

It was chilly. Nick zipped up his jacket, took a large swig from the first can, and then placed it on the ground next to him. He looked up into the night sky and struggled to steady his focus. The lager was certainly helping him to become drunk, but it wasn't making him any less pissed off. Yes, he was still seething at Danny as well as at himself, but something bigger than that was getting to him – it was frustration that circumstances enabled people like Danny to act the way he did, fucking over other people with such arrogance and apparently without a care in the world. And then Tricia – living with no regard to anybody else at all, even her own son. How could people like that even exist? All of that really did make him angry but as he sat there drinking and thinking and staring up at the stars it occurred to him that what frustrated him most of all was being powerless to do anything about any of it.

But then, was he powerless? Maybe he just didn't have the guts to do anything about it. Why did he always have to let people walk all over him? Of course, sometimes it was the right thing to do ... and of course he didn't have to let them always walk over him if things got really serious. There were always options, extreme ones if that became necessary. He soon finished the first can. He scrunched it up, threw it down the garden, and then started on the second one. He already knew that he would be going back into the house to top up again after all.

*

10. Hugh

Jason had been very excited about the fact that an old college friend was coming to stay with him for a few days and had been banging on about it for ages. The friend, Hugh, was from South Wales, and during the build up to his visit Jason had bored Nick and Martin to death regaling them with stories of his Hugh's shared adventures during their time together at Bath University. All the same, Nick and Martin had allowed themselves to be talked into joining Jason and Hugh for a drink in central London.

Nick took a very quick disliking to Hugh. There was an unwarranted arrogance about him. He struck Nick as the sort of bloke who would make a big show of shaking hands with the owner when entering his local Indian restaurant - as if knowing the owner made him something special, without it occurring to him that everyone else there probably knew the owner just as well as he did. Basically, he was very much like Jason.

They were three pints in, and Hugh had been holding court for most of the time while Jason laughed a bit too much at his 'hilarious' anecdotes. Stories of conquests of females formed much of Hugh's repertoire and he'd just paused for breath after telling of his latest success with an apparently 'gorgeous' young 'blonde bit' with an 'amazing bod' that he had met when they were both working out at the gym.

"Cool, brilliant. Well done, mate. Fair play," cooed Jason. "Good place to pick up fanny, the gym."

"Is that where you met Emma then too?" Hugh said to Jason.

"God, no! I pulled her at a club."

"Yeah, I thought probably not."

"Ha-ha! Fuck off, ya bastard!" Jason had the slightly-hurt-but-trying-hard-not-to-show-it look that he displayed whenever the boss Tony Clarke put him down at work. He decided to deflect. "What about you, Nick, where did you meet your missus?"

Nick was snapped out of a semi-slumber. "Oh, er, Alyson? Yeah, nothing spectacular - I just sat next to her at the canteen where I used to work. There weren't any seats left, and she was on a table for two, so I asked her if I could join her."

Martin made a rare philosophical contribution to the conversation. "It's funny how little things like that can completely change the course of your life, isn't it?"

"True, enough," said Nick, "and I'll bet that most of the time we don't even realise that things like that have happened."

"Yeah," said Jason, "if you hadn't met Alyson, you might not be living on your council estate!"

Nick shook his head. "Nothing wrong with living there; I've got a lot of friends in our road."

"Still got your chav problem though?" Jason sneered.

"Oh, yeah, she's still there, unfortunately."

"Nick lives on a chav estate surrounded by chavs acting like chavs," Jason explained to Hugh.

Nick had to defend his neighbourhood. "You can't call everyone who lives there a chav, Jason. Most people are decent and honest and do proper jobs. There's only a couple of scum families like that woman opposite me. They are the chavs, and they cause misery for practically everyone else. It's the decent working-class families that you call chavs that are actually the victims of the real chavs. They are more victims than the likes of me because I'll be moving on from there one day but lots of those families will be there all of their lives. You should be sticking up for those people, not lumping them in with the scumbags."

Nobody knew what to say to that at first; Martin and Jason weren't used to Nick getting serious about that kind of subject - it was bordering on the political. The only person even less likely to make such a statement was Martin.

Martin then made such a statement.

"You're right, Nick. These people are human beings. I was brought up on a council estate; my parents still live there. They're decent people, most of them. It's not right for people to look down on them."

All four members of the group then looked at their shoes until Jason broke the silence.

"Yeah, well they might not all be chavs, but I bet most of them have got criminal records."

Nick frowned, shook his head, and rolled his eyes. "Don't be daft, of course most of them haven't got criminal records. Anyway, so what if they did? Anyone can get a criminal record for something; it doesn't necessarily make them a bad person."

"Well, I haven't got one, Hugh hasn't got one, Martin hasn't got one, you haven't got one."

Nick looked at Jason slightly smugly. "Says who?"

"What - you haven't, have you?" said Jason, his eyes popping out.

"Might do."

Suddenly Jason and Martin were all ears and even Hugh didn't seem to mind not being centre of attention for a bit.

"There's not that much to tell really," said Nick, lapping it up. "One of the people I shared a house with when I was student was a really good artist. He made up a fake twenty-pound note - just for the fun of it, I think. Then everyone kept telling him how good it was and that he should try spending it for a laugh. So, he made a couple of photocopies and took them to the college bar, and it worked.

"Then he made a load up. I don't think he spent many, but he got caught cashing one in at an amusement arcade.

He'd given a few to me. I hadn't spent any of them but when the police raided the house, they found them in my room, and I got done as well as him."

"Wow, so what did they do to you?" asked Jason in wide-mouthed admiration.

"I got fined four hundred quid. A bit tight, I thought, as I was a skint student who hadn't done anybody any harm, when there are thousands of morons out there mugging and stabbing people all the time and always getting away with it."

"Good on you, mate," said Hugh.

Martin held out his hand and shook Nick's.

"Well, it was an interesting experience," said Nick. "I wouldn't choose to go through it again though."

And with that he sauntered off to the toilets, leaving his impressed fellow drinkers to no doubt talk about him in his in his wake.

When Nick returned a couple of minutes later, he could see that Hugh had managed to turn the attention back on himself and was in full flow with an animated anecdote. Nick took his place in the foursome just in time to catch its booming punchline of, "… and there was this fucking great coon stood at the top of the stairs!"

Hugh guffawed.

Nick, Martin, and Jason stared wide-eyed at one another.

Jason put his arm around Hugh's shoulders. "Er, mate. We don't really say that kind of thing in London."

Hugh looked about him from Nick's bemused face to Martin's and then to his friend Jason's. His big grin disappeared. "Oh, er, sorry mate. No problem."

"Yeah, it's 2010, mate - not the nineteen fucking seventies!"

And then they all laughed … rather awkwardly. They needed a new conversation topic. Jason took the initiative.

"Anyway, Nick, have you still got a thing going for that Annette bird?"

Nick rolled his eyes. "Ha-ha, Jason, don't be such a twat!"

*

The second public meeting of the Hewens Park Residents' Association didn't go well.

Word had got about that the committee - or more specifically Brian and Nick - were going to arrange for the hedges around the park to be cut down, and that wasn't a popular move.

As he stood watching people flood into the church hall in bigger numbers than ever before Nick felt uneasy. There was an unpleasant atmosphere about the place and, as ever, there was chuntering and chatter but very little laughter.

"They are not happy," Susan confided to him.

"Why not?"

"They think you're going to cut down the hedges."

"What makes them think that?"

Susan shrugged.

Nick refrained from asking her why, if she knew that that was what people thought, she hadn't told them it wasn't true. But then he caught sight of the frowning faces of her dad, Bert, and his mate Derek shuffling their way into the hall. They'd probably fuelled the rumours rather than quashing them. They might have even started them. Idiots.

Bert and Derek took their seats on the stage, as did Susan. Brian was still mingling.

Aki was the last committee member to arrive. He smiled and shook hands with Nick. "Okay, Boss?" he said.

Nick smiled back. "I'm good; you?"

"Mustn't grumble, mustn't grumble." And he too took his seat.

The next person to walk up and shake Nick's hand was a policeman. As promised at the last meeting, Brian had arranged for an officer to be present to take questions from the hall and listen to people's concerns. It wasn't Chief Inspector David Ball and nor was it Sergeant Alan Rose, who had attended the launch meeting; it was a younger man than either of them. He introduced himself as P.C Nicholls, and after exchanging a few pleasantries with Nick, he took his seat with the committee members.

Then the time had come to start the meeting, and it was Nick's turn to give the introductory speech. There was standing room only: every single seat was taken, and people were crammed in, standing at the back and along the side of the hall. It was a cool September evening, but it would soon be warming up in that room.

It took Nick, with some help from Brian, a minute to get the crowd to be quiet, and then he began.

"Welcome, everyone. And thank you for coming. It's really good to see so many of you here. For those who don't know me, my name is Nick Hale and I'm …"

"WHAT'S ALL THIS ABOUT YOU CUTTING DOWN THE HEDGES?!" yelled a very angry-looking middle-aged woman in the front row.

"Sorry?" said Nick.

"YOU HEARD"

"No, sorry - I didn't catch it," he lied.

"The hedges … around the park. Why are you cutting them down?"

"Why is who cutting them down?" Nick was enjoying playing along.

"You lot!" She gestured at the committee, and as she did so a swell of murmuring was apparently backing her.

"No, we're not cutting any hedges … are we?" He turned to face his fellow committee members.

Brian shook his head, Aki shook his head, Bert stared intently ahead, Susan looked at her feet, and Derek just looked angry - as always.

"Well why did you say that you was then?" the woman continued.

"We didn't," said Nick. "You must have been misinformed."

"YES, YOU DID!" an angry man in his early sixties joined in. "At the last meeting, HE DID!"

The man was pointing to Brian.

Brian stood up.

"I did mention that I had seen that done successfully elsewhere," said Brian.

"SEE, what did I tell you?" said the angry man.

Nick responded. "But Brian asked if that might be something that people here would like, and it wasn't. So, we all agreed that it wasn't something to consider."

"So, it's not happening then?" asked another woman, from near the back.

"No, no, of course not," said Nick. "That's the whole idea of the residents' association, to find out what people want to do and to try to do that … and nobody wanted to do that, so it was never going to happen. That was very clear."

"What a load of bollocks," moaned the angry man. It wasn't obvious to whom he was aiming the observation, but at the same time loud debate broke out all over the hall. Nick let it run for a while. From the snippets that he could make out people were blaming others for misinforming them while others were insistent that the hedge cull was definitely what 'he' said 'they' were going to do last time. Most of the bile seemed to be aimed at the committee, and the angry mob seemed even more angry that the thing they had turned up to fight wasn't happening than they had been when they thought that it was. The woman at the front suddenly stood up and left the room and that sparked a shuffling angry exodus. After a couple of minutes maybe a third of the hall had emptied.

Nick addressed the remainder.

"Well, that's cleared out a few … it'll be a bit more comfortable in here now!" He could have left it at that but couldn't help but go on a little more. "That's odd, isn't it?

Neighbour From Hell

You agree that something very definitely isn't happening, and somehow the word gets out that it is. We'll have to make sure that we are even more clear next time … if that's possible."

And so, the scene was set. The big topic was done with, but the mood was still hostile, and another fractious meeting was in store. Most of the remaining people - there were maybe fifty or sixty of them - had very little to contribute, but almost anything that any of them did say was negative … yet more moaning. Poor P.C. Nichols took the brunt of much of it. However well he tried to diplomatically respond to their concerns, the moaners couldn't get over their fixation with going on about how the police never took any notice of them. Their collective sense of irony seemed to be rather lacking.

But that was all a week before, and now the members were at Aki's house nearing the end of a committee meeting. They were sitting in a circle in the small living room on a selection of chairs brought from various parts of the house and had just about finished off a second round of teas and biscuits that Aki's wife Molly had cheerfully provided.

The meeting had followed very similar lines to all of the previous ones, with Nick and Brian doing most of the talking and any contribution from others usually being negative - especially if it came from Derek or Bert. Nick was getting ever more frustrated.

The topic that they were onto was public meetings and how to make them more positive.

"Any more suggestions?" said Brian.

Nick had a thought. "You know how at the meetings we sit at the front, separated from everyone? I wonder if that contributes to the kind of 'them and us' impression that some of them seem to have. Maybe we could try a different layout, with us sitting in the middle in a circle - like we are now, or something like that?"

Bert was the first to react. He tutted loudly and shook his head.

"So, do you have any ideas that you'd like to contribute, Bert?" said Nick. He could feel the bile rising.

Bert shook his head.

"But you are prepared to criticise whatever else anyone suggests?" said Nick.

Bert glared at him. "It's my right to say whatever I like."

Nick snapped. "Well, why don't you ever say anything useful then, instead of just moaning at everyone? What are you on this committee for? What have you actually done in the four months that we've been doing this, other than complain?" He couldn't stop himself. "You are a fucking waste of space - a fucking whinging loser!"

He cast his eyes around the circle at five pairs of wide eyes staring back at him.

"I'll tell you what, I'm not going to bother either. I'm sorry everyone else, but I've had enough of this. Bert, you are a fucking idiot."

And with that Nick picked up his things and walked calmly out of the door.

He walked quickly home. He picked up Alyson and they went straight to the pub before Brian or anyone else could come to try to change his mind.

Nobody from the committee phoned or texted Nick that night and nor did they during the following working day. In the evening though he answered the doorbell and was surprised to see Susan Henwood standing there. He invited her in, and she sat nervously with him and Alyson in their living room.

"Apologies for walking out like that yesterday," said Nick. "It's just that there's only so much ..." he was about to say 'whinging' but he checked himself, "erm, negativity that I can cope with."

"Yes, that's what I came about. I really hope that you're not leaving - I mean, we all do - it just wouldn't be the same without you; I'm not sure that it would work."

Nick tried to disguise how much it pleased him to hear somebody say that. "Well, thanks. It's good of you to say that, but you have to ask whether it's worth the effort when all we seem to get in exchange is complaints." He had to think carefully before saying the next bit. "Look, I know he's your dad, but Bert really is the worst of the lot. What's the point of him being on the committee if all he ever does is moan? It's very frustrating for those of us who actually want to do something to make things better."

Sue nodded her head.

"I know, that's always been his way - he likes to say it like it is, but …"

"Look, sorry to interrupt," said Nick, "but that's exactly the point. He doesn't 'say it like it is' at all, he just says it from what he chooses to be his viewpoint, which is always negative. Like I say, I'm sorry, and I know that he's your dad, but frankly that kind of attitude is the mark of a loser, which is why I said that to him. That was me saying it like it is - something that he doesn't do. He, and to an extent Derek, and half of the people who come to the public meetings don't do anything useful at all. Well, worse than that, they drag the whole thing down and get in the way of anything good coming out of it. Sorry."

Nick felt bad being so blunt to Susan, but he also felt good for doing it - much better than he would have done if he'd just apologised, which could so easily have been his response.

Susan looked hurt or maybe worried, Nick couldn't be sure.

She cleared her throat. "Look, I know that he can be difficult - believe me, I know. But it would be a shame to throw it away just because of him. You've really helped to get things going, and you're so good at the public meetings when you speak to everyone. None of the rest of us can do that. And I think you actually love that bit if I'm honest." He glanced over at Alyson as she said that, and they exchanged knowing smiles.

"Well, I'm glad you think that that works well," said Nick, suppressing a smile himself. "Brian's pretty good at the public speaking bit as well though …"

Susan gave a half laugh. "Yes, he is but he's you know … a bit, er, well - you say things that make them laugh and that."

"You mean that he's a bit dull?"

"Well, yes, he's sort of formal. I'm not sure that they really like that."

"I'm not so sure that they like me all that much either!" said Nick, still succeeding in hiding how chuffed he was that at least one person did appreciate his contribution.

"Can I get you a cup of tea, Susan?" asked Alyson.

Susan declined but the conversation moved to slightly forced small talk between the three of them before, after another ten minutes or so, Susan decided that she must be going.

"Well," said Nick, "I'll think about my future part on the committee, and I'll let you all know." (He already knew what that part would be.) "But thank you for coming to see me, and I appreciate what you say."

"Thank you too. I do hope that we see you at the next meeting."

"And do pass on my apologies to your dad, although I still think that he should be apologising to everyone else."

"Yes, he's not had an easy life. I think that's what makes him bitter at times."

"Maybe he'd be happier if he didn't take it out on other people then … perhaps he might make a few more friends."

Susan smiled a sad smile and the three of them said their farewells.

"She seems nice," said Alyson.

"Yes, she's OK. She said more words tonight though than in all of the meetings put together."

"You really don't like her dad though, do you?"

"He's probably OK underneath. He's just so fucking miserable ... it really gets on my nerves."

"Well, you made that clear enough!"

"Do you think I was too harsh then?"

"No, you did well - for once! I was proud of you."

And with that back-handed compliment Alyson gave Nick a kiss.

"Maybe I'll have to be nasty to people more often," said Nick.

"Well, not to me - and if you play your cards right, I might just be very nice to you later."

*

A death so many years before its time is always tragic, but for this to have happened at such a time in her life is utterly heartbreaking.

*

Nick checked his watch as he half trotted up the front stairs of Countrysafe's head office to the second floor, on which he worked. It was ten to eight - absurdly early for a Monday morning start, especially after a tiring long weekend in Brussels with Alyson, followed by a few beers in the local on Sunday night.

Slightly out of breath, he made his way across the near-deserted office, picking up a plastic cup of free coffee from the machine on the way and then slumping down at his desk to drink it.

It was Tony Clarke's fault that Nick was here feeling knackered, hung-over, and a bit nervous. Nick and Alyson had got home from their trip early in the evening and, after eating a Chinese takeaway, Nick was enjoying his second can of lager before they were to head out to the pub to round off the weekend, when he'd received a text from Tony.

> Can we catch up first thing in the morning? My pod at 8?

It was clearly an instruction rather than a request and so Nick had replied with the only real option.

> OK.

And it *was* OK, but it ate at him as he worked his way through the weekend's final four pints at The Star. Was it something bad … or something good? Either way it was probably something interesting. It ate at him during the night as well. When he and Alyson had got home, they were exhausted and went straight to sleep. But that hadn't stopped him dreaming and waking up three or four times in the night before sinking into a deep sleep just in time for his 6:45 alarm brought him harshly into the new week, feeling completely shit.

He swigged back the last dregs of his coffee and looked at the time on his phone. It was 7:58; might as well go and face the music.

The butterflies were rising in his stomach as he made the thirty second walk to Tony Clarke's pod. Tony was sitting there already going through his emails. His desk was uncluttered and immaculate, as ever, and he wore a pristine expensive suit, also as ever.

"Good morning," said Nick, a little weakly.

"Ah, hi Nick!" Tony returned, standing up as he did so. "How was Brussels?"

"Brilliant! Bit knackered though but had a good time."

Tony came around to Nick's side of the desk. "Shall we go to Jim's office?"

Jim West was Countrysafe's IT director, Tony's boss. He had a large corner office, the only real office in the entire building. His direct reports, such as Tony, sometimes used

Neighbour From Hell

the office as a meeting room or a place in which to conduct confidential conversations. This really must be something important - whether good or bad. The butterflies fluttered all the more as Tony and Nick made their way to the office, exchanging stilted further pleasantries about Nick's Brussels weekend.

The door to Jim West's office was open and Nick followed Tony in to see to his horror that Jim West was sitting at his desk! Nick had only spoken to him a handful of times previously in his seven years with the company.

"Morning, Jim," said Tony.

Jim West stood up; he had clearly been expecting them. "Good morning gentlemen." He walked around to the front of his desk. "Take a seat." He was indicating his oval meeting table that had six chairs around it.

Nick sat on one side and Tony and Jim sat down on the other.

Tony spoke. "Thanks for coming in early, Nick. We are going to be announcing some changes this morning. The portfolios are being re-structured. Some teams will move around, a few are merging, and there will be a couple of new ones created. Some members of the management team will be changing roles and unfortunately one or two roles will no longer be present in the new structure." He then paused and cleared his throat. "You are to be the new head of Financial Systems."

Nick felt his eyes expand to saucer-size. Jim West was beaming at him.

"Congratulations, Nick. Tony's been telling me good things about you."

Nick just nodded back at him thinking, "Don't shake my hand, it's covered in sweat."

Tony continued, "It's a grade three role, so you'll get all the extra benefits - proper bonuses, health cover, and so on. It's all in there," he added, handing over a cream-coloured envelope.

Then Jim West spoke again. "We'll sort you out properly when it comes to pay review time. But there's a couple of grand rise in there for you in the meantime."

Back to Tony Clarke. "There's going to be a general announcement in the auditorium at ten-thirty. I'll introduce you to your new team after that."

The two men then looked at Nick as if expecting him to say something. He tried to think of something.

"Well, er, I don't know what to say."

Tony tried to help him out. "Do you have any questions at this stage?"

Nick thought for another five very long seconds.

"Er, yes, what's happening to Jeff Wilmore?"

Jeff Wilmore was the current manager of the team that Nick was about to take over. He was around sixty years of age and although not somebody that Nick had had much to do with, he was in his experience a very nice guy.

Tony and Jim exchanged glances and then Tony spoke again. "Jeff's moving to a different role; we spoke to him on Friday."

That didn't sound particularly positive. Nick tried another question.

"Has anyone else got a promotion?"

Tony answered. "One or two. Did you have anyone in mind?"

Yes, he did. "No, not really … what about Jason though?"

Tony gave a brief wry smile and then shook his head.

"No, Jason didn't get promoted. Don't speak to him about this yet; wait until after the announcement. The same goes for your team or anyone else. We want to do this properly."

Then Jim West stood up and extended his hand for Nick to shake.

"Congratulations, Nick - and well done."

Nick brushed his sweaty palm on his trousers and shook Jim West's hand.

"Thank you."

Tony moved to the door and held it open for Nick.

Nick nodded to first Jim and then Tony and then made his exit.

"Well done mate," said Tony, before shutting the door and returning to Jim West.

Nick didn't bump into anybody on the way back to his pod and he was pleased to find that no members of his team were in yet when he got there. He sat down and buried his head in his hands. His heart was thumping. He was excited but he was also anxious. He liked working with his current team. Shit, what was going to happen to them?! Who would be taking them over? He wondered what they would think about the change …. How would Annette take it? He cursed himself for not asking about them. And Finance?! He didn't know anything about finance. His new team would probably resent him for that, after all Jeff Wilmore had managed them for years. He thought back over the meeting he'd just had. 'Well done', 'congratulations', 'Jeff's moving to a different role', 'one or two roles will no longer be present in the new structure'. There wasn't any 'would you be interested in this role?', 'do you want to think it over?'. It was a cheek of them to assume that he would be delighted, just because they would have been in the same situation. He was actually quite pissed off. Alyson would of course be delighted: promotion, more money, bigger mortgage possibilities - it was just the sort of thing that she loved. Nick didn't call her.

*

The pub was crowded with city types in expensive suits being loud and obnoxious, enjoying their long liquid lunch break. It was a scene that Alyson loved being a part of. She loved Thursday lunchtime too as it had become a tradition that, unlike every other day, when she would eat a sandwich at her desk, she went out with her friend for food and sometimes a drink. They had been doing it for a number of years.

Alyson placed her menu down on their table. She was ready to order.

"Let me guess," said Simon. "You are going for the extra small salad with no dressing, followed by a glass of still water for dessert?"

"Ha-ha! Well, we *are* having the wine, aren't we?"

"Yes, and a bottle each it seems, rather than a glass, judging by the price of it."

"Well, you did offer."

"So, I'm right – it's the salad, is it?"

"I need to get in trim for that skiing trip."

"That's months away!"

"It'll soon be here. Anyway, it's your fault for giving me the idea."

"I suppose so. Are you looking forward to it?"

"Yes, I think so – definitely looking forward to getting away from the shit."

"I thought he was coming with you!"

"Ah, ah. ...Anyway, how *is* the lovely Veronica?"

"Ooh! Touché."

*

"FUCK YOU, YOU FUCKING CUNT - I'LL FUCKIN' 'AVE YOU!"

Nick jumped up from his desk, turned off the light, and peered out of his bedroom window to see two members of the scum grappling with each other in the middle of the road. Under the pale glow of the streetlight, he could see that they both already had blood on their faces. Others were scattered around watching and shouting, some rooting for one side or the other, but none joining in or trying to break up the fight. Tricia looked on nonchalantly smoking a fag and sitting on her doorstep, a vodka bottle at her side. Then Nick saw something glinting - one of the two that were fighting had a knife held at the side of the other's face.

Shit!

The one holding the knife wore a black hoodie and seemed to be getting the upper hand as the two of them grappled. The other one had a light-coloured hoodie that appeared beige under the streetlight.

"I'll fucking do it, I fucking will!" It was the beige hoodie; he'd freed his hand and he too had a knife that he was now holding above the other's head.

Fuck!

Charlene came out of her house and in a scene that could have come straight from *Eastenders* yelled at the fighters.

"Oi, you two - stop it. Leave it Aaaaaaht!"

If Nick wasn't so concerned, he would have been tempted to append the words 'it ain't werf it!'

He thought about calling the police. But that would take too long.

Shit!

What could he do?

He didn't need to do anything.

Smack! The black hoodie crumpled to the ground. He was out cold. An onlooking member of the scum had delivered a fierce right hook squarely on the side of his jaw. Victory to the beige corner.

The victor trudged off along the street followed by the scum member who had delivered the punch, and a number of others. The vanquished lay sprawled on the road with spectators standing over him looking vaguely concerned. Charlene came running over to him. Nick thought about whether to go out to them or even whether to call an ambulance. But then the boy sat up. He stayed there on the ground for a couple of minutes wiping blood from his mouth while Charlene fussed over him, his 'mates' stood around and Tricia stayed smoking in her doorway. The Charlene fussing seemed to do its trick, as well it might, and with some help from her the boy was soon standing up. He then walked away groggily with the remaining members of the scum in tow. Charlene went back home, Tricia disappeared into her house, and about one minute after all had cleared away a police car showed up, probably summoned by a frightened elderly neighbour. After a brief look around the policeman got back into his car and drove on - whether in pursuit of the combatants or on to another call, Nick couldn't know.

Nick sat back down. He was shaking. He composed himself and then went downstairs to get himself a can of Stella. He mused how different parts of his life moved in such disparate worlds. This morning he was sitting in the office of a director of a corporate organisation talking restructures, portfolios, and his remuneration package. This evening he was watching two yobs trying to knife each other to death in the street. He hadn't yet told Alyson about his promotion. He wouldn't be telling her what he'd just witnessed either.

In fact, Nick didn't talk to Alyson much at all that evening. They superficially watched TV together while Nick carried on drinking, his mood carried on darkening, and Alyson continued doing work on her laptop.

When Alyson went to bed at eleven o'clock, Nick took his drinking outside. It was cold. He shivered and zipped up his jacket. Colin wasn't there. Nick was glad about that; he didn't want company.

Nick was disturbed. As the evening had drawn on the reality of the knives had sunk in, opening up old wounds that he normally managed to keep buried deep – always there and always ready to be painful, but not often on the surface, and hopefully not visible to anyone else. He pictured his school friend Rob, who died in a knife attack. He moved on quickly to being mugged at knifepoint himself as a student. That was still disturbing; it was still humiliating.

He could never face something like that again. He would have to do something about it. He *could* do something about it. …He *had* done something about it. He put his hand into his jacket pocket and his fingers felt the cold metal of the handle that was in there. It didn't make him feel any better. He got up to get himself another drink.

*

"That's it - go on, start killing each other then. None of us are going to be shedding any tears. Should fucking use that knife if you're so fucking brave. Fucking COWARDS! Ha, if only…"

*

11. Geoff

The day after Lee the builder had alerted Nick to Danny's abandonment of the Bond, Lee's friend Lawrence brought it around to Nick's house on his flatbed, as promised. Lee came with him, and they placed the car back onto Nick's lawn where it had been four months earlier, before Danny had got hold of it.

"Fucked you over, did he?" said Lawrence.

"Yes, I'm afraid so," answered Nick, looking slightly sheepish.

"Yeah, they always do - especially that one."

Lee and Lawrence both refused to take any payment for their efforts despite Nick's attempts to persuade them.

Once the Bond was there, Nick felt uncomfortable every time he cast his eyes on it, and he hoped that Danny did too. He'd chosen as yet not to confront Danny as making an enemy of him, and more to the point, of his obnoxious wife and their four teenage sons was likely to cause more harm than good.

After a few weeks of the car being parked up, partly prompted by more than strong hints from Alyson, he decided to look into what to do with it next. Several people had mentioned to him somebody called Geoff Lanning, a mechanic and car restorer who specialised in classic Triumph cars. As the Bond was Triumph based and Geoff Lanning's garage was quite local, Nick had decided to give him a call. Nick found that people in the classic car fraternity tended to be nerdy, or miserable, or know-alls (like Danny), or sometimes perfectly decent balanced reasonable people. He was pleased to find that on first impression Geoff Lanning appeared to fit into the final category. He'd listened to what Nick had to say about the

Bond, asked a few sensible questions, not saying anything patronising, and arranged to come and have a look at it.

When Geoff Lanning subsequently turned up exactly when he said that he would, Nick was even more impressed. The only disappointment was that he came not in a classic Triumph, but in a five-year-old Mazda truck. Geoff Lanning looked around the Bond, checking it over, much the same as Danny had done all those months before. Except that it was completely different from what Danny had done. Geoff took his time looking around the car, under the car, and in every nook and cranny of the car. He made notes in a notebook, and he said very little. When he'd done all of that he asked a few more sensible questions about what Nick knew of its history and what level of restoration he was interested in. He said that the car would need a 'fair bit of work' but that it was all there and that there was nothing particularly complicated about it. There was nothing showy or judgmental in his attitude. He asked Nick to give him a few days to price up the work after which he would call.

"I have to warn you though: I can give you a quote, but it'll be a while before I could do the work - I've got a bit of a backlog of restorations, quite a few months' worth."

Nick was a little disappointed with that but said that it would be fine. And three days later Geoff Lanning did indeed call. He said that there were a number of options to talk through and that maybe they should meet up to have a look at them on paper. He and Nick then arranged to do just that the following weekend.

*

Nick played a lesser role than normal in the third public meeting of the residents' association, with the planned speaking parts being taken up by Brian Hart, Pauline Fielding, and P.C. David Nicholls. It gave him an opportunity to, relatively speaking, relax, and to observe the participants from a more neutral perspective. Brian gave the opening speech, but Nick didn't really listen - he just sat in his position on stage with the rest of the committee and P.C. Nicholls, observing his public. And as he scanned the room what he saw at first was the usual bunch of angry wankers sitting there looking disgruntled and itching for an excuse to complain. But as he continued to observe he became aware of something more than that in some of the faces. Maybe the look wasn't anger at all - it was resignation, from downtrodden perhaps reasonable people who had suffered at the hands of the likes of Tricia and Billy Grindle all of their lives, and who would be doing so for ever more. He reminded himself of his speech to Martin, Jason, and Jason's friend Hugh defending these people; he was here to represent them, to help them. It was a noble cause. Or was he just here for himself? At the end of the day the residents' association only existed because he'd wanted to get Tricia kicked out of her house.

Nick found himself drawn to the face of a woman in the front row. She was short, in her late forties, had wispy light brown hair, and she wore glasses; Nick recognised her as Billy Grindle's next-door neighbour. She was staring straight ahead and looking particularly angry. Nick could feel that she was itching to say something. Hopefully, she would be giving Billy Grindle some stick. Her opportunity came when Brian's rambling thankfully drew to a close and he invited the audience to ask any questions. She got straight in there, no faffing around with putting her hand up or any other such formalities. She spat out what she had to say:

"What I want to know is, why wasn't I invited to this meeting?"

That threw Nick, it wasn't what he was expecting at all. It confused Brian as well.

"What, *this* meeting that we are in here now?"

"Yes! Why wasn't I invited?" She had gone red in the face and was clearly furious.

Neighbour From Hell

"Well, you are here aren't you?" suggested Brian.

The woman's expression turned from angry to deeply insulted … and angry.

"ONLY BECAUSE SOMEONE TOLD ME ABOUT IT!" she screamed. "I didn't get an invite."

"Well, we put leaflets through everyone's door. You do live on the estate, don't you?"

"Yes, you know I do - on Connaught. And I didn't get a leaflet, and you know that too."

The confused Brian glanced over at Nick.

Nick had delivered all of the leaflets himself, and he distinctly remembered going to this woman's house - as well as of course to Billy Grindle's, next door.

"I delivered a leaflet to your house," said Nick, calmly.

The woman glared at him. "Well how come I didn't get it then?"

"I don't know but I can promise you that I did. I went past that pale green and white caravan in your drive and pushed it through the front door on the side of the house."

The woman ignored that evidence. "It's disgusting how you lot pick and choose who you want to attend these meetings. I'm sick of it."

Nick bit his tongue for a moment before having an idea. "Well, I can promise you that nobody is excluded, but if you would like to have more influence on things then why not put yourself forward for the committee when the next chance comes up."

The woman tutted and shook her head. "You lot are all just as bad as each other. I don't know why I bother."

The bile was rising in Nick; he wasn't just angry with this stupid woman, it was also the rest of the morons in the room, none of whom were challenging her. He could feel the tension from the other committee members; their thoughts had turned back to the meeting where he'd lost his temper with Bert. Nick told himself there and then that he was getting out of this as soon as he possibly could. *Fucking ungrateful bunch of shits!*

Brian told the woman that he would personally make sure that she got the leaflets in future and that he thought it an excellent idea of Nick's for her to join them on the committee when the re-elections came around.

The woman just shook her head.

"You fucking miserable cow!" thought Nick. He so wanted to say it out loud.

The meeting finished at around nine-thirty and a subset of the committee adjourned to The George. For once it wasn't just Nick and Brian, as Aki and Susan joined them as well as Susan's husband Carl.

Billy Grindle was the subject of much of the group's early conversation. It was mostly miserable stuff - tales of him threatening other children with violence, glaring just as threateningly at vulnerable old people, rumours of further thefts at his hands, and of course the frustration that he'd still never been prosecuted for anything. But there was one small bright spot. One of the topics that P.C. Nicholls had talked about was the police 'crime awareness unit' - which was essentially a caravan full of leaflets that people could visit to talk to a police officer to seek advice about crime prevention - and how it was going to be paying a visit to the estate for a day in the near future. "Apparently they are going to park it for the day right outside Billy Grindle's house," Brian told everyone. They all laughed at that thought and the mood of the group was lightened.

"That's brilliant," said Carl. "Mind you they ought to go after that Bradley Mullen next, he's probably the biggest criminal on the estate, what with his drug dealing and all that."

Susan chipped in. "Do you know he's got another girl pregnant? - Ellen Sheady's daughter from over Cromwell

Neighbour From Hell

Avenue. Pretty little thing. She's only seventeen. That's about the third one that I know of alone."

Nick always bristled irrationally at the sight of Bradley Mullen or even at the mention of his name and this information didn't help the situation. Fortunately, Aki, who had a habit of being a bit random, came up with something else to talk about.

"You know, I had a fox on the roof of my shed this morning."

Thus ensued a lengthy fox conversation, with the members of the group swapping experiences of coming across them on the estate.

"A funny thing that I find about foxes," said Brian, "people - especially the middle classes - love to be able to tell their friends and colleagues that they have foxes in their gardens, and apparently love to have the things around. Until they ransack their bins that is - then they just become vermin!"

That observation elicited polite smiles from all, rather than the guffaws of laughter that Brian was maybe expecting.

"I hope you are not accusing me of being middle-class," said Aki, affecting a stronger-than-usual Nigerian accent. And that comment did get a round of laughter.

"You're alright, you are," said Carl. "You see, all the racism and that that goes on, it's not against the likes of you, you see. It's just the Muslims, cos they are the ones that cause all the problems."

Aki looked back at Carl, still smiling. "I am a Muslim!"

Carl adopted a rabbit-in-the headlights face. "But you're, I mean they are usually, er …"

"Lots of Muslims are black," said Aki, "and white."

Brian quickly stepped in. "There you are Carl; you come for a drink, and you get some free education thrown in."

Carl just looked confused. Aki was still smiling. Brian carried on speaking and was soon onto his favourite subject of life as a local councillor. The same old anecdotes that Nick had heard too many times already were soon trotted out and Nick zoned out to daydream some more of getting away from all of this as soon as possible, only being prompted back into the room when such over-familiar soundbites as 'no respect, the youth these days', 'family opposite me, black as the ace of spades', and 'what about the human rights of the old lady that he robbed' served to strengthen his resolve even further.

*

Geoff Lanning's workshop was seven miles from Nick's home, on the opposite side of Harlesham. He drove there in his Reliant van, and he approached with some trepidation, not knowing how many thousands more that restoring Uncle Frank's old car was going to cost him. The workshop was large - much bigger than Danny's unit - and was surrounded by a fair bit of land. There were about ten cars on the piece of ground next to the workshop, and they were all Triumphs. They ranged from the dumpy but somehow appealing little Mayflower saloon of the early 1950s to the sporty TR7 with its distinctive Harris Mann-designed 1970s wedge-shape lines. All of those cars were in poor states of repair, and most were part dismantled, but they were positioned neatly, and the place had an organised feel to it. In front of the workshop were two more vehicles, a green Triumph Spitfire 1500 that had a large 'for sale' sign behind its windscreen, and Geoff Lanning's Mazda truck. Peering out from the far side of the workshop was the front of a low-loader lorry. Nick drove in and parked up. The workshop appeared closed, but Nick opened a side door next to its large roller shutter main entrance and stepped inside. A maroon 1966 Triumph 2000 was raised on hydraulic ramps and Geoff Lanning was working underneath it. Geoff Lanning immediately stopped working and came over to shake Nick's hand.

Neighbour From Hell

The two men chatted for ten minutes about Triumphs and cars in general before Geoff showed Nick his spray booth, which took up a third of the main workshop and contained a freshly re-painted red Triumph Stag.

"Is it just you working here then?" asked Nick.

"No, I have a lad helping me – an apprentice - but he's not here at the weekends."

They went through to Geoff's office, and he gestured to Nick to take a seat. There was a small pile of unopened letters on the seat and Nick picked them up and absent-mindedly flicked through them. They were all addressed not to Geoff Lanning but to "Giannes Lagoudakis".

"Who is that – the apprentice?" asked Nick, handing the post to Geoff.

"Oh, it's me. I'm Greek - or at least my parents are; I was brought up over here."

"Really? I'd never have known."

"I call myself 'Geoff Lanning' 'cause it's off-putting for people if you have a foreign name. Nobody can pronounce it anyway!"

Nick laughed. "Yeah, you're probably right."

He sat down and looked around the little office. In its centre was a well-worn old wooden desk on which sat a computer monitor and grubby cream-coloured keyboard, an order book, a coaster with a large mug sitting on it (the mug was adorned with a picture of a Triumph Herald and lots of oily fingerprints; it was half-full of cold coffee), a land-line telephone, and a couple of pens. There was a chair each side of the desk - the one that Nick was sitting in and another that Geoff Lanning now lowered himself into. There wasn't much else in the office, a few car body parts were leaning against the walls and various things hung from those walls: job sheets, invoices and the like, a print of a car painting - oddly of an MG, not a Triumph - and the obligatory 'girlie' calendar. The office was illuminated by a single uncovered 60-watt light bulb hanging from the centre of the ceiling and what limited outside light could get in through a high-up dusty heavily-barred window. The office smelled of used engine oil.

Geoff Lanning fired up his computer, opened a file, and then turned the monitor so that he and Nick could both see it. On the screen was a spreadsheet that was named 'N. HALE - BOND EQUIPE' and it contained a long list of items with, in most cases, prices next to them.

"Now, what I've done," said Geoff Lanning, "is that I've listed everything that it needs doing, or that could be done, and I've priced those things up, either for individual items, or for a bunch of things that go together. And what I thought we'd do is, if we go through choosing what you do and don't want done, and then we can work out a price. Where there's more than one option - like here, for example: 'new bumper strips vs. polish existing strips', I've priced up both options, and we can talk through the pros and cons. How does that all sound to you?"

"Yep, perfect," said Nick. He was feeling very nervous, looking at the long list and dreading what the total cost might come to. What would he do if it was way more than he wanted to spend? And how silly would he feel?

"Right then," said Geoff. "Let's just take them in the order that I've got them in here, starting with the engine."

And so, they began working one by one through the rows on Geoff Lanning's spreadsheet. Nick's anxiety increased on a lot of them if they sounded serious or if the price was alarming, but on others he felt some relief if they weren't as expensive as he might have thought or if Geoff made a positive comment about the car's condition.

"OK," said Geoff, "the chassis."

"Yeah, I know - it's shot, isn't it?" Nick was ready for this one as Danny had told him how he would have to re-manufacture the whole chassis from scratch due to the extent of its corrosion.

"No, it's not too bad really. I've seen much worse. The outriggers and side rails are gone, but that's quite normal,

Neighbour From Hell

and you can get new ones cheap enough. The main backbone's surprisingly solid."

That was one of Nick's positive moments, tinged with some regret at the reminder that he should never have let Danny anywhere near Frank's prized possession.

After almost an hour of discussing options, weighing up pros and cons, and a lot of deviating from the subject, they had agreed on more or less the same work as Nick had previously agreed with Danny. There were however some differences: At £3500, Geoff's quote was a lot more expensive than Danny's £2000; on the other hand, he only wanted a £200 deposit to start the work, and he didn't want any of the balance until he'd finished it and Nick was happy with the result. But the key difference was that Nick felt confident that he would actually do the work rather than take the money and then leave the car as a pile of scrap.

"Now, like I said, I'm not going to be able to do it for a while." Geoff Lanning then explained how bodywork repairs and mechanical work were his bread and butter, and that full restorations were background tasks that he did as and when he had time. "I should have that Stag finished in a couple of weeks, and then there are three other restorations after that."

"So, how long are we looking?"

Geoff Lanning took a deep intake of breath as he thought about it for a moment. "You are probably looking at about six months."

Nick again managed to hide his disappointment. "Six months to start the work, or finish it?"

"Start, probably. Then about another six weeks to finish it." He gave Nick a moment to consider that information before continuing. "Take your time and think about it, then just give me a call if you want to go ahead. Then I'll get you on the list. I haven't got any more coming that I know of, so it should be the same time if you come back to me in the next couple of weeks."

Nick had thought about it long enough. He held out his hand. "Let's do it!"

"You sure?"

"Yep, sure. So, what happens next? Do you want the £200 in cash or shall I transfer it?"

"No, no - I don't need that now, not until I'm about to start the work."

And so, the deal was done. Geoff Lanning also agreed to collect the Bond soon after so that it wasn't sitting on Nick and Alyson's front lawn for the next six months. "It'll be under a tarpaulin, mind. I haven't got room in the workshop for it. But it should be safe enough here, we're well locked-up and there's a security firm comes around in the night. We've never really had any trouble."

Nick felt really good as the two of them walked outside into the sunshine - sunshine that glinted off the chrome of the green Spitfire that was up for sale.

"Is that yours or a customer's?" Nick asked.

"No, it's mine. It *was* a customer's, I repainted it for him last year."

"Nice."

"He traded it in for a Stag."

"What, that one in there?"

"No, a yellow one that I'd done; nice one it was. Do you like the Spitfires then?"

"Yes, it's very nice."

"Well, make me an offer if you like."

"Ha-ha! No, thanks - I've got enough cars as it is."

Geoff Lanning then turned and nodded at Nick's Reliant van. "I could do you a deal on the plastic pig. There's always people on the lookout for those, they like to turn them into *Only Fools and Horses* replicas."

"Yeah, I know. Mine's probably the only one left that isn't yellow!"

Then both men turned back to the gleaming green Spitfire sitting there in the sunshine with its soft top down exposing its deliciously 1970s light brown (almost beige) faux leather interior with wood veneer dashboard.

"Have a sit in it; see what you think."

Nick laughed. "I'll have a sit in it if you don't mind, but I won't be buying it!"

"Go ahead; it's not locked."

Nick opened the Spitfire's door and slid himself into the low-slung driving seat. He gripped the after-market wood-rimmed steering wheel and looked around at the very 1970s circular instruments on the dashboard. Geoff Lanning removed the large 'For Sale £5995' sign from the windscreen so that Nick could look out through it.

Nick had got into the idea of driving around in a classic sports car, but the Bond now wasn't going to be ready for another eight months. He loved his old Reliant van but had had it for a while and at times would tire of its limitations and of the sneers of those who didn't appreciate the irony - as well as those who called it a 'Reliant Robin' ... or even worse 'Robin Reliant'! With his legacy from Frank and the proceeds of selling his Porsche, he had plenty of money in what he could justify as his 'car fund'. He also wouldn't need to be shelling out on the cost of Geoff Lanning's restoration of the Bond until it was over. He was sitting in an inexpensive stylish open-top British sports car. The sun was shining. He was in a happy mood. His classic car insurance broker was open for phone business on Saturday afternoons. Internet banking meant that money transfers could be instantaneous.

Nick had a huge grin on his face as he drove his Spitfire from Geoff Lanning's yard - even more so after a couple of miles of winding lanes had identified no more squeaks, bangs, and rattles than could be expected. Just one thing left: what the fuck would Alyson say!

And, of course, what would the scum think of it ... and do to it.

Neal Bircher

*

She took her orange bikini bottoms in both hands, slid them down to her knees and then wriggled them down to her ankles. Then she stepped her right foot out of them, spreading her feet part, and leaned forward onto the work surface in front of her.

*

"Triumph Spitfire, eh? Yes, I remember them," said Colin. "I always fancied a sports car; never had one though."

"Well, there are plenty of them around still," said Nick, through the fence to his unseen neighbour.

"Ha!" said Colin, "I wish. There are lots of things that are around but they're not for the downtrodden working classes."

Then he thought for a moment. "The non-working classes are OK though, like that bitch over the road. I'll bet she bought that little brat a new Playstation with her dole money after she'd smashed up the last one. Fucking nonsense. Still though, Spitfire - nice. Maybe you can take me for a spin in it sometime."

He took a drag on his cigarette and blew the smoke up into the air.

Nick watched the smoke drifting over the top of the fence.

"So, er, how are things - you managing to get more sleep yet?"

"Not really. I kip on the sofa downstairs so I'm away from all the chaos. I don't really need much sleep though. What's good about me being downstairs is I can slip out when I want without disturbing anyone else."

"What, when you go to work early, you mean?"

"No - in the middle of the night. I go out for a walk and a smoke. It's nice and peaceful when nobody's about, just me and the foxes. I see badgers from time to time too, over there by the park."

"Blimey, I never knew you did that. I haven't heard you going."

"No, well I'm quiet, you see. I've only being doing it recently. Sometimes have a bit of a drink as well. … Ah, yeah, speaking of that, do you drink vodka at all?"

"Not really. Alyson does, but not me. Why?"

"I've got some here; 80% proof. There's a Polish bloke at work gets it. I bought a box of six one litre bottles for sixty quid. It's twelve quid just for ordinary Smirnoff up at Savealot. I could get you some if you like, or you could have one of my bottles for a tenner. Treat the missus."

"I'll ask her. Probably shouldn't though, she drinks too much of the stuff as it is."

"Yeah, we all drink more than's good for us, don't we?" said Colin.

"Well, yes - I certainly do!" said Nick.

"So what though, I say. We might die a bit sooner, but it's probably worth it. What would life be like if we couldn't get a bit pissed from time to time!"

"Yeah, you're probably right - the pleasure outweighs the downsides. Not sure that I would say that first thing in the morning when I've had a skinful the night before though."

"Ha-ha! No, probably not. Anyway, let me know. It'll take me a while to get through all six."

"Yeah, I will. Thanks."

"Well, I'd better leave you to it. No rest for those of us who have to work for a living."

"Yeah, you're right. I'd better be going soon too. Sleep well."

"Cheers, mate. Goodnight. 80%, mind - don't forget!"

*

Alyson had gone to her parents' house for a Saturday night out with some old schoolfriends, and Nick was home alone. He'd been to watch Norling F.C. in the afternoon, called in at The Star for a few pints on the way back, and then picked up his usual large doner kebab with extra chilli sauce on his way home. In the kebab shop he'd had a brief conversation with the only other customer - a middle-aged man who was even more drunk than Nick was, about the fact that people only buy kebabs when they've had too much to drink. He'd got home just after nine o'clock and after finishing off the kebab had a shower and was now sitting on his sofa relaxing with a can of Stella. It was just after nine-thirty - almost an hour to kill before *Match of the Day*. He sat back and reflected on his day so far. It had been a bit mixed. He'd enjoyed his freedom: Alyson had travelled 'home' on the Friday afternoon, so, after indulging in a major Friday-beers-after-work session that had gone on until almost midnight, he'd been able to get up in the morning as late as he'd liked and then, after walking to the local shop to buy a few provisions, he'd made himself some lunch before walking the couple of miles to watch the football. Norling had lost three-nil which was disappointing but didn't really bother him. At The Star he'd played pool and lost more games than he won, which annoyed him a bit, but the accompanying lagers and the pleasure of being able to indulge in a kebab without being chastised for doing so more than made up for that particular disappointment. The walk from The Star to the kebab shop and from there to his home was accompanied by torrential rain which Nick rather enjoyed, although it was a bit of a pain to arrive home soaked to the skin. So, yes, very much a mixed day in which good and bad experiences had largely neutralised one another. And now he could just sit with his lager and relax ready to enjoy a bit of football on TV. Except that he couldn't just sit down and relax, because the anxiety was there, eating at him, frustrating him, making him angry.

He went through to the kitchen, cracked open another can of Stella and slumped back onto the sofa. His mood further darkened as he recalled another incident earlier that day, during his hung-over walk to the local shop. 'Savealot' was located on the corner of Connaught Avenue and Harlesham Road - a wide busy route linking the nearby town of Harlesham with, eventually, the centre of London. Connaught Avenue at that point was quite narrow but lined with parked cars on either side. When Nick had been fifty or sixty yards from the shop, just ahead of him on the opposite side of the street a woman pushing a small child in a pushchair had squeezed between two parked cars in order to cross over. Just as she began to emerge from the parked vehicles, a car swooped in from Harlesham Road with a squealing of tyres, and accelerated hard towards her. The woman pulled back her pushchair and the speeding car passed by inches in front of her, the driver seemingly oblivious to her presence. The driver wore dark glasses and had his phone held to his ear; his car was a black BMW convertible. The woman shrieked. Nick turned and glared helplessly after Bradley Mullen, once again full of contempt for this arrogant twat whom he'd never actually met.

And now thinking back over the incident many lagers later he felt even more revulsion at the thought of Bradley Mullen than ever before. He had to do something, something to make himself feel less … less what? Less oppressed, perhaps. He swallowed some more Stella and a hint of a smile returned to his face as he hatched a plan.

He went upstairs and looked out of his front window into the dark street. It was still chucking it down with rain … perfect. And Bradley Mullen's BMW was parked in its usual place, just along the road … also perfect.

Next, he located a torch and went down to his shed where he first dug out an old dark green hooded raincoat that he hadn't used for years, and then rifled through his boxes of nails, bolts, and screws until he found the one that was full of rusty old six-inch nails. He took one of the nails and went back to the house. Then he changed from the blue jeans that he was wearing into a black pair and put on some black shoes and the raincoat. He put up the hood on the raincoat and pulled it tightly around his face. Next stop was the fridge, where Nick got himself another can of Stella. He opened the can, took a long swig, and then placed it upright in the large outside pocket of his raincoat.

After turning off all of the lights in his house, he quietly edged out of the front door. The rain was hammering down harder than ever. Nick felt excited. He walked to the end of his driveway and glanced to his left. The BMW was still there forty or fifty yards away. It was beckoning him, but he turned to the right and started walking. His nail was in his left hand and his Stella in his right pocket. The raincoat's hood was restrictive to his field of vision; he could only really see straight ahead. The walk 'around the block' took little more than five minutes, and then he was right upon the black BMW. Its big headlights sleepily eyeing him as huge raindrops bounced off its shiny paintwork that glinted under the streetlights. Nick hadn't seen another person on his short walk. Bradley Mullen's house - or at least his parents' house - was on the other side of the road, opposite the BMW. Nick glanced over; there was no sign of life. The BMW was parked, as always, half on and half off the footpath. If anybody had come by with, for example, a pushchair, then they would have had to go out into the road to get past. Nick slowed his pace. As he came alongside the car, he had to stoop to avoid a large rain-laden bush overhanging from the garden to his right. He gripped his six-inch nail in his left hand and stared straight ahead as he quickened his pace again, passing the BMW and then a long twenty seconds or so later getting to the hedge at the front of his garden. He turned into his driveway and stopped.

"Bollocks," he shouted to himself, in a whisper. He was cross with himself - he'd chickened out.

He took out the Stella and took another large swig. He let that go down for a few seconds and then drank the remainder in one go. After crushing the can in his hand, he threw it clumsily onto his front lawn. "You're drunk," he mouthed to himself.

Nick's raincoat was no match for the torrential rain - he could feel cold water streaming down either side of his neck. It didn't bother him. He tilted his head back in order to face the sky. "Bring it on!" Emboldened by adrenalin and Stella he was ready to go into battle.

He set off around the block again, walking faster this time. Just after he took the first right turn, he saw a man on the other side of the street walking in the opposite direction. He wasn't alone on the streets in the rain and the dark; that wasn't good. Once the two of them had passed each other, Nick turned to see where the other man was going. He had to turn right around because of his restrictive hood. The man veered to the right, not in the direction of Bradley Mullen's BMW. That pleased Nick. He turned again and continued on his quest. He walked ever faster, with ever more determination. In what seemed like seconds he was upon the BMW. He stuck out his left hand and thrust the six-inch nail against the car's paintwork, making contact just behind the front wheel arch. He pressed the nail hard and continued walking at his same fast pace. There wasn't much sound above the hammering of the rain on his hood and on the car, but he could feel the nail gauging a satisfying furrow in the shiny paintwork. The nail meandered upwards and downwards along the whole length of the door and then clattered across the gap between the door and the rear wing. Nick at first lost some downforce as the nail moved on to the wing, but then he gave it a last stabbing thrust across the top of the wheel arch before pulling away. He quickened his pace still further and made to his front door without looking sideways or back. He got into the house as quickly as he could (he had left the door ajar so that he wouldn't need to faff around with his key) and returned to his living room without switching on any lights. His heart was beating so fast that he could almost hear it.

He took off the wet raincoat, rolled it into a ball. and went out into his back garden. He buried the six-inch nail in the earth in the middle of the lawn, and then stuffed the raincoat behind his shed in the small gap between it and the garden fence. Back in the house he took off his now-sodden black jeans, threw them in his empty bath, and put the blue ones back on. Then he made his way gingerly to the front of the house. The rain was still battering comfortingly against the window, but it was also the only thing moving out there: no people, no moving vehicles, just torrential rain on a shiny black river-like street, and still there over to his left, the shiny black BMW, placid and unmoving and from this distance looking exactly the same as it had half an hour before.

"Yes!"

Nick went downstairs. He hid his black shoes in a cupboard, got himself another can of Stella, and returned to the sofa. He still hadn't switched any lights on, and he didn't switch on the TV either - it was still not quite time for *Match of the Day*. He cracked open the can and held it aloft in celebration. But his mood wasn't all celebratory. His heartbeat was still racing and once he sat down, he become engulfed in anxiety. *What if there was a camera in the car? What if someone had been watching him? Did any of the nearby houses have outward-facing CCTV?*

He tried to comfort himself. *Surely the police wouldn't spend time looking into anything so trivial ... would they? ... Especially not with Bradley Mullen being a known criminal himself ... or on the other hand maybe they would, for that very reason. But then, surely Bradley Mullen wouldn't report it to the police. But what if Bradley Mullen somehow got to work out who'd done it? That would be so much worse than the police!*

It was fair to say that by the time *Match of the Day* started Nick was very much regretting his actions. By the time it ended he had drunk a lot more Stella. He went to bed resolving to never do anything stupid ever again.

Nick woke at around ten o'clock feeling stressed and very rough. He climbed out of bed, stumbled his way to the window and pulled back the curtain. It was unpleasantly bright outside but through blinking eyes he scanned the street. Bradley Mullen's car was not in its usual parking space, he had moved it into his parents' driveway. That made Nick at the same time both excited and more anxious. He'd never seen Mullen's car in the drive before - he must have moved it because he'd discovered the damage. Nick closed the curtain and clambered back into bed.

He soon dozed off again for another couple of hours and awoke feeling marginally less unwell than he had the first time. He ambled over to the window again and opened the curtain. There were three men standing around Bradley Mullen's car! One was Bradley Mullen, wearing his usual dark glasses, another was of similar age to him, and the third was quite a bit older. Nick guessed the other two to be Bradley Mullen's father and brother, although he had no idea as to whether or not Bradley Mullen actually had a brother. They were talking and looking at the car. Nick felt excited again and for the time being the anxiety deserted him. He so much wanted to know what the three men were saying, and he found himself unable to resist the compulsion to find out.

Two minutes later he exited his front door. He was wearing clothes that were as different as he could manage from the ones that he'd had on the previous night. He wore a bright red sweatshirt, pale blue jeans, and white trainers. He also put on his favourite Ray Ban Wayfarer sunglasses. He crossed the road. As he approached the Mullen house, he suddenly felt some reluctance - but not enough to stop him. Two more men were there now; they must have just turned up, one in his twenties, the other quite old … neighbours? He was passing the house. The five men were all looking at the side of the BMW. None of them looked up at him. He almost wanted them to do so, to engage with him, to ask if he'd seen anything. He passed the car. He caught a snippet of conversation, it came from one of the older men: "It's just jealousy, isn't it?"

Nick laughed inside; he laughed at their arrogance and stupidity. He hurried on by. He felt glad, but then again, he still felt stressed. His heart pounded. He was very hungover. He felt sick. He carried on around the block, and then went home and got back into bed.

*

More blue lights joined the show as a police car arrived from the left, followed by an ambulance from the right.

"I have a horrible feeling there's not going to be any need for that ambulance," said Nick.

*

The familiar sound of an argument in the street caught Nick's ear as he was doing his online football bets for the weekend. He looked out of the window just as Charlene and Kevin's front door was flung open from the inside. Nobody came out to start with, they just seemed to be obligingly making their verbal disagreement more audible for their neighbours, as was the custom for a number of couples in the area. Nick couldn't quite make out the actual words, just Charlene and Kevin taking turns to shout at each other. He called Alyson through from her office.

Alyson arrived in time to see Kevin emerge. He turned back to the open door and shouted his farewell:

"Alright, so now I'm going to go and get my dick wet, just like I do every night!"

"Charming turn of phrase," commented Alyson.

Kevin grabbed his push bike that was lying in their driveway and sped off up the road without looking back. Charlene slammed the door behind him, and all went quiet again.

"They are normally OK, those two," said Nick.

Alyson gave a little sarcastic laugh and said, "You and your chav mates," shaking her head. "Don't forget that it's your taxes funding their dole money."

Nick ignored her. "Perhaps that's where we are going wrong," he said. "Maybe we should get to know these people more as human beings. I've never really spoken to any of the scum other than Tricia and Damian … well, and Billy Grindle, I suppose. Might have been better to try to engage with them in the first place."

"Hmm," scoffed Alyson. "'Hug a hoodie', eh?' Well, good luck with that!"

And with that she went back to her office, leaving Nick to continue with his 'investments'.

The following day, being Friday, Nick was in the pub with his colleagues by five-thirty. Jason wasn't one of the most regular members of the beer-after-work-on-Friday club, but when he did get involved, he liked to take charge. And this was one of those occasions. The usual venues for the group were the Pilot, which was a rough centre-of-Norling little bar with Karaoke 'entertainment', and the Carpenter's Arms - an old pub that had catered for factory workers since the 1920s, and then, since the 1970s, smaller numbers of mainly office workers as manufacturing employment in Norling's factories had dwindled to nothing. But they also had other options, and this time, at Jason's suggestion, they were in the Lemon Tree, built in the 1950s to serve the sprawling council estate that was growing around it.

It wasn't a great choice. There seemed to be any number of other Friday night office groups dropping in which, when combined with the more regular locals who were mainly seated at tables, took up almost all of the floorspace. Nick was on his third pint and, like everyone else in the group, had yet to be able to sit down. In the 45 minutes or so that he'd been there he'd flitted around successfully avoiding getting dragged into dull conversation with career types, like Jason, or techies, like Pete Little. That left him with essentially no-one to talk to. Normally Martin would be there, and he and Nick could 'people watch', which meant taking the piss out of everyone. But Martin *wasn't* there, he'd gone away for some kind of family weekend with his sister and parents. So, Nick was left supping his pint on his own on the fringe of the throng of office workers. But then he spotted someone that he recognised. It was a woman from work. He didn't know her well, but he spoke to her from time to time and she seemed quite pleasant ... he also found her very attractive. Her name was Gail Timson.

She was sitting at a table with three others. To her right was a large bald man with a pint of beer in his hand who was in conversation with people on the table to his right. To her left sat another large bald man who looked quite similar to the first one and who was texting on his phone, and opposite her, with her back to Nick, was a young woman with whom Gail Timson was speaking. There were lots of drinks on the table. Gail Timson's conversation looked a bit forced; she didn't appear particularly happy. Maybe it wouldn't be appropriate to interrupt her. What the heck.

"Hello!" Nick waved his hand as well to grab her attention.

Gail Timson looked up and, to Nick's pleasant surprise, burst into a warm smile. "Hello. Don't usually see you in here."

"No, I don't come here that often. We just go for a few beers after work on Fridays and came here for a change. What about you?"

Gail Timson held a large vodka and Coke in one hand, and she brushed her fingers through her long hair with the other. "This is my local. We're here for my 40th birthday."

The young woman that Gail had been speaking to turned to look at Nick.

Gail continued, "This is my daughter, Katherine."

Nick apologised to Katherine for interrupting. She was in her late teens but other than the age difference was the spitting image of her mother.

"That's alright," she replied with a disinterested look and tone that gave no indication as to whether it really was alright or not.

Nick turned back to Gail and was about to launch into a '40th - never?!' type of chat when he became aware that the man to Gail's left was no longer texting and was looking at him quite intently.

Gail noticed too and spoke to the man. "This is, er …" she had to think for a moment, "… Nick. He's into old cars too. He's got a Spitfire."

Nick remembered telling her that but was surprised that she'd remembered.

The man spoke. "Triumph Spitfire, eh?"

"Yes, a 1500 … 1976," said Nick.

The man replied. "Hairdresser's car. I'm more of a Jag man myself."

Nick wasn't quite sure what to say to that. Gail helped him out: "This is Alan; he's my brother-in-law."

There was something of an apology about the way she said it.

Nick put two and two together: if this is Gail Timson's brother-in-law then the other bloke must be her husband. Lucky man.

Nick looked back to Alan who was downing the remains of his latest pint. "So, have you got a Jag then?"

Alan put down his empty glass. "You what?"

"A Jag … have you got …"

"Another pint, Al?" Gail's husband bawled across the table.

"Yeah, Baz - Stella, mate."

"What about you, darlin'?" 'Baz' asked his daughter.

She replied with something that Nick couldn't hear.

"And you?" he asked the birthday girl.

Gail wanted another vodka and Coke … double.

He stood up and pushed his way from the table en route to the bar. He didn't look at Nick.

Gail Timson *was* looking at Nick; she smiled weakly.

"What was that you was saying?" Alan challenged Nick.

"Oh, er, a Jag - have you got one?"

"XJ40 - 2.9 litre straight six, fantastic car." He said it aggressively, as if Nick had accused him of not owning one. Then he turned his attention to Katherine. "You coming to QPR tomorrow with me and your dad, Kath?"

Feeling a little unsettled, Nick turned his eyes back to Gail Timson. She looked apologetic again, or maybe just uncomfortable.

It was time to make his exit. It was probably a good thing that nobody had invited him to sit down. "Well, I'd better circulate. Have a good birthday."

Gail nodded and smiled again. But her eyes weren't smiling.

Nick gave a little wave and turned away.

"Al, give us a hand with these, mate." Barry Timson had four Stellas in his two hands. He still didn't look Nick in the eye.

Nick downed his pint and then took refuge in conversation with Pete Little and Jason. He needed another drink. There was something wrong with the world.

*

Neighbour From Hell

Nick came bursting in through the front door with a huge grin on his face.

"Best Christmas present ever!" he announced to Alyson.

He'd just been out delivering Christmas cards to neighbours and, in a little P.R. initiative, as well as posting cards through doors of people who were friends, he'd also included Tricia, who got a really cheap card, and Charlene (and Kevin), who got a slightly better one.

"What have you bought me then - something expensive, I hope."

"Better than that!"

Alyson looked up from her sofa; her expression said, "Get on with it then."

"Well … Tricia's leaving!"

Alyson's face lit up. "Seriously?"

"Yep!"

Alyson jumped up and the two of them high-fived. They even hugged.

Alyson sat back down. "How come? How do you know?"

"I've just seen her. She says that she's fed up of it around here. She's doing a house swap on January 15th."

"Oh my god! That's brilliant. I've wanted that for so long." It was as much as Alyson could do to stop herself from crying.

"I had to laugh when she said she was fed up," said Nick. "We've obviously been making her life a misery or something."

"January 15th?" said Alyson. "Isn't that when we're going skiing?"

"Yeah, it is, isn't it? That'll be a good weekend. We'll have to have a drink or two over there to celebrate!"

"I think we should do that now, don't you?"

"Good idea," said Nick, as Alyson took a bottle of Cava from the fridge. "And if you play your cards right you might get a shag later as well!"

"Speaking of which," said Alyson, "did you hear those bloody foxes last night?"

"No, I don't think so."

Alyson pulled the cork on the Cava, which flew across the kitchen and bounced off a window. The Cava fizzed and Alyson quickly poured some into a glass to catch the spillage.

"About three o'clock, it was - mating or fighting or whatever it was that they were doing. Sounded like someone was murdering a child. I had to get up and shut the window. I couldn't see them out there though. Ha - I thought I saw a bloke coming out of Tricia's house for a moment, but it was only Colin on one of his walkabouts."

"Well, don't wake me if you hear them again tonight, will you."

Alyson handed him a glass of Cava.

"It didn't sound as if we'd be doing much sleeping from what you said."

She clinked her glass against Nick's and kissed him on the lips.

*

"Haha! Yes! The bitch is going, the bitch is going! Good riddance, fatty! And good luck to your new neighbours - poor sods. Fucking yes, yes ... YES!"

*

12. Anette

Alyson was pissed off because skiing had turned out to be crap. Making a fool of herself in front of a bunch of strangers and getting covered in bruises in the process was not her idea of fun.

Nick was pissed off because Alyson had, as ever, chosen the most expensive restaurant in town. It wasn't particularly the cost of such places that he objected to, it was more that, to him, the more expensive a restaurant, the less pleasurable the experience. To Nick, expensive restaurants were synonymous with small portions, obscure weird food, tedious poseur customers, snooty waiters, and slow service.

Alyson was pissed off with Nick moaning about how long the main course was taking to arrive.

Nick was pissed off that Alyson had ordered a really expensive bottle of wine … as if either of them could tell the difference between that one and the cheapest on the menu. Just who was she trying to impress exactly?

Alyson was pissed off that Nick had ordered a pint of lager in addition to the nice bottle of wine that she had selected. It was as if he was deliberately trying to show her up at times.

Nick was pissed off because the menu was in French. He didn't have a problem with the restaurant writing their menus in French - they were in France after all, but it did make the selection and ordering process that little bit more painful. And, more importantly, whilst he was keen for his food to arrive, he still wasn't completely sure of just what he was going to be getting.

Alyson was really pissed off that Nick had been arguing with the waiter. It was hard to imagine anything more embarrassing ... other than perhaps trying to learn how to ski in front of a bunch of strangers.

Nick was really, really pissed off that the waiter had come back with a message from the chef telling him that he should reconsider his request to have his steak 'well done'. He was the customer, wasn't he? And he knew more than some head-up-his-own-arse French cook how he liked his own food. Fucking cheek!

Alyson was livid that Nick had made a suggestion that she'd put on a bit of weight of late. That was the last thing she wanted to hear at any time, least of all whilst trying to enjoy a meal in a nice restaurant. She'd had half a mind to walk out and leave him to it but chose not to give him the satisfaction. Yes, she was aware that she'd put a couple of pounds on her hips, but it wasn't as if she was fat, and she would soon lose it again - she always did. But of course, if she went on a diet, it would be her breasts that would lose it before her bum; it always was. Life was unfair like that. Nick was such a shit.

The main course arrived and the two of them ate in silence. The food was good though, and Nick was particularly pleased with his steak, which came quite well done, in spite of the chef's protests. He finished before Alyson - as always - finished his glass of wine, and then continued with his latest pint of lager. His phone beeped, and he looked at it.

"Who's texting you at this time of night?"

"Jason ... work stuff."

Nick started texting back.

"Doesn't he know that it's Saturday night ... and you're on holiday?"

"I'm just reminding him."

Alyson shook her head and tutted. But her annoyance was dissipating - at least Nick wasn't work-obsessed like that sad wanker Jason.

Nick's phone beeped again. He read Jason's response and smirked.

Alyson rolled her eyes. "Go on then, what's he saying now?" And she peered over towards the phone.

"You don't want to know!"

Alyson made a grab for the phone; the wine was encouraging her to disregard restaurant etiquette.

Nick held it out of her reach. "Ah … ah!"

"Don't be mean."

"OK, OK - I'll read it out."

He held the phone in his right hand whilst keeping Alyson at bay with his left.

"Alright, this is it: 'Sorry mate, forgot you were on a dirty weekend. Give her one for me!' And then a couple of winking emojis."

Alyson sat back down on her seat and took a large swig of wine. She thought for a moment.

"Well, are you then?" she said.

"Am I what?"

"Going to do what he says."

"Oh! Dunno … might do, if I can be bothered!"

"Yeah, right!" She poured herself another glass of wine and then downed most of it in one go.

Nick took a large swig of his lager and sat back, relaxed. This made something of a change from a normal Saturday night at the local - and what a weekend so far! There was the mountain scenery, the party atmosphere, the clean air … and the skiing itself was fantastic. After just one day of ski school, he wasn't yet any good at it, and quite possibly never would be, but the falling and larking around with a multi-national bunch of strangers was one of the biggest laughs he'd ever had. OK, this evening's meal hadn't been a complete success, but now he was starting to feel pleasantly drunk, and it was even sounding as if he was on a promise as well! He could get used to this skiing lark; he was already sure that he would be doing it again.

"Fuck, this is good stuff! Am off my face! Another one of those please, barman. Gotta be up at the crack of DAWN … Who cares! Good stuff. Really good fucking stuff."

*

After polishing off their second bottle of the posh red French wine, Nick and Alyson stumbled hand in hand through the snow-covered streets to one of the village's three night clubs. There they met up with other members of their ski school and all shared exhilarated accounts of the day's dramas shouted over a loud mix of current and eighties dance tracks, accompanied by much laughter and continued excessive drinking. They got back to their chalet at about three o'clock, ripped off their clothes and jumped into bed.

The invigorating effects of alcohol, adrenalin, and fresh mountain air combined with the liberation of being away gave their lovemaking an exuberance exclusive to holiday sex and rare special occasions. Alyson had already orgasmed once and was about to do so again. This time Nick would be joining her.

"Shall I put on a condom?"

He knew what the answer would be.

"No … don't stop!"

Alyson screamed Nick's name as the two of them climaxed in noisy unison, both happily oblivious to the effect on anyone trying sleep in the neighbouring rooms.

Nick looked down into Alyson's blue eyes and at her big smile. They kissed and then stayed lying there holding onto each other's bodies and both feeling their two racing heartbeats gradually slowing back down. When his breathing was close to returning to normal, Nick kissed Alyson once more and then rolled his body gently onto his side. Alyson turned to face away from him, and he put his arm around her. He kissed her on the back of her neck.

"Love you!"

"Love you too!"

There was an alarm clock on Alyson's bedside table. Nick focused his eyes on it: 04:13. They wouldn't be getting up in time for ski school in the morning.

*

Oh my god, Nick. I don't even fucking know who you are anymore!

*

The long weekend was soon over, and after three days of excessive booze, sex, and exercise, combined with very little sleep, an exhausted Nick and Alyson trudged their way to the taxi rank at Heathrow Airport. They were ushered to a black cab and were both annoyed but too tired to argue when the driver started ranting when he found out that they lived only five miles away. The previous time that that had happened Nick sarcastically apologised and promised the cabbie that they would move to somewhere further away before next flying anywhere in order that if he picked them up again, he would get a larger fare. This time Nick and Alyson just looked at each other knowingly. This bloke wouldn't be getting much of a tip, that was for sure.

The taxi turned into their estate.

"I wonder when we'll get to see our new neighbours," said Nick "… and what they'll be like."

Both had something of a deja vu moment as they recalled the near-identical situation returning from their Isle of Wight weekend two years before.

"Well, they can't be any worse; I pity the poor sods *she's* moving next to," said Alyson.

"I wonder if we'll ever see her again."

"I bloody hope not!"

The taxi pulled up outside their house, and all was quiet in the street. There was no sign of the new neighbours, which itself was a good sign. The taxi fare was £12.70; Nick handed over £13 and didn't look the driver in the eye.

The taxi sped away and as Nick and Alyson began to wheel their suitcases into their driveway the door of the house opposite opened - and somebody came out with a black sack full of rubbish. That somebody was Tricia. Nick's jaw dropped. Alyson muttered "fucking hell."

"Awright, mate!" Tricia called to Nick, waving her hand cheerfully as she did so.

"Give me your keys," said Alyson to Nick. She had never spoken to Tricia and had no intention of starting now. Nick gave her his keys and walked back out to the road.

"Hello. You OK?" Nick asked Tricia.

"Well, mustn't grumble."

"So, when is it that you're moving out - it's soon, isn't it?"

"Ha! It was going to be, but it's not now."

"Oh, dear. What happened?"

"They changed their minds, didn't they? Don't want to do the swap now."

"Oh, dear. Sorry to hear that." That was something of an understatement.

Tricia cackled. "You'll have to put up with me for a bit longer."

Nick wondered how much 'a bit' meant. He turned and headed back towards the house. A brilliant weekend had suddenly turned to shit. And now he was going to have to tackle a tired, emotional, and very pissed off Alyson.

*

Neighbour From Hell

"Come on then, let's see some photos," demanded Annette Price, as she pulled up a chair next to Nick's behind his desk.

Nick took out his phone and the two of them peered into it. He enjoyed feeling Annette's closeness - he always did, but it had been a long time since the two of them had last been 'really close'. He started at the most recent photo and then flicked backwards through the others. There were bar scenes, a couple of pictures of Nick's tentative first-time skier pose, and beautiful snow-covered mountain scenes. He paused on some of the better ones to allow Annette a closer look; he didn't pause on any of the few in which Alyson appeared.

When he flipped to the end of the ski photos, a picture of the Bond came up next. He had visited Geoff Lanning's workshop a couple of weeks before to have a look at its progress, as he had done from time to time throughout its restoration.

"Oh, and that's the Bond. Starting to look good, isn't it?" he said.

"Yeah, I like the colour. It looks smart."

"Yes, I chose that. It's not exactly an original colour for them, it's just a really dark blue, but I thought it suits it."

"It does. When's it going to be finished?"

"A couple of months or so. It's mostly done really, other than the engine. And that's not in it at the moment - he's re-building it … well, overhauling it anyway. Do you remember how much of a shed it was to start with?"

"Yeah, sort of."

"Let me show you."

Nick opened up an album called 'Bond' on his phone and started going through photos of the Bond in its original tired condition and shabby white paintwork as it was when he'd inherited it. Annette feigned interest.

"Who's that?" asked Annette, referring to a man standing next to the Bond when it was parked up on his front lawn.

"That's Danny."

"What, the Danny who ripped you off?"

"Thanks for reminding me."

"I didn't know he was black!"

"Well, he's not really, he's Asian."

"No, I mean all of that time you used to go on about him and moan about him pissing you about, I just pictured a white bloke in his fifties for some reason … with a grey beard. You never said that he was black, well - brown."

"Didn't I? Well, it doesn't really matter; he's a wanker either way."

"Danny's not a very Asian name though, is it."

"No, he's got a much longer Indian name. I think he just uses 'Danny' because it's easier for customers."

"Or he uses false names because he rips people off."

"Yeah, thanks again."

Annette laughed. "Oh, don't be so sensitive," she said, playfully slapping Nick on the shoulder.

*

Alyson had dinner ready for the two of them the minute that Nick got in from work. Quite often when she worked from home she was bored by the middle of the afternoon and did something that wasn't work with the rest of her time, such as shopping, phoning her mum, watching TV, or - as was the case today - cooking a meal. She had even phoned Nick at work to ask him what he wanted to eat, which was unusual. She'd also seemed keen for him to come home and been particularly attentive and smiley when he'd got in. Nick wondered what she wanted.

Alyson did most of the talking during the meal, but she spoke more quickly than normal and seemed ill-at-ease. She topped up their wine glasses - another rarity; they didn't usually start drinking until much later in the evening.

"Nick, there's something I need to tell you."

Neighbour From Hell

Here we go.

"… OK - go ahead."

"Well, you know that time on the ski trip when we had unprotected sex? Well …"

A few hours later Nick and Alyson were sitting at a table in The Star. Nick was staring into his pint. He was pleased that he'd asked her about putting on a condom that night in the Alps. She wouldn't have minded at the time if he hadn't asked - might have preferred it even - but given the consequences, she would now have been able to hold it against him whenever it suited, for evermore.

They were into their third round.
Alyson spoke.
"We're going to have to stop drinking like this soon, aren't we?"

"Well, *you* are!"

"Very funny."

"I'm not sure I could cope with not coming here about five nights a week."

"Well, we are going to have to move away before too long, aren't we? Who'd want to bring up a child surrounded by chavs and racists."

"Hmmm, I suppose so."

The door flew open with its usual loud creak, and in came Len Phillips and a blast of cold air. Len nodded at Nick and Alyson as he made his way to the bar, unbuttoning his coat at the same time. They'd kept themselves to themselves so far and both hoped that Len wouldn't come and join them.

Alyson turned back to Nick. "How many times did we have sex that weekend?"

"Five." He'd been thinking about the same thing himself.

She frowned. "Have you been keeping notes?"

"Yep, it's all in a spreadsheet!"

"Very funny." She slapped him but she was smiling.

Len called over. "Are you two playing pool tonight?"

Nick made a dismissive gesture with his hand. "Not tonight, thanks."

Len nodded and turned to Darren who had just finished losing at pool and was selecting songs on the jukebox. "Darren?"

Darren gave him a thumbs up.

Alyson continued. "But only the Saturday night without protection?"

"No, the next morning as well."

"Ah yes. I wonder when it happened."

Nick thought for a moment. "Probably the Saturday night, I reckon."

Alyson nodded. "Yes, probably."

"... Would be nice to think so," said Nick, "that was a good session!"

Alyson smiled and nodded. Then she leaned over and kissed him. They had never kissed in The Star before.

Nick looked into her eyes. "We should re-enact it some time."

She was still smiling. "Yes, we should."

Nick thought for a second. "It only takes ten minutes to get home ... five if we run."

"I'm not running in my condition!"

"Seven then, if we walk fast."

"Do I get to finish my drink first?"

"Do you want to?"

Alyson took his hand and squeezed it - another first for their local pub.

They kissed again and then got up, quickly putting on their coats, and left, neither looking to see whether anyone was watching them.

*

13. Alyson

The fire started slowly. The ingredients were all in place: fuel - a crumpled cotton dressing gown discarded next to the bed; heat - a cigarette butt, smouldering at 900 degrees centigrade; and oxygen, present in more than sufficient quantities in the air. The few flecks of cotton that were in direct contact with the cigarette butt's remaining glow of tobacco heated up and blackened, giving off a tiny wisp of grey smoke. The process then spread to the cotton flecks' immediate neighbours, causing a hot dark mark to form on the garment, at first not even a hole, and not more than half a centimetre in diameter. The dressing gown didn't though provide a sufficiently flammable fuel source to sustain any further growth of the fire with such a limited heat source, and it would have died out causing no more damage than a small mark on the garment, if not for the presence of some spilt vodka, or 'an accelerant' to use fire investigation officer terminology.

*

Alyson was fine with the fact that Nick had gone to a football match on a Tuesday night, and she would also be OK with him going for a drink afterwards. She was also pleased that he'd asked her beforehand rather than just telling her that he was going; he was being better with things like that since she'd become pregnant. What she wasn't fine with was the gathering of the scum outside Tricia's house. It stressed her as much as ever, and the fact that she still couldn't get over it stressed her still more. They didn't tend to do it so much in the winter, especially not on a cold evening. So why did they have to choose to do so on a night when Nick was out? She turned to drink, like she always did; she really did try to resist, but it was the only thing that worked. But this time it didn't work, and when Nick got home at close to midnight, she was not only drunk, but more stressed than ever. Nick came through the door, bringing with him a rush of outside air from the cold January night, and Alyson flew at him.

"Those fucking yobs were all over the road again while you were out enjoying yourself!"

Nick, who'd had a few drinks himself could tell that Alyson was drunk and he did his best to calm her, but she was having none of it.

"Why don't you do anything about it, Nick? Why don't you stand up to any of these people?"

Nick reminded her of the work that he had done with the residents' association. But that didn't help.

"A lot of fucking good that's done, hasn't it? Why do you let all of these people walk all over us?"

A few months before, after a few too many lagers, he'd told Alyson about scratching Bradley Mullen's car. It had proved to be a mistake, as she was livid, and it would undoubtedly prove a mistake to bring it up again. But he did it, all the same.

"Well, I scratched that drug dealer's car, didn't I?"

"Yes, you did, and that was one of the stupidest things you've ever done. How did that help anything?"

"Well, it made me feel better," said Nick as he made his way to the fridge to get himself a can.

Alyson carried on. "Rob Stockdale stands up to them, and they take notice of him."

"That's because he'll beat them up. We don't have that option ... we're a different type of people."

"So, what do we do then? What are you going to do when one of those scumbags comes running at you with a knife?"

Nick stood facing Alyson. He was drunk and he was exasperated. There had been so many times during his and

Neighbour From Hell

Alyson's eight years that he had come close to doing what he was now considering. But every time he'd managed to resist. There was never a good time to do it, and now was *absolutely* not a good time to do it. He couldn't stop himself. He reached into his jacket pocket. He took something from it and placed it down with a 'klump' on the solid pinewood coffee table in front of him. Alyson glared at the object.

"What the fuck is that?"

"What does it look like?"

"It looks like a fucking gun, Nick!"

"Exactly."

"What the hell are you doing with that?"

"Well, you asked me what I would do if one of those morons came at me with a knife and …"

"Where the hell did you get it, Nick?"

Nick composed himself. "Look, I'm sorry - I've been meaning to tell you for years." He sat down on the sofa, but Alyson remained standing, staring at him in disbelief. "You know how my mate was murdered when I was seventeen …" he cleared his throat "… and about that time at college when I was held up at knifepoint … well, I decided to protect myself in case something like that ever happened again."

"When? When did you get it?"

"Right back then, when I was at college."

"And you've never thought to tell me that you've got a gun?"

"Look, I'm really sorry. I was always meaning to, but there never seemed to be a right time."

"Too bloody right, there wasn't. Get rid of it, Nick. Get rid of it - NOW!"

"Make your bloody mind up - do you want us to defend ourselves from that lot or not?" Nick thought, but fortunately didn't say.

"Oh my god, Nick. I don't even know who you fucking are anymore!" She picked up her vodka glass and downed the remaining contents. "Right, I'm going to bed. And I want that thing out of my house now. It had better not be here in the morning."

Alyson stormed out of the room, slamming the door behind her, and stamped her way up the stairs.

Nick stayed where he was and cracked open his can.

"Fucking hell!" he muttered to himself.

He swallowed a mouthful of lager.

Not for the first time, he pondered how the bullies always seemed to come out on top. Why *couldn't* he be more like Rob - the good elements of Rob? Rob had strength and size on his side, but also – partly due to those qualities - the ability to not concern himself with consequences. Of course, he also had less to lose.

Bullies and wankers were getting to him ever more: Danny, Tricia, Billy Grindle, all the rest of the scum, career twats and miserable whingers at work, the moaners and racists in the public meetings, Bert Walsh, Bradley Mullen, "…wastes of fucking space, the lot of 'em!"

Of all things though, today it was being promoted that was making him the most morose. Why was that? He knew some answers to that question. It frustrated him that people should assume that he would be delighted about it. Was that all they thought of him – that he could do OK in the cosy safe dull world of the corporate ladder? Did they not realise that there was so much more to life? Maybe they did. Maybe they realised that and were just doing exactly the same thing about it that he was – absolutely fuck all! That's right, he was drifting along in his career just going wherever it took him without doing anything to steer it where he wanted, or even to work out *what* he wanted. Things just happened to him. It was the same with his relationship with Alyson: it drifted along and just happened – no planning, no consideration as to whether it was the right thing to do. And now he was drifting into parenthood … *they* were drifting into parenthood – no planning, no consideration ….

And next they were going to be moving house – to somewhere better for a child to grow up. It wasn't necessarily a bad thing, but it wasn't his idea or his choice. Alyson had spoken to her parents who had then offered them a contribution of a hundred thousand pounds. How fucking nice of them!

He turned back his thoughts to the scumbags – the Tricias, the Billy Grindles, the Dannys – who made other people's lives a misery without any care of consequence. Rob could punch any one of them, but not Nick – he wouldn't, he couldn't. He took his half-empty lager can and slung it hard against the far wall. Then he went through to the fridge and got himself another one.

*

The fire spread in a line along the vodka spill on the dressing gown. A small flame appeared at the head of that line, moving slowly down the crumpled garment, emitting a still small but growing plume of grey smoke as it did so. After a few minutes it had travelled the six or seven centimetres that took it to the carpet-covered bedroom floor. There was a lot more of the vodka spill on the floor, soaked around the carpet's polypropylene fibres and spread out over an area the size of a dinner plate. The flames quickly covered that area and were now larger, several centimetres tall. As the temperature around them began to rise, so the larger flames spread back to the crumpled dressing gown which ignited and was soon engulfed, with flames licking around the side of the bed and starting to spread to the duvet cover on top of it.

She snored in her vodka assisted slumber. Her lungs were starting to draw in smoke that irritated them with its heat and slowed her oxygen intake. She coughed but didn't awake.

The fire's growth accelerated as it drew in air through a window that had been opened just an hour before to allow cigarette smoke to escape. Flaming molten droplets floated across the room, falling onto soft furnishings, and causing mini fires to flare into life. The fire was jumping around the room in deadly little dances. The smoke was real now, it thickened and blackened and rushed along under the ceiling. Had there been a smoke alarm in the room then it would have triggered by now.

Her sleep deepened as her lungs continued to fill with heat and poison.

The air rushed in from the window; the flames spread across the ceiling; the room grew ever hotter.

*

There were no yobs over the street this time, but that didn't make any difference. Alyson was cross with herself. She was home alone again, as she'd told Nick once more that it would be OK for him to go out. She'd told him that she would be fine. She'd managed to hide from him for all this time how stressful it was being alone in the house in the evenings, and she wasn't going to change that now. She'd done well. She'd wanted to get used to it, and not to be so weak - it would get better in time. But that was why she was cross with herself: it hadn't got better; it had got worse. She was emotional because she was pregnant now, but that wasn't the reason, was it? No, she was sure it wasn't - it would have made her even more angry if she'd thought that that was the case. No, what had made things worse was the hope that had been snatched away. That bitch over the road had promised to go, but then hadn't done so. So, the yobs went on, the menace went on, the stress went on. Not a world to bring a child into.

Over time on these evenings alone she had dispensed with her warm-up glass or two of red wine and started going straight to the vodka. She still had her cigarettes, lighter, and ash tray in a kitchen drawer. The maintenance of that secret stash was the nearest thing that she had to a coping strategy. But she had to stop all of that now; it wasn't right. Just one drop tonight though. Nick would be cross if he knew. *Fuck him.*

She watched some TV, flicking from channel to channel, from shit programme to shit programme. The vodka was going down well. The hours slid by. It was eleven o'clock; Nick would be a few hours yet. She went to her kitchen drawer and took out a cigarette. Just the one. She put on her coat, went out into the back garden, and lit up. She breathed the smoke deep into her lungs and then blew it out into the night air, watching it float away and disappear into the darkness.

When she came back in, the house felt so warm, and Alyson felt comforted. It was time for bed. She went up to the bedroom, stumbling on the stairs and emitting a nervous giggle. The bedroom curtains were open, so she didn't turn on the light. She placed her vodka bottle, glass, cigarettes, lighter, and ash tray on Nick's desk. Next, she quickly stripped off her clothes and threw them into a pile at the foot of her bed. She grabbed her dressing gown but then fumbled around and struggled to get the sleaves untangled. *Fuck it - who needs clothes!* She let it fall to the floor. Then she went over to the window and opened it a little to let out the smoke that she was about to produce. It was unlikely that anyone would see her naked form in the window, but she was too drunk to care if they did. She lit up another cigarette, sat down on Nick's office chair, and glared with hatred at the house across the street. She poured herself a glass of vodka. The draught through the open window felt uncomfortably cold on her naked body. She lit one more cigarette from the butt of the previous one and then downed her glass of vodka in one. She stumbled over to the bed, near empty vodka bottle in one hand and freshly lit cigarette in the other, and flopped down on her back. She let the vodka bottle slip to the floor. The room was spinning. Her cigarette tasted good; the smoke smelled nice. The draught from the window was now just a cool breeze in the hot room. Alyson smiled. She hadn't been so drunk in ages. She felt good. *Fuck 'em!* She felt free. She took a long drag and then started to laugh.

*

"The bitch! The Fucking fat bitch! Why didn't she go? She was supposed to fucking GO! She's gotta go; she's got to go; she's got to fucking go. She's fucking going. Fat fucking COW. She's going, she's going. She's fucking going."

*

Alyson awoke from her nightmare with a start and sat bolt upright. She was coughing. She could smell smoke. She was disorientated. A terrible feeling of dread overcame her. She knew that she was still drunk, and she was furious with herself for drinking so much. But the dread was something much more than that - she had a feeling that she was dying. She was hot and she was sweating profusely. Bright orange light flickered aggressively around the room. There was noise, lots of noise - a rushing sound, and voices. She felt next to her for Nick. He wasn't there. She called out his name. She panicked. She threw herself out of the bed and fell straight to the floor. She pulled herself up, she was gasping for breath. She scrambled her way to the window. The smoke was choking, and the heat was overwhelming. There were people in the street. Was that Nick sitting on the footpath?

*

"I could do it. Won't take much. Shit. No-one will know. Fuck, I'm pissed. Ha! What the fuck! Who cares - nothing to lose anyway. SHIT. Ha! Problems just gone away … well … could be …unless…. What the fuck. What the FUCK."

*

Waves of flame swept along the whole length of the ceiling, radiating intense heat onto everything below. As they heated up, items with combustible surfaces - a fabric armchair, a wooden dressing table - released further flammable gases into the air until, when the temperature hit 500°C, 'flashover' occurred: The armchair and dressing table simultaneously ignited in an explosion that blew out the windows and brought down the ceiling. Huge flames then licked around the outside of the building and shot up into the roof space. The whole bedroom was ablaze. There was no chance of anybody getting out of there alive.

*

"Ha-ha-ha! Feels good. Yeah, feels OK. Freedom! No-one about. Ha-ha! Fuck 'em. FUCK the lot of 'em. Sweet dreams, eh? Sweet dreams! Bollocks to it; bollocks to it. Need a drink. Need to get some kip. Yeah, sweet dreams. Bollocks! What the fuck. What the … SHIT! It's good; it's good; it's OK. Sweet fucking dreams… Fuck! Fuck! FUCK!"

*

Nick was sitting down on the kerb exhausted. He hadn't really done much - he and Rob Stockdale had tried to get to the house, but the sheer heat made it impossible. His lungs ached, his skin was singed, and the heat had drained his energy. He'd taken his seat just in time to see the explosion. If he and Rob had still been at the front of the house they would have been showered with red hot splinters of glass. Rob was still standing, he wandered around in the middle of the road looking dazed. Charlene and Kevin were out in the street in their night clothes, huddled with their children. Ted Davies was there too, and others were arriving. Nick put his head in his hands; he felt sick. The windows of all of the houses began to illuminate with big blue sweeps of light and that unmistakable sound of a fire engine's motor was once more present. There was no need for sirens at this time of night.

Then he heard Alyson scream his name, "NICK!"

He got up and ran up his driveway. Alyson was standing in the doorway looking dazed. They threw their arms around each other.

"Oh, my god!" sobbed Alyson. "Is there anyone in there?"

Two fire engines came to a halt between them and the fire, and their crews disembarked.

"I don't know," said Nick. "Quite likely Tricia. Charlene said that Damian's at his dad's for the weekend."

The firemen executed their well-rehearsed routines with incredible speed and had two hoses trained on the fire in no time. There was a loud crack as, unseen by Nick and Alyson, one of them smashed open the front door, making short work of Nick's handiwork with the door frame.

"I woke up with the heat," said Alyson. "I thought I was dying. Our room's full of smoke."

She and Nick embraced again.

"I just put some clothes on and ran outside when I woke up," said Nick. "Sorry, I probably should have woken you."

More blue lights joined the show as a police car arrived from the left, followed by an ambulance from the right.

"I have a horrible feeling there's not going to be any need for that ambulance," said Nick.

Alyson pulled back from him, she'd only just noticed the damage to his skin.

Neighbour From Hell

"Shit, what happened to you? Are you OK?"

"Why, what's wrong?" asked Nick; he hadn't really noticed.

"Your face is all red and your eyebrows aren't there. Shit, Nick - we need to get that looked at!"

"Oh, no, it's OK. Rob and I tried to get there but the heat stopped us."

The flames were soon subsiding from the gallons of water being played onto them, and where Tricia's bedroom window had been there emerged a black smoking hole. Nick and Alyson looked on with lumps in their throats.

There were more people in the street. Lights had come on in all of the houses around. Colin emerged and wandered to the end of his driveway. People were arriving from all directions, most were on foot, but some even came in cars. Dopey Dave turned up. "NO!" he yelled. "I love you, Tricia!" Soon a concerned looking Brian Hart was walking into Nick and Alyson's driveway. It was becoming a bigger social gathering even than one of Tricia's 'parties'.

*

"Hahaha! Not laughing now, is she? You're NOT laughing now, are you, eh?! Fat COW. Not good for you all those fags, you know! Ding dong, the bitch is dead, the bitch is dead. Here's to peace and quiet for the rest of us. Cheers!"

*

Tricia's body was carried from her house at eleven o'clock on the morning. Police tape was tied across the front of her yard and a uniformed policeman stood guard behind it. Underneath the sinister gaping hole where Tricia's bedroom window had been, the word 'SCUM' was still visible in those big white spray-painted letters on the brickwork - a photo opportunity for the various journalists who turned up during the course of the day, keen for an 'angle' to report on. An acrid stench filled the air.

Police scene of crime officers and their counterparts in the fire investigation team arrived in numbers. Before entering the house, they each donned a white protective suit, the likes of which most onlookers had only seen before on television. And those onlookers continued to arrive as well. A steady stream of cars dove slowly by, their occupants straining their necks to take in as much of the scene as they could. Others cycled and then stopped for a few minutes looking blankly at the house and the police and fire officers before heading on their way, curiosity sated. But most arrived on foot and then stood around, some chatting, and some taking photos. These were mostly other residents of the estate; several members of the scum were among their number. Billy Grindle hung around for a few hours. Dopey Dave didn't appear.

Early in the afternoon Kevin and Charlene turned up from a friend's house. They went into their home and emerged a short while later, Charlene carrying a small suitcase and Kevin a rucksack, departing without speaking to anybody.

Later, some workmen arrived in a lorry and draped large tarpaulins over the house. First, they covered the part-collapsed roof and then the whole of the front of the building. The gaping black hole could no longer be seen, the word 'scum' could no longer be seen.

The show was over.

*

"Bloody coppers - haven't got a clue. Haven't got a fucking clue. I could have done that - probably been quite good at it. Me, in the police. Ha! Ah well, their loss. Just have to sit and laugh at them instead. Ha-ha! Not a clue. No chance. Not a FUCKING clue. Bunch of fucking mugs."

*

"I was thinking of going to the football this afternoon," Nick mumbled.

Alyson didn't look up from her laptop. "I thought you were supposed to be getting rid of all that crap from the shed."

"I took it to the dump a couple of weeks ago," he replied, matter-of-factly.

"You didn't tell me," she huffed.

"You didn't ask."

Then the scene of fragile domesticity was broken by a rare interruption from Nick and Alyson's doorbell. Alyson sighed loudly as if whoever was at the door had deliberately chosen that specific moment in order to disturb her concentration, and she thumped the laptop down on her sofa. She soon returned, with two serious-looking men following her.

Nick recognised one of the men as a policeman who'd spoken to him on the day after the fire, a week before. That man introduced his colleague and explained that they were talking to people again to try to clarify the sequence of events that night.

"Sure," said Nick, and invited them to sit down.

The two policemen accepted that invitation and then one of them went matter-of-factly through some questions while the other took notes.

First, they went over the night of the fire with essentially the same questions that they had asked Nick, and - he presumed - any other witnesses, previously - what had woken him, what he had done next, and so on. But they also went on to other things such as whether Nick had ever been in Tricia's house, whether he had a set of keys to the house, or if he knew of anyone else who did.

Alyson looked on, with an increasingly annoyed-looking expression before chipping in, "So, are you saying that someone killed her?"

The two policemen turned towards her.

"No, we are not saying that at all," said policeman number one. "We just need to establish exactly what happened that night."

"So, what's all this about her keys then?"

Policeman number two answered this time. "It's just routine. We believe that Mrs Gorman had a spare set of keys, and they haven't been found in the house, so we'd like to account for them."

That was the first time that Nick or Alyson had heard Tricia's surname, or known that she had ever been married.

"Well, you seem to be accusing him of having them!"

Nick then stepped in to first calm Alyson down and then explain that he had indeed seen Tricia's spare keys when he had fixed her door, but that that was the only time. He then described the 'World's Best Mum' key fob for them. He got the impression that they were familiar with the description.

The policemen stayed on another few minutes before thanking Nick for his time. They didn't have any questions for Alyson. As they departed policeman number one made the standard 'If either of you think of anything else ...' comment and then wrote down his contact information on a card that he handed to Nick.

Nick glanced at the card in his hand – 'D.S. Ferriby' and a landline phone number – then closed the front door behind the policemen and returned to the living room.

"Bloody cheek!" snapped Alyson.

"They are only doing their job," said Nick.

Alyson then returned to her laptop shaking her head.

"Yeah, I think I *am* going to go to the football," said Nick.

"Do whatever you want," said Alyson.

"Yes," thought Nick, "I will!"

Then Alyson had another thought. "What happened to that gun of yours?"

"I hid it - like you wanted."

"They are not going to be finding a bullet in Tricia's body, are they?"

"Don't be ridiculous."

*

As Nick started on his second lager in the back garden, he heard Colin take his place at the other side of the fence. He listened as Colin pulled up his chair and then lit himself a cigarette. He thought that he would give Colin time to take his first drag before alerting him to his presence, and only spoke when he smelled the first particles of smoke drifting through to his side of the fence.

"Good evening!"

Whilst both Nick and Colin had carried on with their garden drinking/smoking exploits throughout the winter, they hadn't done so as often as before and as a result hadn't bumped into each other here for some time.

"Hello Nick," replied Colin sounding quite surprised. "Spring must be here!"

"Well, we're halfway through March. The year's going quickly."

"Yeah, it must be nearly a month since that business over the road."

"It is. Did the police come and speak to you? They came round here about a week afterwards."

Colin took a long drag on his cigarette and then exhaled a plume of smoke that wafted up into the night sky.

"They came around while I was out. I can't tell them anything useful though. I told them that on the night - I didn't wake up until after they were there. At least I got out there in time to see that Charlene in her night dress though. Did they say what they were looking for?"

"Just routine, they said. Probably just got to make sure that she wasn't murdered."

"Hmm," said Colin. "I'm sure plenty must have thought about doing that."

"They asked about her spare keys - you know, the ones that she tried to give me. Glad to say that I didn't have them!"

Colin took another long drag, and then let out the smoke slowly and deliberately.

"Are you thinking of going to the funeral?" asked Nick.

"Am I fuck!" Colin then took yet another drag. "Anyway, how's your missus getting along? Is she starting to show yet?"

"She's fine, thanks. Yes, starting to look a bit fat."

Colin chuckled. "Well, make sure you keep getting your leg over while you can; you won't be getting much of that for the next few years."

"Thanks."

"So, what are you going to do - turn the back room into a baby's room? Cos you've got that as an office, haven't you?"

"Well, we're not sure. Actually, we were thinking about maybe moving."

Colin paused before replying, "I see. That's nice."

"Yeah, Alyson's mum and dad said that they might help us out a bit and you know …"

"Alright for some. Where are you going?"

"Don't know really at this stage. We haven't really talked about it much yet."

That wasn't true - he and Alyson had talked about it a lot but all of the areas they were considering were much more upmarket than Nick wanted to admit.

Colin was taking yet another long drag on his cigarette, and so Nick carried on.

"Anyway, we must be overdue another visit to the football club – see if your favourite barmaid's still there!"

"Yeah."

"And if we do move then we'll have to do that, or at least meet in a pub, as we wouldn't be able to have our back garden chats anymore."

"Yeah, we'll have to do that," said Colin. And then after one more long pause he continued, "Shan't be coming out here so much, anyway though. I'm trying to cut down on the fags."

"Ah, well done. How's it going?"

"Not great so far. I'm going to have to do it though - besides anything else, they're so bloody expensive."

"Well, best of luck with that; probably a good idea."

"Yep," said Colin, before taking a last quick drag and then dropping his cigarette butt to the floor and squashing it under his shoe. "I'll try to make that the last one tonight. Right, I'm off to get some sleep. Onwards and upwards, eh?"

"OK. See you soon. Sleep well."

*

14. Roy

There were ten people at the crematorium for Tricia's funeral, Nick and Alyson, Charlene and Kevin, Damian, a woman called Anne - who was apparently a former social worker, and two dishevelled-looking middle-aged couples that Nick and Alyson presumed to be relatives.

Nick had said to Alyson that he thought he should attend, "to represent the residents' association and because, well, you know …" and Alyson had offered to come along with him.

Proceedings were carried out in a perfunctory manner by an elderly priest, and a eulogy given by Anne.

Anne, who was in her late sixties, had first known Tricia as a child, more than thirty years before. She talked of a mischievous but smiley girl brought up in poverty and suffering 'many hardships' that brought about the two of them first meeting. In time, having suffered 'abuse at the hands of more than one person,' Tricia had been taken into care at the age of thirteen. She had had a 'troubled' time in care before finding herself alone in the world when she turned eighteen and her care support ended. Anne's professional involvement had ended at that point but the two of them had remained in touch during Tricia's 'further struggles' throughout her twenties, about which Anne was non-specific, but seemed to hint at drugs and possibly prostitution. But then things had taken an upturn for Tricia, as at the age of thirty 'she fell in love with the man that she went on to marry', and with whom she had two 'beautiful children' - twins, Damian and Danielle.

That revelation was a bit of a shock to Nick and Alyson but a bigger one was to come.

Tricia was a 'proud and happy' mother, according to Anne, but that happy period of her life proved 'all too

Neighbour From Hell

brief' as her marriage broke up and Tricia was left to fend for her children alone. And then came the lowest and saddest time in Tricia's life as she had to face 'what no mother should ever have to face - losing her own daughter, at just eight years of age.'

Anne was speaking as if all who were present would know Tricia's life story, which it was quite likely that other than Nick and Alyson they all did. She paused to compose herself. Damian stared straight ahead, as he had done throughout the speech. Nick did likewise. The whole room was in silence. Anne cleared her throat. She talked of the sadness that she had seen in Tricia's eyes over the years but also of the kindness that she had seen Tricia demonstrate to others, and to Damian in particular. She said that sometimes it might have been masked by her troubled exterior, but that underneath Tricia had a heart of gold and only wanted to do the best by her son.

"Whilst Tricia's life was still far from perfect, it was recently the most stable that it had been for a very long time, and with Damian developing into a young man, she had much to look forward to. A death so many years before its time is always tragic, but for this to have happened at such a time in her life is utterly heartbreaking.

"Tricia has been taken from this world far too soon," said Anne, "but if she was able to speak to us today, all she would ask is that we look after Damian, as she would have continued to do if she was still here. And I am sure that I speak for everybody in this room when I say 'Of course, Tricia, we promise to do that for you.' We'll miss you, Tricia. Rest in peace, and God bless."

As Anne made her way back to her seat there was not a dry eye in the room. In fact, the tears were flowing freely, many of them from Alyson.

*

As Nick returned home from his last ever Hewens Park Residents' Association committee meeting, which was held in Susan's house, he felt a mix of sadness and euphoria - but mostly euphoria. He'd given a little speech about how good the experience had been and how glad he was that they'd done it. And to an extent he meant it. It had certainly been an experience and an education. Brian had made an attempt to persuade him to stay on for another year "just in case you don't move away after all", but Nick assured him that he and Alyson would indeed be moving on in the coming months. Everyone, even Bert, had wished him well, and as he exited the house, he certainly did feel sad to be leaving. But five minutes later as he entered his own home the euphoria had completely taken over.

Nick skipped through the porch, observing a large clear recycling sack full of clothes in there as he did so, and then burst in through the front door.

"Hi, Honey - I'm home!"

"Hello. Did you have a good meeting?"

"Of course. What's that big pile of rags doing in the porch?"

Alyson was sitting on her sofa eating a piece of toast. She smiled at his comment.

"They're baby clothes - from Michelle."

"Oh, er, that's nice of her."

"Yeah, they'll all be going to the charity shop."

Nick got himself a can of lager.

"She had some news," said Alyson.

"Yeah, what?"

"Rob's left her."

"Shit! Really?"

"Yep, got some bird pregnant apparently. So, Michelle's kicked him out and he's gone back to his mum's."

"WHAAAT! Bloody hell."

"I always thought he was a bit of a pig."

"What? I thought he was supposed to be your hero!"

Neighbour From Hell

"Ha, Ha."

"Well, that's one thing settled: he's never going to get around to doing that roof tile now, is he."

"He was never going to anyway, was he?"

Nick took a big swig of lager.

"No, I don't suppose he was. Let's hope that the neighbours in our next place are more reliable."

"They will be. They definitely will be."

"Seriously though, that's a real shame for Michelle."

"I know. I felt really sorry for her. Let's hope it works out for her in the long run. Anyway, what happened at the meeting?"

"Nothing exciting … it's just so good to know that I'll never be going to one again."

"It certainly is."

"Here's to freedom!" said Nick, holding his lager can aloft. Alyson clinked an imaginary glass against it. She had a big smile on her face.

*

Nick and Alyson had been making a real effort to cut down on their drinking and as a result it had been more than two weeks since either of them had been to The Star when, on a Thursday night when Alyson had driven over to visit her parents for the evening, Nick decided to pay the place a visit. On the familiar ten-minute walk from his house, it occurred to him that other than when he and Alyson had been on holiday abroad, that two-week gap was the longest that he'd missed out on the pleasures of The Star for several years. And he was looking forward to getting back, he'd missed it. Len would almost certainly be there, as probably would Richard and Carol. It wouldn't matter whether they were present or not though, there would certainly be somebody that he could speak to, and quite likely play pool with as well. And if not, he could put some songs on the jukebox and have a relaxing pint alone with his thoughts. He smiled as The Star came into view; he was excited to be back.

He walked, as ever, straight past the door to the lounge. It looked surprisingly dark in there behind its frosted windows, and then he came to the door to the bar; it would no doubt be creaking loudly, as always, to announce his entrance. He pushed the door, but it didn't open. He then pulled on the handle, and then pushed again. But no, it seemed to be locked. He peered in through the door's frosted glass, but the bar, like the lounge, appeared to be in darkness. Nick looked at his watch, then he stood back from the door and looked up to the upper floor of the building. He then looked around him to see if there was anybody about, but there was nobody - just lots of cars rushing by on the busy Harlesham Road. He shook his head and checked his watch again. Then he made his way around to the back of The Star where its small car park was located. There were no lights on in any of the rooms of the large old red brick building, and in the car park there was just one vehicle - a battered old white Mercedes Sprinter van that always seemed to be there and that he presumed to belong to one of the neighbouring businesses. He circled the entire building and then, scratching his head, made his way back to the Harlesham Road and back in the direction from where he'd come. He thought about going home but decided instead to detour via The George. He was worried about The Star - had somebody died? He hoped that it wasn't anything as bad as that. Maybe it was getting a refurb. If so, then that might take away a bit of its character, but he had to admit that it was long needed. Hopefully, someone at The George might know what was going on.

The landlord of The George was able to tell him what had happened.

"It's closed down. Last day was last Friday."

"What, you mean for a refit or something?"

"No, it's gone for good. The brewery gave him three days' notice, apparently. They had a bit of a party there on the last night; went a bit mad, so I heard."

"Shit!"

"Yeah, bit of a shocker, isn't it?"

"Yeah, yeah. That's very sad to hear. Do you, er, do you know what's going to happen to it?"

"Getting turned into flats, I believe."

Another customer then drew the landlord's attention, so Nick found himself a table to sit down alone and drink his pint.

His first thoughts were of the most memorable times that he'd had at The Star - drunken sing-a-longs to the jukebox, the fight with the travellers when Rob had come to the rescue, and a time when one of the bikers who drank there had taken his Harley into the function room and performed donuts on the dancefloor that had filled the place with tyre smoke and set off the fire alarm, causing everyone to have to de-camp to the street. But his thoughts then turned to the people: Len, Len's sidekick Darren, Richard & Carol, even the obnoxious Doug, and countless others that he knew only through meeting them at The Star. He wondered when he might see any of them again - possibly never in some cases. He came over misty-eyed as he took a long drink of his pint. He wished that he'd known about that last night party; he wondered who had been there. He and Alyson would certainly have gone had they known. He went to text Alyson to give her the news but decided to leave it until later.

Nick left The George after the one pint and made his way slowly home. He continued to think about the people from The Star, and he thought about what a mix of people it was. It wasn't just him who had met people there that he wouldn't have met otherwise - the same no doubt applied to everybody else who drank there. Class and age barriers didn't exist in The Star, and what about race? He smiled again as he thought back to the moment that he'd witnessed Len and Rob, both of whose views were 'old fashioned' at best, enjoying a beer-bonded conversation with black man Harry and turban-wearing Sikh, Ranj.

Nick had a lump in his throat. It felt as if he had lost a good friend, and that his community had lost something so much more.

*

What's the matter? You all wanted rid of her, didn't you? Someone had to do your fucking dirty work.

*

Nick nervously pressed the buzzer for flat 3. It felt somehow improper visiting Charlene, especially as he'd told Alyson that he was just taking the Spitfire for a spin ... but it also felt exciting. He waited a long twenty seconds, but there was no response. He pressed the buzzer again, a little longer than the first time, and then waited again - probably for a minute. He felt a mixture of disappointment and relief that there was still no response and he turned to walk away. But then a voice crackled through the intercom, "Hello, who is it?" asked Charlene.

"Hi, it's Nick ... Nick Hale."

"... Who?"

Nick was immediately regretting coming, although it didn't surprise him that Charlene didn't know who he was. She'd probably forgotten what his name was - if she'd ever known it in the first place.

"Nick, from Hain Avenue ... the house opposite you."

"Oh, right." Then followed a buzzing sound and a large click.

"Come on up," crackled the intercom.

Nick climbed two flights of bare concrete stairs, his footsteps echoing around a bright and airy stairwell.

Charlene was standing at an open door. Her hair was wet, and she had a large towel wrapped around her.

"Sorry mate, I'd forgotten what your name was."

She gestured for Nick to follow her into her flat and led him along a small passageway to a large modern-looking kitchen.

Nick was surprised at how clean everything was.

He handed over a parcel.

"This came to your old house this morning; I thought I'd drop it around."

"Aw thanks mate", Charlene gushed with exaggerated gratitude. "It's New Look, I must not of updated my address on their web site."

She undid her towel to give her hair a quick rub. Underneath she was wearing just a bikini and a deep tan. She placed the towel back loosely around her shoulders and then nodded out of the window.

"Been playing in the pool with the kids."

Alfie and Francesca were running around a blow-up paddling pool on a patch of communal grass.

"Can I get you a cup of tea or something?"

"Erm, no it's OK thanks."

She picked up a packet of cigarettes, put one in her mouth, and turned the packet towards Nick.

He shook his head.

Charlene picked up a disposable lighter and lit her fag. She took a long drag and then blew out a plume of smoke. She wafted the smoke away with her hand. "Sorry ... do you want a beer?"

"N ... OK then, why not! Thanks."

She walked over to the fridge, slipping her towel off as she did so - a little more slinkily than was necessary - and placed it on a chair. She first closed the kitchen door and then opened the fridge. She brought over two cans of Foster's and resumed her position standing with her buttocks supported against a work surface, facing Nick, who was also standing. To Nick's left was the kitchen sink, underneath the window that overlooked where the kids were playing. He and Charlene clinked their cans of Foster's together.

"Happy New Year!" said Nick.

Several awkward minutes followed filled with lager supping and bland slightly forced conversation. Having established the likes of the flat being nice, the old place not having changed much (in less than three months), and that they were both in good health, they came to a lull. They both looked vaguely out of the window and took long swigs of their lagers before Nick resumed the conversation.

"So, er, Kevin not about?"

Charlene continued to gaze out of the window. She gave a little smirk. "He's long gone …"

Nick wasn't quite sure what to say to that, so he took another swig of his lager instead.

Charlene then turned back to face him and smiled. "I'm well out of that one, mate."

And with that elephant released from the room the chat became more relaxed. Her kids were getting on OK at the new place; he still had that green sports car; she was hoping to go to Lanzarote in the summer; he fancied having another go at skiing. The subjects of Alyson's pregnancy or the imminent house move didn't arise.

Nick and Charlene each started a second can of Foster's. Charlene lit up another cigarette; she took a deep drag and then handed it to Nick. He took a drag, managing to avoid coughing. They both blew out their smoke at the same time.

And then they were kissing - gently at first and then harder and faster, each of their tongues eagerly exploring the other's. Charlene threw her cigarette into the sink and her arms around Nick's neck. He slipped his hands from her shoulders slowly down the sides of her body to rest on her hips, which were as beautifully toned close up as they'd looked from afar when she used to sunbathe in her front

Neighbour From Hell

yard. He paused there for a moment before sliding his right hand tentatively inside the front of her bikini bottoms. She seemed to approve, and the kissing got still more intense. Nick eased his middle finger inside Charlene and caressed her; she was as aroused as he was. She broke off the kissing and let out a long sigh. "Ah, that's nice", she whispered in his ear.

Then Charlene let go of Nick's neck and brought her hands onto his shoulders. She had a look of concentration on her face. He brought his hands back onto her hips. She pushed him slightly away, and then moved her right hand down to feel the front of his jeans. She smiled. She didn't utter any words, but her expression said, "I see that you are pleased to see me!" She kissed him on the lips again, and then swivelled around, turning her back to him. She took her orange bikini bottoms in both hands, slid them down to her knees and then wriggled them down to her ankles. Then she stepped her right foot out of them, spreading her feet part, and leaned forward onto the work surface in front of her.

Nick gazed at her slender body. There was no white patch where the bikini had been, she was perfectly bronzed all over to a colour not very different from the garment that she had removed. He leaned forward and kissed the back of her neck. Then he stood back upright, undid the buckle of his belt and in one movement pulled out the belt and threw it onto the floor behind him.

And then the kitchen door flew open!

"Mummy, Alfie won't let me play in the paddling pool!"

In the few seconds that it took Francesca to run over to her mum and put her arms around her Nick had shot to the other side of the room and was already putting his belt back on. By the time he'd looked up from completing the task Charlene's bikini bottoms were also back in place.

"Well tell him not to be naughty or I'll come down and smack his bum."

"I want a biscuit."

Nick looked on. Francesca was oblivious to what had been going on; thank goodness she hadn't turned up a minute later.

Charlene patted the top of Francesca's head. "You've already had lots of biscuits."

"But I want a chocolate one."

Nick coughed politely. "I, er, I probably should be going."

Charlene held onto Francesca with one hand whilst opening a cupboard to extract a packet of chocolate digestives with the other.

"Yeah, mate. Thanks ever so much for that."

Nick made his way to the kitchen door.

"You OK seeing yourself out?" asked Charlene whilst handing Francesca two chocolate digestives.

"Yeah, yeah, fine," said Nick. "I know the way."

"Thanks again mate," she called after him.

"No problem … see you around."

Nick made his way quickly down the concrete stairs and then departed through the front door with magnified versions of the feelings of disappointment and relief that he'd felt at the same spot half an hour before.

He got into the Spitfire, composed himself, and checked his phone to see that he didn't have any messages. He decided to text Alyson.

Back in a few mins. QO?

She got back surprisingly quickly.

Don't mind if I do!

This could be a first: start with one woman and finish it with another. He fired up the Spitfire and drove home fast, with a big smile on his face.

Nick didn't have Charlene's phone number, nor she his; it was unlikely that he would ever see her again.

*

"Got away with it, haven't I? I've fucking got away with it! Feels fucking GOOD. Take that, you lot - the fucking lot of you. Haha! Onwards and upwards. Fuck the LOT of 'em. Ha! Onwards and fucking upwards."

*

"Oh, you'll love it around here," said Nick and Alyson's elderly new next-door neighbour, Roy. "Much nicer than Norling, and very quiet. Not so many of our ethnic friends either. There's a few of course, but they tend to be professional people - doctors and that kind of thing. You know - people who contribute to the community."

*

Nick felt more nervous than he had expected to. He'd had nine months picturing this moment in his mind but now it was really about to happen, and he was pacing around outside. He even found himself nibbling at his fingernails for a moment. It was a big moment in his life. He was feeling good: he and Alyson were settling nicely into their new home in leafy suburbia and his new job was going well. This would be the icing on the cake. He looked at his watch, just as he had done a minute before, and another minute before that.

And then Nick heard that unmistakable sound: a large vehicle with a diesel engine was approaching. He walked quickly and expectantly to the end of his driveway and arrived at the same moment that Geoff Lanning brought his low-loader to a stop.

The Bond was beautiful. Although Nick had been dropping in to check on its progress, and Geoff had sent him photos from time to time, this was the first time had he'd seen the finished article. It truly was a thing to behold. It took Geoff twenty minutes to carefully extract the Bond from the low-loader, and all the time Nick looked on in awe, marvelling at its beautiful deep shiny paintwork and at its chrome parts sparkling in the sunshine.

When it was done, Nick and Geoff shook hands. Geoff looked pleased with his handiwork.

"Would you like to drive it?"

No, for some reason Nick didn't feel ready to. He let Geoff park the Bond carefully in the driveway for him. When it started up, the soft perfectly-tuned burble from its thin exhaust gave him a warm feeling inside. Uncle Frank would have been very proud.

Nick walked around the Bond. He opened and closed everything - the doors, the boot lid, the bonnet, the glove box. He did a lot of nodding. There was a tear in his eye. There wasn't much to say.

"It's like a brand-new car," he managed.

"Happy then?" ask Geoff, needlessly.

"Very," said Nick. And then, "I'd better give you some money."

Nick went into the house and retrieved the cash that he'd prepared and placed in a brown paper envelope. It was the whole £3500; Geoff Lanning hadn't in the end taken a deposit in advance and nor had he increased the price from his original estimate, even though some things had proved more of a challenge than had been envisaged.

Nick handed over the brown envelope.

Geoff nodded, folded it in two, and placed it in the pocket of his overalls.

"Did you want a receipt?" he asked.

No, of course Nick didn't want a receipt. When Geoff Lanning had been so cool as to take the three and a half grand and put it in his pocket without even counting it, how could Nick ask for something so dreary as a receipt.

They shook hands again.

"Well, in the nicest possible way, I hope not to see you again soon," said Nick.

And then Geoff Lanning departed to leave Nick alone with his new pride and joy.

Nick couldn't be more pleased with how the Bond had turned out. It had been worth all of the stress and expense. He loved it. Alyson would be back from her mum's very soon. He had every confidence that she would love it too.

*

Whilst Nick was making the last quarter of his second pint last as long as possible, Colin was draining the remains of his fifth. It was three months since Nick had moved house, and he and Colin were catching up for a drink and for Nick to return a drill that he'd borrowed when he left. Nick had picked up Colin in the Spitfire from near his house - not *at* the house, as Colin had told Janet that he had to go into work for a bit, not that he was going for a drink - and they had driven five or six top-down miles in the evening sunshine out into the country to a pub called The Black Horse. It was a popular place in the summertime, a big old-fashioned red-brick pub that sat at the top of a valley, enjoying a view over lakes and woodland as far as the eye could see. Anyone new to the place would hardly believe that they were so close to London and even still inside the M25. When Nick and Colin arrived at eight o'clock the car park was full, and they'd had to park in a lay-by outside. They'd then chosen an outside table to enjoy the last of the sunshine. It was three hours later now and the sunshine was long gone, along with most of the customers.

Nick shivered as he placed his glass back down on the table with just a half an inch of ale left. He had been looking forward to having a catch-up with Colin, but the evening had so far been something of a disappointment. Colin was tired, as often, but he was also edgy, and the conversation had struggled to flow. It lacked the joviality of their old late-night chats through the garden fence. But the two pints of strong real ale - he wouldn't normally have more than one if he was driving but Colin had persuaded him - had worked their way in, and Nick had latterly become more relaxed.

They had talked about a lot of things, but inevitably Tricia's fire had been one of their subjects. And Colin now came back to it again.

"They'll never find who did it you know ... no chance."

"You don't think so?" said Nick.

"No chance; too fucking stupid, the lot of them. They didn't even find her keys, did they? They'll never know who did it."

Nick wasn't sure that he wanted to continue the subject, but he went along with it for the time being.

"That's if it was anyone of course," he said.

"Ha - 'course it was. She had it coming to her, didn't she?"

At that point Nick decided it really was time to leave it. He fixed his eyes on his beer glass while he tried to come up with a change of subject, hampered by the knowledge that Colin was glaring at him expectantly. It took him thirty seconds.

"Yeah, probably. By the way, make sure we don't forget that your drill's in my boot when we get back."

Colin nodded and then did move on from the fire, returning instead to another favourite topic of his that he'd already covered twice that evening.

"That Charlene though - wouldn't you just?!" And he smiled - a leering smile, not a happy one.

Nick had resisted saying anything the previous times, and he still knew that it was best not to, but the beer had lowered his resistance and he was tempted.

Colin went on, "I wonder if that tan went all over ... or were there any white bits."

Nick looked straight ahead rather than at Colin, who was slightly to his left, and said casually, "It's all over."

There was a pause before Colin smirked and then said, "Yeah, and how would you know that?"

Nick paused too, before answering, "I've seen it … it's definitely all over."

Then he turned his head to Colin, who was eyeing him intently.

Colin spoke. "Seriously?"

"Yep, seriously."

"You didn't …?"

Nick smiled. "A parcel came for her a few weeks ago, so I took it round to her new flat …"

He stopped to take a sip of his beer, about half of the tiny remainder.

"And?!" Colin prompted.

Nick was a little perturbed by the intensity of Colin's interest, but he continued.

"Well, she invited me in - she was only wearing a bikini; we had a couple of beers, and well …" He let Colin's imagination fill in the rest.

"You bastard!"

It wasn't completely clear whether Colin meant 'you bastard' as in 'fair play to you' or whether he really did mean 'you bastard'. In his head Nick went with the standard football pundit response to any one way or the other question, which was 'probably a bit of both'.

Colin continued, "So, where was her bloke while all of this was going on?"

Nick had an answer to that one. "That's all over. At least that's what she said - they're probably back together again by now."

Colin shook his head. "You bastard!"

Nick was already regretting his revelation. He thought about explaining how his encounter with Charlene hadn't gone quite as far as he'd perhaps so far implied, but then he considered that revealing more detail might do more harm than good.

Colin seemed to ease up. He sat back in his seat and drained the half pint or so that was remaining in his glass. He put the empty glass down on their small round table with a satisfied-looking smile on his face. Then he stood up and placed his hands on the table, leaning over so that his face was right in front of Nick's. Colin was still trying to give up cigarettes and had managed not to smoke any so far during the evening, but his breath still smelled of stale smoke, as well as of stale beer.

Nick could see that there was something under Colin's left hand.

Colin laughed.

And then he lifted that hand to reveal a set of keys - a Yale key and a mortice lock key, attached to a ring with a grubby large white plastic fob in the shape of a star, adorned with the words 'World's Best Mum' in pink script.

"See ... all you college boys aren't so clever as you think you are."

He laughed again, and then stood upright, his eyes trained on Nick's.

"I'm off for a piss."

He turned and walked slowly and casually off into the pub, leaving the keys on the table for Nick to do with them what he wished.

Nick watched Colin disappear into the pub. He broke into a cold sweat and shivered again. He stood up and looked anxiously around him. There were no other customers left - not outside anyway, and the car park was empty. Should he stay, or should he go? He decided to go. Leaving Tricia's keys untouched on the table, he walked briskly along the short tree-lined driveway that led from the pub's car park to the lane outside. He stumbled over the pot-holed tarmac surface whilst the overhanging trees whispered eerily at him in the gentle breeze. His pace quickened, as did his heartbeat. His Spitfire was the only car left outside in the dark bumpy layby. He tripped as he got to it and fell against its boot lid. He steadied himself there and thought of the big electric drill that was lying in that boot - the drill that belonged to a murderer.

He turned around and stood, waiting for Colin. His hands were sweating, and the sound of his heartbeat was close to drowning out his thoughts, but not quite - some were still able to flash through his brain.

The fire was started with vodka - Colin could get hold of big bottles of strong vodka.

"What with that fucking lot and everything else I haven't had a decent night's sleep for months."

"I thought I saw a bloke coming out of Tricia's house for a moment, but it was only Colin on one of his walkabouts."

"... make the most of it; you won't be getting your leg over once the baby's born!"

Colin had hated Tricia right from the start.

"She's anyone's for a bottle of Vodka!"

He was always so adamant that it was murder, not an accident.

"Keep hold of them if you want; you never know when you might want to come over."

Colin knew what Tricia's key fob looked like when Nick had mentioned the "best mum" words.

My God, was he actually shagging Tricia?!

But why kill her? ... Shame?

"Shit, you'd have to be really desperate, wouldn't you?" ... "Yeah, really desperate."

SHIT!

Colin was taking his time.

What would he do when he got there? Colin was strong - he was bad-tempered - he was a fighter; 'Red Card Reid' - he was in a foul mood - he was pissed - he was a murderer.

It seemed as if the occasion for which Nick had carried that gun around for so many years might have arrived. Unfortunately, the gun was wrapped up in a polythene bag underneath his shed at home.

Maybe he should leave.

"That's the problem with you, Nick - you never stand up for yourself."

"That's the problem with you, Nick - you let these people walk all over you."

"Grow some balls, Nick."

Perhaps Colin was bluffing. Maybe he would come back laughing his head off - it was all a joke.

Colin came back. He was smoking. He was stumbling. And he was laughing.

But it wasn't a jovial laugh, nor this time was it a leering laugh. No, it was a mocking laugh.

He stopped just a few feet from Nick, and faced him.

"So, what are you going to do then?"

Nick had no idea what he was going to do - either now or longer term.

Colin carried on, "I'll tell you what you are going to do: you're going to do fuck all! That's what you're going to do.'"

He took a long drag on his cigarette.

"You're going to do fuck all, because if anyone finds those keys on me then I'll say that I got them from you. And that means that they'll have to investigate both of us – and they won't find any evidence either way. But you're not going to tell anyone that I've got them anyway because I'll tell them about Charlene, and that'll mess up your cosy little middle-class life, won't it?"

"There are lots of things that are around but they're not for the downtrodden working classes"

He blew out some smoke.

The two men stood facing each other. Nick was tense, Colin less so.

Colin spoke again.

"You didn't know that I'd sunk to that, did you? You didn't know that I was fucking her."

He shook his head, apparently incredulous at Nick's naivety/stupidity.

"A bottle of cheap vodka and she'd do anything I wanted."

He took another drag, and then laughed.

"Fucking pig ugly though … not like your Charlene.

I'll bet you're laughing at that, aren't you - you get the dolly bird, I get the pig.

She laughed at me too ... and tried to blackmail me. She's not laughing now though, is she?"

The two of them eyed each other warily. It was Nick's turn to speak.

"Are you saying that you actually ..." he couldn't quite bring himself to say the word "murdered" "... killed her?"

Colin drew on his fag once again, but it seemed to be more for effect than to give himself time to think. He blew the smoke in Nick's direction.

"I didn't particularly plan to, but the opportunity arose. She'd spilt vodka all over the place and she was snoring away there -" Colin's eyes glazed over as he pictured the scene "- like the big ugly sweaty pig that she was."

He shrugged his shoulders and came out of his gaze to again look Nick in the eye.

"Just put my fag down on her dressing gown. I didn't even know for sure whether it had caught. It was smouldering a bit, but I went home and went to bed. I was out like a light. Good stuff that Polish vodka, sent me off to sleep and ... well, apparently vodka doesn't really burn unless it's at least 60% - and that stuff was 80%. I didn't wake up until you and Rob were making a racket out there, trying to be fucking heroes."

Nick shook his head slowly, keeping his eyes fixed on Colin's.

"What's the matter?" said Colin, "You all wanted rid of her, didn't you? Someone had to do your fucking dirty work."

Nick looked Colin in the eye. "What about Charlene and her kids next door?" he said, softly.

"What about her? She lived, didn't she ... lucky for you!"

Nick had nothing else to say. Whatever was going to happen next?

Colin dragged on his fag a final time and then squashed it under his foot, in the style of a gangster in a film about the Krays or the Mafia: Colin Reid - last of the famous international playboys.

"What's the matter ... cat got your tongue?"

Colin laughed again and then leaned forward and flicked Nick's nose.

Then came the fist. One fast clean jab that hammered straight into the jaw, not guided by any technique, but fueled by years of pent-up frustration. Nick winced in pain, but Colin crumpled to the ground; Nick had knocked him out cold.

Nick shivered, more through shock this time than cold or nerves. His hand was in agony; he wondered if he had broken a knuckle. He stood looking down at Colin who was lying on his side in something akin to the recovery position. Nick watched him for a good minute; he groaned a little, but he didn't stir.

Nick looked up and down the lane. There were no vehicles approaching from either direction. There was also nobody leaving the pub. He cast his eyes back down at Colin's prone form. Colin groaned again and shuffled his feet. It was probably best to get out of there before he came to ... assuming that he was going to come to.

Nick turned away from Colin, walked around to the Spitfire's door, and then climbed in. He'd left the roof down, and so hadn't bothered locking the car. He put on his seatbelt. His heart was still racing and his hand throbbing with pain. He looked into his mirror, but there was no Colin rising zombie-like to grab him from behind. He shuddered and then started the engine. He pulled slowly from the bumpy lay-by and out onto the lane beside it, and then slammed his foot to the floor. The Spitfire's tyres squealed in protest and pieces of grit scattered over the road surface. Nick changed into second, floored it again, and then threw his fist the air, yelling

"YEEEEEESSSSSSSSS!" as loud as his voice could muster.

*

ABOUT THE AUTHOR

Neal Bircher's acclaimed first novel, *Love Sex Work Murder*, was published in 2015. After the novel's success he went on to publish his grandfather Gordon Heynes' WWII memoir, *I Felt No Sorrow – This Was War (Burma 1942-45)*. Since its release in 2019 the book has sold consistently well; its proceeds are donated to charity.

Neal Bircher has also written for radio, live comedy, and a variety of motoring publications.

contact@nealbircherbooks.co.uk

Facebook / Neal Bircher Author

Printed in Great Britain
by Amazon